THERE WILL BE BLOOD

THERE WILL BE BLOOD

WAR OF THE ANGELS™ BOOK FIVE

MICHAEL TODD   MICHAEL ANDERLE   LAURIE STARKEY

LMBPN Publishing
PMB 196, 2540 South Maryland Pkwy
Las Vegas, NV 89109

First US edition, February 2019

eBook ISBN: 978-1-68500-382-1
Paperback ISBN: 979-8-89354-733-7

DEDICATION

To Family, Friends and
Those Who Love
to Read.
May We All Enjoy Grace
to Live the Life We Are
Called.

The temperature in Paris was cooler than normal, and the breeze cascading across the park in front of Notre Dame made it downright cold. Still, the city was gorgeous. It sparkled under bright blue skies and the joy of waking another day without an incursion. The residents had reached a point in time where some counted the days, while others counted the hours between the appearance of more demons. However, across the world, they had seen a longer stretch of peace than at any time in recent years. What the Damned and the military tried to remember, though, was that it wasn't an end, just a pause.

Outside of the nearly-finished fort protecting both a section of the city and the cathedral, Katie and Pandora stood huddled together. Katie smiled. "What do you think? Do we give them a speech, or do we send them on some insane run and *then* thank them?"

Pandora thought about it. "You know how much I like it when we torture these guys…but they *have* been pretty cooperative during their training. I say we give them a moment of kindness and let them enjoy a little praise, at least from you. You're the nicer one."

Katie chuckled. "Damn right I am, but only when it's deserved."

They turned around and looked at the Damned soldiers, who were standing in ranks waiting for their next directive. They had all assumed a military posture, hands stiffly beside them, fists clenched, and knees bent just enough to avoid passing out—not that any of their demons would let that happen. They held their heads high and stared straight forward, remembering the incident where they'd all had to do three hundred pushups because someone looked Pandora in the eye. They had been out there all night. It was amazing what a little pain and sleep deprivation did to a person's motivation.

Pandora stood to the side and Katie took front and center. "At ease."

The group shifted in unison, bringing their arms behind them and relaxing slightly. She looked at each of them with a smile. "We are a hodgepodge now, aren't we? Some of you have decided that Paris is the place you want to be, where you want to stand on the front lines and protect this beautiful city, while others have responded to our call and will be following us to Romania to train their Damned. No matter which place you serve, it will be both exciting and terrifying at the same time."

Katie put her hands behind her back and began walking back and forth in front of the ranks. "I wanted to take the time to congratulate you all on completing your initial training. If you could see what I have seen, you would be more than proud of yourselves. This first section of training has been exhausting and frustrating, and maybe it even felt hopeless at times. But you guys have pulled through it and are actually starting to look like a bunch of soldiers."

Pandora smiled and interjected, "But it's not over."

Katie laughed, glancing at Pandora. "No, ma'am, it is not. As Damned, you have to be on a constant training regimen. You have demons in you who can push you to the next level, but even without their help, you are expected to be the toughest, strongest, fastest, and fiercest of all of the soldiers. You are expected to run head-first into the battle and never think twice. The good thing is, you are Damned, and as such, I know you'll get it. I know you'll be incredible."

Pandora walked up in front of the soldiers and took a bow. "You have had the pleasure of learning from the finest teacher in history. And who, Grant, may I ask, am I speaking of?"

Grant, a Damned soldier, came to attention again. "That would be *you*, ma'am!"

Pandora laughed. "Damn right. At ease."

Katie rolled her eyes and tapped Pandora on the shoulder. "Uh, you *do* realize that in your 'greatness,' as you put it, you have managed to sexually harass every single one of them except Yuri."

The soldiers grinned and held back chuckles. Pandora put up one finger and leaned toward Katie. "I got Yuri when you weren't looking."

Katie blinked at her, unimpressed. "Great. Just great."

Pandora shrugged and looked at the soldiers. "Besides, I

was a goddamn demon until like two seconds ago. I'm not a role model, am I, troops?"

The troops, smiling, yelled in unison. "No, ma'am, Drill Instructor!"

Katie huffed and shook her head, kicking her foot through the grass. "Not a great teacher, either."

Pandora put her hand to her ear. "What was that? I couldn't hear you over the praise my soldiers were sending me telepathically."

Katie laughed. "I *said*, 'Not a great teacher, either.'"

Pandora nodded, putting her hands behind her back and looking at one of the soldiers. "Do you *believe* her? Them's fightin' words."

Katie smirked as Pandora clapped her hands to call her Angel Armor. As it snapped to Pandora's body, she pointed at Katie with a mischievous grin. "I challenge you to a grudge match."

Katie leaned her head back and laughed, clapping her hands loudly in front of her. The team took a step back as her armor slapped onto her. She looked at Pandora with bright blue eyes. "You're on."

With their wings spread wide, the angels flew into the air, positioning their shields and swords. They laughed wildly as they sparred, putting on a good show for the soldiers below. Katie swung her sword at Pandora, who blocked it with her own, then leaned toward Pandora with a grin. "Pick up the pace, Grandma. We don't want to look bad in front of the kids."

Pandora threw her off and lunged toward her, laughing wildly as she beat on Katie's shield with her sword. The Damned below broke ranks, watching and cheering as the two battled. It was the kind of morale boost everyone needed.

Baal stroked his ever-growing stringy black goatee as he walked down the halls next to Beelzebub. He glanced at his companion, who was walking a lot more lightly than normal toward Lucifer's chambers. There was a strange partial grin on his face, and he didn't seem to have a worry in the world about what was about to happen. Though Baal was concerned any time he got called to chambers, he was more concerned with how smug Beelzebub was acting, as if he thought he'd never had anything to fear. That was not how hell worked, even for the higher-ups.

The demon servants bowed in fear as they passed, Baal pulled out the scroll that had been sent to him. "You are ordered to Lucifer's chambers for a meeting of the Council of Eight. You are to be prompt, and be aware that you are there to listen to his Greatness, speaking only when called upon to do so."

Baal rolled it back up and gripped it tightly. "This is the second time the Council is meeting in his chambers and not in the meeting room."

Beelzebub shrugged. "You know Lucifer. He isn't much for leaving his comforts. The meeting room is across two levels of hell, and usually he is not present for meetings held there. He sends his minions with any messages. This time he must have something to say."

Baal sneered, looking over his shoulder and down the hall behind him. Azazel, Belial, and Asmodeus were all far behind them. Their faces were down, hiding their expressions. Baal sighed and gazed at Beelzebub. "That's what I'm afraid of. He might be on one of his crazy kicks again."

Beelzebub shrugged as they reached the door to the chambers and passed through into the huge room. "He always has the best ideas when he is on his crazy rants."

Baal snorted as they headed toward the center. "Or he rips someone's dick off and tosses it to the demon dogs."

They stopped when they reached the center, looking up at Lucifer, who whispered in a servant's ear and then shooed him off. Both Baal and Beelzebub graciously bowed to the Dark King, and they remained folded over until he responded, just as he liked. Lucifer took positive notice of their arrival. "Well, it looks like the two of you are the first ones here. Maybe you have learned a lesson or two."

Just then the other three walked in, hurrying up beside Baal and bowing. Lucifer's face fell, and he waved them up. "I appreciate you all coming so quickly, not that you really had a choice. First, I would like to put the rumors to rest. Earth is still off-limits."

The demons tried to hide their dismay. Lucifer raised his hand to shut them all up. "But I am formulating a plan, the details of which you don't need to know. In fact, it might be safer for you if you do not."

The demons all clapped at the Dark Lord's words since he was obviously looking for praise. Lucifer smiled smugly and leaned back on his throne, crossing one leg over the other. "Oh, and I would also like to make an announcement. If you don't like it, I can work with you to alter your opinion." He zapped a nearby servant with an energy bolt in the crotch, and the demon squealed and limped off.

They glanced at each other suspiciously. Lucifer smiled at Beelzebub. "Your brave partner in crime, Beelzebub, has been re-inducted into the Council of Eight...although at the current time there are only five of you. Trust me when I say he will be of great use in coming days as the battle for Earth and hell escalates."

Baal and the other three nodded happily at Beelzebub. Lucifer sighed and waved his large clawed hand. "All right, I'm done with you. You may leave. Just keep your eyes open for my next summons and make sure you are on time. I don't like waiting for anyone."

The demons quickly turned and headed out of the chambers. Lucifer stroked the skull on the armrest of his throne and glanced to the side, only to find Mania sitting perfectly still with no expression on her face. He reached out and stroked a piece of her inky-black hair. "My dear, you are moping again. What's wrong?"

Mania straightened her shoulders and shifted her eyes to Lucifer. "Not moping, just emotionless at this moment. Trust me, it is a nice change from what I have been going through."

Lucifer tugged on the lock of her hair. "Tell me your thoughts."

Mania swallowed and decided she already pissed him off plenty, so she might as well ask what was on her mind. "I guess I was just wondering why Beelzebub was promoted if his plans failed. Calvin and Sofia are still alive, Sofia is no longer infected, and the demon responsible has infected one of Katie's soldiers."

Lucifer pulled his hand back, sensing that Mania was still very upset about what had happened to her. He took a deep breath and shrugged. "I guess I would say it is mostly because I want to keep an eye on him. He is not to be trusted, and I cannot just sit around sensing his movements at all times. The truth is, he grew wily during his time in the caves. He learned much and perfected his slithering and skulking skills. That may lead to some really bad actions on his part."

Mania pursed her lips, then lifted her chin and glanced around the throne room. It was apparent that his answer had not pleased her. She cleared her throat. "I do not like him, and he did nothing to avenge my honor, even with instruction. But you know best. May I go? I would like to lie down for a bit."

Lucifer stared at her for a moment and nodded. "Don't be gone for too long."

***

"Ha! You wish. You just brought me out here to the woods to con me into loving you even more than I already do," the tall, fit blonde woman said as she walked down the wooded path.

The guy with her chuckled and shrugged, tapping the long, curved walking stick he was using on the ground. "Hiking in Sonora, Texas is known for its aphrodisiac effects."

It was a perfect day for a hike. The temperature was moderate, the sky blue, and there was no one else on the trail. The two walked gingerly up a small hill and bore to the left. The woman began to slow her pace, staring off the trail.

The guy poked her with his walking stick. "What? Did you finally find the enchanted part of the forest?"

The woman smiled. "Maybe. That, or I found a bear's den and we will shortly be eaten."

He wrinkled his forehead, stopping next to her. "Is that a cave?"

She grinned and nodded, grabbing his arm and pulling him off the trail. "Come on, we can take a rest there—and maybe more if you're good."

He laughed and jogged with her, approaching the cave and pushed her gently against the jagged rocks at the entrance. He pressed his lips to her neck and she giggled, pulling him close. As she stared into the darkness of the cave something changed, her mood plummeting. The guy reacted the same way, pushing himself away from her.

She stared at him for a moment, her face twisting, then pulled her hand back and slapped him hard across the face. "That's what you deserve."

The guy stumbled back and shook his head. "What the fuck was *that* for?"

The woman gritted her teeth, feeling unnatural anger flowing through her. "Don't stand there and act like you haven't been thinking about my sister this whole time. You are in love with her, not me. It's so very plain to see."

The guy's eyes flashed angrily, and he put his hands in the air. "I knew you were fucking crazy. Your sister means nothing to me. In fact, I find her even more annoying than you most days."

The woman scoffed, throwing her hands up. "Oh, *that's* how you think about me? Then why don't you just go? The woods would be much nicer without you in them."

The guy narrowed his eyes and breathed heavily. "FINE! Find your own fucking way back."

He turned and began marching off through the crunchy leaves. When he got about halfway to the trail, he glanced up, spying something from the corner of his eye. His mouth opened, but he couldn't get a sound out as a giant bat dove from above the canopy of the trees straight for him. He took off running, then tripped over the fallen branches of a tree and fell to the ground.

He covered his head with his hands and clenched his eyes shut, waiting for the giant claws to latch onto him. After a few moments of nothing, he released his clenched muscles and turned over, looking around him. There was no bat anywhere near him. In fact, there was nothing out of the ordinary at all. Even the anger he had been feeling just a moment before had completely dissipated. It was as if he had dreamt the entire thing and was now awakening to reality.

He sat up, rubbing his head and brushing the leaves and dirt off his clothes and hands. Just moments before he could have sworn that the day had been gray and dreary, everything around him lifeless. He hadn't noticed at that moment because the anger flowing through him had blinded him to everything else, but thinking back, it was almost as if a cloud had come into the forest and wrapped completely around him.

Now, though, looking up through the canopy, there was nothing but bright blue skies with a few fluffy white clouds floating overhead. The temperature was cold, but nothing too terrible. Just a normal beautiful, chilly, winter day, just as it had been when they arrived. His girlfriend's cries snapped him from his haze.

She ran toward him, her arms out. "Oh, my God. Are you all right?"

She knelt in the leaves beside him, picking twigs and leaves out of his hair, then cupped his face and stared into his eyes. "Tell me you're okay. I couldn't bear it if you weren't. I don't understand what happened between us over there just now."

The guy shook his head. "I'm okay. I don't either. Everything was so gloomy, and the anger and fear inside of me came out of nowhere."

She nodded. "I know. I don't think you are in love with my sister, not even for a second. But standing by that cave, it was like all the fears I've ever felt my whole life came flooding into me at once. I was terrified that you were going to leave me; that you didn't love me. Then the anger came and… well, I'm so sorry. I didn't mean any of it. Not a single word."

He put his hands up to her face as well and leaned forward, kissing her deeply, then pulled back and shook his head. "I didn't mean any of it either. I don't think you're crazy, and I would never leave you out in the woods by yourself. I felt the anger and fear too; it was like a blanket wrapped tightly around me."

She stood up and took his hand, helping him to his feet. He wrapped his arms around her tightly, glancing back at the creepy cave. "Let's get out of here."

As they walked away, a low wind whipped out of the opening of the cave and black smoke oozed over the floor of the forest.

2

Lucifer clenched his fists in front of his face and gritted his teeth. He growled louder and louder, his body shaking as he pitched a temper tantrum. He threw his hands out and finally roared at the top of his lungs, shaking the chambers. Plumes of dust fluttered to the floor and pebbles of lava rock bounced off it. The demon standing in front of him shivered.

Lucifer sighed and looked at him. "I don't understand women! You try to please them, and they are assholes. You try to motivate them, show them they are stronger than their lost crows, they are assholes. You try to show them you love them even with scars, and what do they do? They complain about how you gave them a damn scar to begin with."

The demon just stared, unsure of what to say. Lucifer sighed and leaned back in his chair, one eye peering at the servant. "What can I do to please Mania? She's obviously still upset, although there was a moment when I thought she had gotten over it. Then the whole Beelzebub thing came up, and she is back to being prickly. Dammit, how am I supposed to please her and keep hell running at the same time? I swear, those humans with more than one lover are insane. They must attempt suicide at least once a week. I know I would. Not that it's any better down here in hell."

The servant swallowed hard, seeing that Lucifer was actually looking to him for an answer. His face brightened and he put his finger up, but then shook his head, realizing his idea was terrible. He just shrugged instead. "Unfortunately, your Greatness, I have little experience with this. I really don't know what to tell you."

Lucifer eyed him and growled. Getting up quickly from his throne, he stomped toward the servant, who cowered in front of him, shaking. "What good is it to have all of you around if you are too stupid to know how to fix my problems?"

He snarled loudly, quickly pulling his sword from his side and swiping it at the demon. It cut through one of his legs, and the demon screeched as he fell to the ground. Lucifer sighed and sheathed his sword. "Someone clean this up."

As he sat back down in his chair another demon, glancing nervously at the hapless one-legged servant on the floor, cleared his throat. "I'm sorry to disturb you at such a fraught time…"

Lucifer snarled. "What? What do you want from me? Everyone wants something from the lord of hell."

The servant looked at the others, who nodded and waved their hands at him to proceed. The demon took a deep breath and stood up as straight as his curved body could. "Um, Beelzebub is requesting an audience with you. He says it is important."

Lucifer slammed his hand down on the chair arm and then rubbed it over his face, closing his eyes. "Again? This is the second time he's done this. Does he not know what it means to be the ruler? I am not here to constantly be bothered by the insolent idiots who surround me."

The servant nervously raised his finger. "If I may, your Darkness? You reinstated him on the Council to keep an eye on him. Perhaps if you listen to him, he won't go do anything stupid."

Lucifer opened one eye and looked at the servant. "I guess you're right. I suppose *you* aren't completely useless. Send him in."

The demon scurried off, toward the tall main doors. He grunted as he leapt, latching onto the round ring of a door handle and throwing his body back. The door creaked open a bit and the other servants ran to help him, creating a chain to get the door open. Beelzebub ignored them as he entered, hurrying to the center of the room and bowing deeply.

Beelzebub knew exactly how to handle Lucifer. "Your Greatness, it is a pleasure being in your light once again. Thank you for your gracious welcome to the Council. You are the most amazing and intelligent ruler in all the dimensions of the world."

Lucifer raised an eyebrow and smirked. One thing that he did like was a good butt-kissing. Having his minions tell him how wonderful and powerful he was, was exactly what he needed to feel better. Normally Mania would have filled that quota already for the day, but she had decided to run off and do her brooding elsewhere. Just the thought of this made Lucifer bitter, and his smirk faded.

He rolled his hand in the air, holding his head up with the other. "What do you want, Beelzebub?"

Beelzebub cleared his throat. "I understand that the demons on topside were unsuccessful at ridding the Earth of both Calvin and his bride. I wanted to give you my sincerest apologies for their failure."

Lucifer shrugged. "Wasn't much you could do except tell them their role. You were in hell, and have not been allowed to go to Earth since we set that plan in motion. You should have been a better leader, but I cannot fault you for their mistakes, even if Mania does."

Beelzebub winced at the sound of her name. He knew if it were up to her, he would have been expelled to the deepest parts of hell already, with no chance of return for centuries. He was more than a little glad to see that she was not at his side, although he would never say that out loud.

He nodded his head in thanks. "I have a suggestion, though, and I hope that Your Grace will allow me to elaborate on it."

Lucifer lifted an eyebrow. "Go on."

Beelzebub swallowed hard, trying not to show his nerves. "I suggest that you allow our demons to go back to Earth. In fact, I believe you should be sending them there purposely."

Lucifer narrowed his eyes, and Beelzebub patted his hands in a downward motion to deflect the coming outburst. "Let me explain. Our demonic energy was growing thicker and harder by the second. It was so thick in that dimension that you could almost feel the evil coursing through the air. If we were to push the demonic energy, it might quite possibly wake another Leviathan. They could be a strong force for our cause on Earth, as well as exacting our revenge on both Calvin and his bride."

Lucifer sighed and shook his head. "That all seems well and good from the outside, but I don't believe it will work. Two of them are already dead. Juntto flipped sides completely and is now trying to kill all of us. Baylahn is an idiot, just swimming in circles forever, not actually realizing he's doing so. And the others? Who knows what they'll do? It's a tricky game."

Beelzebub nodded. "I completely understand. But…as we speak, one of the most evil and terrifying of them all is beginning to awaken on his own. Kabbus stirs, Dark Lord. If we could give him a push, and a little direction…"

Lucifer sat up, tilting his head to the side. "Yes. Kabbus. I nearly forgot about him, but he, like you, dwells in the caves of that dimension. I like this. It has merit."

Beelzebub ignored the jab about living in the caves and bowed his head. "Thank you. I will do whatever I can to see this to a quick end."

Before the demon could turn, Lucifer flung out his arm, pointing his crooked talon at him. "If this goes wrong, it's your ass."

Korbin leaned up against the window's frame, shaking his head at Calvin. "Come look at this craziness."

Calvin walked up, brushing cracker crumbs off his

chest. "Ha. Leave it to Katie and Pandora to put on a show for their troops."

They had a full view of their sparring bout out the window. Korbin smiled. "They did a good job training them."

Calvin strolled over to the window on the adjacent wall. "And you did an excellent job with the fort."

Korbin meandered over, looking at the almost-completed fort in the distance. "It's not there quite yet, but it will be done soon. I can't take all the credit, though. The team has really put in the work."

Calvin sighed. "I thought for sure it would be done by now. Then again, I have really nothing to base that on, considering we built the last one like three times and in a hurry."

Korbin nodded. "Yeah, the French are using a lot higher quality tools and materials to build this wall, ultimately because their budget is bigger. So, it takes a bit more time to secure the wall the proper way. No use in building with all this expensive stuff and having the wall come down the first time a demon blows on it. So yeah, not done yet, but we are getting really close to the finish line."

Korbin walked over to the table, picking up his coffee mug and taking a sip. Calvin turned toward him and crossed his arms. "You look happier doing this than you did leading the teams. Not garden-in-the-middle-of-nowhere happy, but you're happier."

Korbin shrugged. "I don't know if I would say 'happier.' I loved leading the team back then. There was always something going on. Now that I'm older and have a wife and a memory of what normal is like, leading the team sounds like a big hassle to me."

Calvin chuckled. "Yeah. It definitely is that, especially now that we're paired with the military."

Korbin laughed. "Even more paperwork. But yeah, I really like doing this. Now, don't get me wrong, I wish every day that we had been able to beat these demons a long time ago. I wish that building these walls wasn't necessary. But unfortunately, it is. The demons got stronger, and we weren't able to get ahead of them. Since we need the forts, I'm glad I am part of it. I know being on the team and fighting is doing something good for humanity, but there is a lot of bad to it too. With this, I am setting countries up to save lives. That feels really good. Really rewarding, in the end. I just hope the forts all hold up and really help."

Calvin smiled. "Good. It's about damn time you felt good about something you were working on. You always took the negative to heart so bad, I thought you would never recover from it."

The phone rang, and Korbin put his hand on the receiver. "I might not, but at least I can feel proud of the work we are doing in the meantime. The rest will just be ghosts of my past, haunting in the background."

Korbin picked up the receiver and put it to his ear. "This is Korbin."

General Brushwood sounded exhausted. "Korbin. Good to hear your voice. I got some pats on the back from the Council for the good work you've been doing on these forts."

Korbin smiled. "Thanks, but it's not just me, it's the whole team."

The general chuckled. "Well, thanks to all of them. I called to get an update on the French fort. I know this one is taking a bit longer because of the supplies and structural issues, but I figure it should be getting close."

Korbin tapped his fingers on the desk. "For sure. We are definitely getting close. Most of the bunkers are finished. The armory is ready to store the weapons, and the walls are close. We haven't brought the weapons to the armory because there is construction going on around it. We wouldn't want to accidentally blow that section of the fort up because someone fucks up."

Brushwood sighed. "Uh, no. That would be a very bad thing. It's one thing when a demon kills our allies, but if we accidentally killed them with their own ammo? That would warrant a change of plans on your part. Let's try to keep people safe."

Korbin smiled, shaking his head. "Trust me, General. I do not want to have gone all this time, having killed that many demons, and die because of a block falling on a missile. That would not be a hero's death."

The general grumbled, "No, it would not. But I trust you. You've done well so far. Even saved a bunch of lives in that battle at the last incursion. We are getting ready now to plan the next few places to go after you get done in Romania. Every time I go to the council, we receive new requests for forts."

Korbin glanced at the fort over Calvin's shoulder. "They are definitely a must-have right now. They may have to get bigger as the war progresses."

The general grimaced. "Yep. And hopefully, the smaller countries will be able to afford to do them as well. Right now, I have a request from both Russia and Brazil for forts —one ice bowl, and one tropical paradise."

Korbin smirked. "I don't know how many volunteers I'll get for Russia, but I have a feeling we will get Brazil built in a day. Everyone will want to tag along to that one. Still, we'll have to talk to Timothy to get an idea of where incursions are likely to happen next. We want to focus on those places first, then move on to the less-affected areas."

The general agreed. "We already know they are going to target you wherever you go, whether through big incursions or small ones. Either way, you are right; we need to protect the most vulnerable and populated locations first. I'm sure the Council can hash that out among themselves once we get the stats from Timothy. I'd rather have *them* fight it out."

Korbin sighed. "I wish it wasn't an issue."

Brushwood was quiet for a moment. "Me too, Korbin. Me too."

Juntto leaned against the wall in the main room of the gaming convention. People were everywhere, and he was feeling the need for some Hygge and a *Doctor Who* marathon. He had just gotten there, but he couldn't stop watching. It wasn't much of a surprise that he had morphed into his nerdy guy form, not wanting to draw too much attention to himself. Besides, he had decided not to compete in the games anymore. He didn't want to risk the team getting a win taken back because they found out he was Juntto.

The phone in his pocket rang and he pulled it out, looking across the room at Angie with her team. The general spoke when he answered. "Juntto. Where the hell are you? It sounds like you are at a rave or something."

Juntto raised an eyebrow. "I am not sure what this 'rave' is, but I don't think that is where I am. Angie has one of her game competitions today, so I have tagged along. There are a lot of loud noises here."

Brushwood lifted both eyebrows and shook his head. "You guys are into the strangest stuff."

Juntto chuckled. "You don't even know the half of it."

The general frowned. "I don't think I want to know, either."

Juntto laughed. "Don't worry, General. Angie says that having privacy and secrets in a relationship is important. I won't rain our laundry on you."

The general paused. "Oh, you mean, 'Air your dirty laundry?' I appreciate that. But hey, I wanted to call and check in with you. I like to get confirmation on status from my guys-in-waiting. Are you still ready to go whenever I call on you?"

Juntto looked down at his fingernails and then around the room, not seeing a single pair of red eyes. "Sure. I mean, I don't know what is going on with the lack of incursions. They said at the base they have just completely stopped. For me, that's worrisome. If nothing else, I am overprepared to leave on a moment's notice. There has to be something brewing out there that we just aren't seeing."

Brushwood groaned. "I agree. Demons don't just give

up like that. There is more to this than meets the eye. I am glad to know you are ready to go whenever I need you. Thanks for that."

Juntto nodded, looking around again and talking more quietly into the phone. "I even have my Juntto-sized weapons stored in the closet. Angie said not to put them there because one could fall on her, but she never goes into that closet. I wanted them to be easily accessible so that if I needed them in a hurry, it wouldn't be a hassle."

The general laughed. "Be careful. A woman's wrath can be worse than a demon's."

Juntto curled his lip. "Yeah, I felt that when I didn't fold the fitted sheet and just threw it in a ball in the closet. How do you even fold those things, anyway?"

The general laughed loudly. "The secrets us men will never know. I'll keep in touch with you, though. Have fun out there, and try to relax. There will be plenty of fighting in the future."

Juntto hung up and walked through the room, stopping and glancing at the cosplay competition going on. Standing in the middle of the floor, waiting to go on stage, was a kid done up as Juntto.

Juntto laughed and ducked into the side hall, transforming to his normal size and color. As he exited, ducking through the doorway and moving through sideways, the kid looked up, excited. "It's you! Let's get a picture together!"

3

Baal and Beelzebub lounged in the cushioned chairs in Baal's study and stared at the fire, thinking about what Beelzebub had accomplished by going to Lucifer. Baal was surprised, and a bit cautious, but who wouldn't be about a demon like Beelzebub? He was conniving on every level.

Beelzebub stuck his glass out and snapped his fingers, and one of the servants ran over to fill it. He let out a deep breath. "It was that simple. A few compliments, and then showing him that the idea was perfect. Of course, we will have to make sure we follow through on it. We can't drop the ball like so many of your cohorts have done."

Baal rolled his eyes. "You do realize that those guys had no idea what they were doing, right? Anyway, it doesn't matter; we are in charge of this. So what is our plan of attack?"

Beelzebub took a big gulp of his drink. "You need to learn to slow down. It's not like Earth is going anywhere anytime soon. In my many years of being a demon…"

Baal tuned him out, narrowing his eyes at him across the space between them. He was being incredibly cocky, and he didn't seem to care one way or another that Baal had any ideas. He was acting incredibly suspiciously, and Baal could trust nothing that was spewing out of his mouth.

Beelzebub got up and walked over to the fire, still talking. "…and that's how it's done. Anyway, since I was just put back on the council, I've got to use my momentum."

Baal blinked at him, waving his hand at the servant and setting his glass down. He leaned forward, pressing his palms together and tapping his snout. "Okay, so what exactly is their plan? Do they want an incursion over Kabbus' resting place? Do we have a specific location for it?"

Beelzebub turned swiftly to Baal. "You aren't going to give this up. Fine, let's talk about it. No, they do *not* want it over his resting place, and even if they did, it would be a very stupid idea. One wrong move and we would have that beast haunting our lives. Besides, we don't want everyone to know where he is at this point."

Baal nodded. "So more of a diversion tactic that he will sense. How about New York?"

Beelzebub shook his head, taking a drink. "New York is played out."

Baal thought about it. "Maybe Washington, DC?"

Beelzebub stared at him for a moment, a smirk beginning to move across his lips. "Normally I would say that was insane. We have protected Washington in the past because we have so many allies there, but fuck 'em. Hit the humans there. *That* will make a damn statement."

Baal chuckled. "That will make a statement to more than just the people in the US. That will make a statement to every country in the world: we are not afraid to hit them where it hurts."

Beelzebub laughed. "I love your sense of evil. It's so refreshing. Besides, the president of Russia will love it. He's had it in for America forever."

They both chuckled for a moment, then simmered down to a thoughtful quiet. Baal looked up. "So, what kind of demons should we send?"

Beelzebub smiled evilly. "Actually, I started thinking about that before we ever had this conversation. I mean, that is the fun part, isn't it? The crazier the demons, the more ferocious the attack."

Beelzebub put his glass down and turned, opening a portal. He waved to whoever was on the other side. "Well, come on. Don't be pussies. Get your asses in here. Let Baal have a look at you."

Baal stood up and watched closely as demons began moving into the room and formed a line in front of the fireplace. He put his hands on his hips and shook his head. "You have outdone yourself this time, Bee. 'Prepared' is something I never thought you would be, but *damn* if I wasn't completely fucking wrong."

To the far right of the standard-issue beasts were two tiny EMP demons. Beelzebub walked over and leaned down to pet the little Chihuahua-looking beasts. "Our Freaks on a Leash were still out there running around hell. Guess these little bastards slipped away last time."

Baal laughed. "They are very useful. We saw that in the last fight. And as far as I know, we haven't given the humans enough time to come up with protection against this type of thing."

Beelzebub smirked. "But wait, that's not all. Besides our normal hordes of idiot flesh-hungry demons, we also have these."

He waved at the portal, and Baal turned as a rhino carefully trotted through, trying not to mess up the floors with his heavy body. Baal cackled madly, clapping his hands. "Aren't you just adorable!"

Beelzebub put up his finger. "Hold on, not quite done."

Baal turned his head, and his mouth fell open. Four big, mean bastards came stomping through, bent over so as not to hit the ceiling. "I thought we lost all of them to the deep recesses of hell?"

Beelzebub smiled. "Apparently, these four guys survived the attack on the fort and got back through to us. They have been waiting at my cave, but I haven't been there in days."

Baal shook his head and stood up straight, slowly clapping his hands. "Bee, you've really done it this time. You have put the work in, and it shows."

Beelzebub grinned as he opened another portal and showed the demons out. "Stay there. I'll come for you soon. And dammit, corral the dogs. Their teeth hurt."

The portal closed, and Baal crossed his arms. "The only question I have is, what about the fucking angels?"

Beelzebub shrugged. "We'll see what happens when Kabbus is finished with them."

Katie stuck her hands in the pockets of her raincoat. Its collar framed her face, and she also wore a pair of slim black ankle-length pants, a crisp white button-up blouse, and a pair of black flats. Her hair was pulled to the side and tied with an elastic band. She carried a small pack over her shoulder. Pandora was right beside her, wearing a black button-up with four buttons undone and a pair of tight jeans, plus black heels. Her makeup was dark, and her hair had been teased into a high bump in the front. She strode along with her hands in the pockets of her trim peacoat.

They walked down the steps behind the crowds and waited on the platform for their train on the Paris Métro. Katie glanced at Pandora and took a deep breath. "I'm really surprised you're up for a trip to the museums. Figured you would be bitching about there not being enough action."

Pandora shrugged. "To be honest, I just want to see how many of the things in these museums I have touched in my lifetime. I can also point out to you how many of the small statues were actually dildos. You would be shocked."

Katie laughed, shaking her head. "For some reason, I really don't think I would be. Given what I've seen since becoming Damned, nothing surprises me anymore. People are freaks. And here I thought the slutty girls on campus were the wild ones. They wouldn't survive in your world."

Pandora pursed her lips proudly. "Damn straight. I would eat those girls, chew them up, and spit them out. They would never be the same."

Katie wrinkled her nose. "I don't know, they probably wouldn't taste too good. Rode hard and put up wet."

Pandora pulled her jacket closed and smiled. "Girl, that

was my saying for about a century. I kind of chilled out, though. You know, wife shit."

Katie laughed. "I can't even begin to picture you as a wife. That is so strange. Although I suppose you being a wife to Lucifer was a lot like being a wife in the forties. Shut up and take care of the kids."

Pandora rolled her eyes. "Yep, just like it. Oh! I wonder if the museums will have any Atlantean stuff in them?"

Katie furrowed her brow. "You would think not, because they would have no idea where it came from."

Pandora tilted her head from side to side. "Yeah, but maybe they have it and just don't know it belonged to them."

Katie smiled. "Probably not, but we can definitely check it out."

Katie looked to her right and then behind her, clearing her throat. She pulled her hand out and rubbed her chest, feeling a tingling sensation that was spreading to her bones. Pandora glanced at her from the corner of her eye. "What's going on? You getting the vibe?"

Katie cleared her throat a second time, pulling on the collar of her jacket. "Yeah. My angel senses are tingling again. I can feel it. Something isn't right."

Pandora and Katie stood still as the people loaded onto and unloaded from the train. They shifted their eyes right and left, making sure to keep their senses open for anyone that might be trying to come up behind them. They stood there watching as each person passed by, but they didn't see anyone with red eyes or any reason for them to be in danger.

After the passengers had changed places and the train

left, the platform was basically empty. Pandora looked at Katie. "You still feel it? Even with everyone gone?"

Katie nodded, turning around. "Yeah. But not everyone is gone."

Sure enough, walking from the shadows was a group of French guys wearing long black shirts, all with five o'clock shadows, and all darting their eyes back and forth. Pandora stepped up next to Katie. "Why do I feel like I'm either going to get into a gun battle or I am going to sing and dance my way through this fight like *West Side Story?*"

Pandora's comment made Katie choke out a laugh. "Or a mime is going to come out of the shadows and give us a hard time in his beret and striped shirt."

Pandora nodded. "I hate mimes. They are so freaky with their weird glass boxes. A mime comes, and I get to take him the fuck out. Boop! Thrown right in front of a fucking train. Mime *that*, bitch."

Katie shook her head as the guy in the front came closer, tilting his head and smiling at them. He had both hands in his pockets, and his eyes roved up and down their bodies. Pandora pulled her hands out and slowly balled them into fists at her sides. "French men are supposed to be sexy, but this one is on the rape-y side of things."

Katie nodded. "I couldn't agree more."

The guy in the front smiled widely. Katie looked around as a few people came down the steps and stepped to the front, waiting for the train. A kid in noise-canceling headphones stood closest to the guy, flipping through his phone with no clue what was happening around him.

The creepy guy stopped and smirked. "*Amis du diable!*"

He pulled a knife out of his pocket and flipped it open.

As he reached for the kid, Katie stepped in front of him and shook her head. "No, no."

The other guys in the group moved up behind him, pulling out their switchblades and swiping them back and forth. Pandora rolled her eyes and her shoulders, not impressed by them at all. The first guy lunged forward, stabbing under Katie's arm and pushing the knife into the kid's side. The kid dropped to the ground and the guy backed up, laughing loudly.

The group of guys pumped their hands, shouting, "*Amis du diable!*"

The rest of the people backed up against the wall, Pandora stepping in front of them. Katie looked at the guy's knife and smiled. She reached up and tapped her back. The guy looked at her strangely, narrowing his eyes. Katie laughed, slowly letting her coat fall to the ground. On her back was her angelic sword, hidden from the others' view but easy to get in case she needed it.

Pandora laughed. "You never go out without protection. I like it."

Katie nodded at the guy's knife and slowly pulled her sword out and held it in front of her. "That's not a knife. *This* is a knife."

The front guy went to lunge and Katie sprang into action, shifting to the side. She flipped her sword up in the air and caught it by the blade, not cutting her hands. She whipped the hilt of the sword through the air, slamming it into the guy's head. He swayed for a moment, but she lunged toward him, kneeing him hard in the stomach and then punching him in the balls. Grabbing his crotch, he screamed, dropping his knife and falling hard to the ground.

Katie kicked the knife toward Pandora and jumped into the group of guys. She grabbed two of them by the necks and slammed their heads together over and over until they were unconscious. As she dropped them, another ran toward her, but she threw her leg out behind her and kicked him dead in the stomach. He flew back, hitting the wall. Pandora threw the switchblade at him, and it caught his sleeve and pinned him to the wall. He groaned, his head falling forward and his eyes rolling back.

The guy on the ground moaned. "My balls, they are in my belly."

Katie stared at the last guy standing, kicking the first guy in the face as she passed. The guy was nervous, holding his knife with a shaking hand. She walked up to him and put her mouth by his head, breathing heavily on his cheek. "I would let you go, but you don't seem to understand you can't attack people. So...goodnight."

She stood back and smiled as Pandora put him in a chokehold. She covered his mouth and held on as he struggled, finally passing out. Katie hurried over to the kid and nodded at him, looking at the wound. "You'll be okay. The medics are on the way."

Katie looked up at Pandora. "What were they saying? '*Amis du diable*?'"

The kid coughed. "Friends of the devil."

Katie looked at the kid and back at Pandora, who nodded. "He's right. Friends of the devil. Who knows where they got that from? It's probably just another group of crazies who want demons to take over the world.

It was nighttime in DC, but the US Capitol building was still in full swing. With the drama in the country going on and the state of the government, that was becoming the norm. Outside the building and around the corner stood two congressional aides, vaping.

One of the aides blew out his vapor and shook his head. "Man, I tell you right now. I love fucking sausage on my pizza. Sausage, onion, green pepper, and maybe even some mushrooms. Thick crust."

The other guy shrugged. "Definitely doesn't sound bad. What about pineapple?"

The first aide wrinkled his nose and shook his head. "Are you fucking kidding me? That shit does *not* belong on a damn pizza."

The other guy fist bumped him. "You might actually be okay for a liberal. I personally believe that pineapple on pizza is a pure and simple travesty. An abomination."

The first guy nodded. "Okay, I can see how we could get along…away from the media, of course."

The second guy shook his head seriously. "Oh, man, of course. There have to be rules. We can't let people in on the fact that we don't actually hate each other. The country wouldn't know what to do if it knew we might all get along."

They both laughed and turned to walk back to the entrance. Stopping in their tracks, they watched as a giant demon stalked past, its huge feet leaving cracks in the Capitol steps. Right behind him was a rhino demon, swinging its horn and snorting loudly. The two guys looked at each other and screamed, taking off for the building's back entrance.

The time had come; the moment that no one in DC had faced before. Demons had come to Washington, DC and let's just say that they were not fucking around.

The congressional aides pulled two of the guards outside frantically, trying to convince them that there really were demons. The guards laughed and looked around, doing a double-take, their mouths dropping open. Across the mall, on the opposite side of the Reflecting Pool, a rhino demon slammed into the Washington Monument. The base cracked, and the stone split all the way up to the top. To their right, rhino demons raced around the mall, digging up the dirt and slamming into the Smithsonian's buildings.

Sirens wailed wildly as cop cars came to a screeching halt to the right of the Capitol. They climbed out, their guns pointed over their doors, their faces wild with fear. The guards and the two aides turned their heads and watched, stunned, as a large demon stomped forward and let out a loud roar. It leaned down and grabbed what looked like a small Chihuahua in its large hands.

Rearing back, it threw the dog-demon hard, slamming into the cop car. The dog-demon fell to the ground, shook his head, and then exploded. An EMP blast blew out of it, and one by one, the lights went out around the Mall.

4

New York City was lively and wild as usual. The lights were blazing, the nightlife was bumping, and cars were backed up down the streets. You could hear horns blaring for miles and sirens wailing in the background. Inside Angie's place, though, the lights were all out, the sounds were muffled by the thick glass walls, and no one except Angie and Juntto was home. Quiet was the last thing it was inside the condo, though.

Down the halls and through the living room, Angie's high-pitched moans and Juntto's low deep groans echoed. They went on and on, with a few giggles thrown in here and there. Suddenly the moaning stopped dead as Juntto's phone blared *Donkey Kong's Country* song.

Juntto groaned in frustration, fumbling around in the dark. He hit the lamp, knocking it in the floor with a loud crash. Angie fell back on the pillow and sighed, shaking her head. "Just let it ring. We are kind of in the middle of something. Whoever it is, we can call back."

Finally, Juntto got his hands on the phone and looked at

34

the Caller ID. "I can't. I promised I would answer at any time and any place."

Angie sighed again, and Juntto put the phone to his ear. "This Juntto."

The general paused on hearing his labored breathing. "It's General Brushwood. Did I catch you at a bad time?"

Juntto sat down on the bed. "No. Just...uh...working my muscles."

The general paused and then continued, having decided not to ask. "Sorry to call so late, but we have a problem."

Juntto perked up. "What is it?"

Brushwood sighed. "There has been an incursion in DC. They've never had one before, and from the sound of it, these demons are not fucking around. Apparently, the Washington Monument is on the verge of collapsing, and they brought their EMP demons. The lights are out in that area, and the city relies on technology for communication, much of which is near there."

Juntto stood up and tripped across the room, looking for the light switch. "Washington Monument...is that the pencil?"

The general chuckled. "Yes, Juntto. The giant pencil in Washington, DC."

Juntto groaned as he stubbed his toe. "So much for the incursions stopping. I can be ready in ten."

The general was pleased. "There will be a car waiting out front for you. Make sure you are small enough to ride in it. Thanks, Juntto."

As he hung up the phone, he finally found the light switch. He flipped on the lights and squinted, blinking to get used to the bright lights. Angie looked at him with a smirk. He had transformed into a smaller version of a human with dark hair and a chiseled body, and he was wearing what could only be described as a male version of the gold slave bikini Leia wore in *Star Wars*. A chain dangled from one of his wrists, and there were small red marks all over his chest.

Angie sat up in the bed, her hair wild around her and her makeup smeared across her cheeks. Juntto's eyes moved over her, and he smirked. She was dressed—well, half-dressed—in black, with one black glove on her hand. The bed was completely tangled, sheets and blankets everywhere. In her hand she held a green "lightsaber" dildo. She clicked it off and set it down on the bedside table.

With another sigh, she shrugged. "Sometimes this job is a bit too much. We were just getting to the good part. I have to admit, you make a much better Slave Leia than she did in the movie."

Juntto gasped, putting his hand to his chest. "Don't ever let any of the nerds hear you say that. They may create a large fire and sacrifice you to the *Star Wars* gods. They used to do that in my dimension, only to the real gods. It wasn't pretty."

Angie smirked and crawled across the bed to the end. Juntto morphed into the body of Luke Skywalker from *Return of the Jedi*. He sat down on the edge of the bed and put his hands on Angie's face, pressing his lips to hers. She closed her eyes and sighed as he kissed her.

She opened her eyes as he pulled back. "You do not know the power of the Dark Side. I must obey my master."

Angie smiled. "I will not turn, and you will be forced to kill me."

Juntto held back a smile. "I'm sorry all of this happened, but the Force is strong in me, and I have to go where I am needed."

Angie lay back, letting out a deep sigh. Juntto crawled toward her. "Luckily, this *Star Wars* thing has lasted for generations. It will still be here when I get back."

Angie leaned up and kissed him again. "I know. And I know you have to go. I'm not mad at you, I promise. I just really thought for a hot minute we were going to get all the way through some alone-time before something called one of us away. Did you say something about the pencil?"

Juntto nodded. "I did. There is an incursion in Washington, DC. They apparently have destroyed the pencil, and they've let loose an EMP. There are no lights in that area, and most of the technology close to where they set it off is out. Not sure how long it will take for them to get it back. Either way, I am the man for the job, so I have to get there as fast as I can."

Angie reached up, pushing a piece of hair back from Juntto's face. "I know. I am not happy about it, but I understand there is nothing that you can do about it. We will just have to pick up this experiment later. I have to say, I think this might be a successful one to add to our bag of tricks."

Juntto smiled and jumped up. "As long as we don't do that princess and toadstool one again. That one was cool until I saw us in the mirror. You look very strange in a mushroom hat."

Angie laughed. "I have to admit, it wasn't as fun to ride the princess as I thought it might be. Plus, pink isn't really your color, and you are not the frost giant to pull off blond hair."

Juntto changed back into himself, although shorter and less stocky than normal. He hurried over to the closet and retrieved several duffel bags, then pulled out the Juntto-sized weapons, grunting as he put them in the bags.

Angie sat up, narrowing her eyes. "Didn't I tell you not to store those things in the closet?"

Juntto cleared his throat. "Uh, I had nowhere else to put them, and you don't use this closet."

Angie pursed her lips. "Who do you think puts away your clothes?"

Juntto grinned. "I'll find a better place when I get back."

Angie rolled her eyes and crossed her arms. "Mmhmm. Be careful."

Juntto hurried over and gave her a big kiss before grabbing his bag and heading out of the condo. Downstairs, he ran out the front, nodding at a few of the people waiting to catch a rare glimpse of Katie. She was rarely in New York anymore. A car with tinted windows pulled up and Juntto climbed in, lugging his weapons with him. The car went down a couple of inches from the weight.

He closed the door and nodded at the driver. In the passenger seat was an agent, there to brief him. "Your flight will be heading straight to DC. When you arrive, you will be taken directly to the center of the events. Did you bring your weapons?"

Juntto slapped his bags. "Sure did. I have my large machine gun and my spear. I just have to twist the spear together and I'll be ready. I also have some human-sized weapons in case I have to shrink and use them. I don't have an endless supply of bullets for my gun, though."

The agent glanced at the huge bags and raised an eyebrow. "No, I suppose it takes a bit to make bullets that large. So, I am assuming this is not your normal size?"

Juntto laughed. "Not even close. Unfortunately, with the weapons in here, if I show you my true size, I may blow the tires right off of your car."

The guy cleared his throat nervously. "Not necessary; I get the idea. Either way, we will get you loaded in. There is food on the flight for you if you need it, but the flight between the two cities is very short, so it shouldn't take long to get you there. If you need anything else, you can contact General Brushwood."

Juntto nodded and sat back, watching the city speed by. The agent in the front turned back around, and they rode the rest of the way to the airport in silence. When they got there, some of the crew tried to help Juntto with his bags. He turned to find three men grunting as they tried to lift a bag off the ground. Juntto laughed and walked over, grabbing the strap and lifting it without any problem. "Let me help you."

He put it in the cargo hold, the plane creaking as he dropped it in. He brushed off his hands and headed to the stairs, looking back at the agent, who was watching him board. He nodded and headed into the plane, excited to smell the scent of fresh donuts on board. "Oh, good. I could eat a house right now. Being Leia is exhausting."

The room in Paris was dark, only a small candle flickering on the other side of it. The curtains on the windows were pulled shut tightly to keep any light from the city from creeping into the space. Pandora and Katie were still separated, sleeping in their own beds across from each other. Katie slept soundly, her pillow pulled over her head. She had never realized that Pandora was a snorer since she'd usually slept inside of her. Still, the space was nice, so she wasn't going to complain.

Outside, there was very little movement except for the roving watch that passed the apartment building once an hour. They were almost done with their shift since it was very early in the morning, and the next watch came on a couple of hours before everyone else had to report for duty. The ground was frosty from the cold night air, but the wind barely blew at all. It was a beautiful night in Paris, but Katie and Pandora were both happy to be sleeping. They'd had a long day of sparring with each other and the new Damned.

The vibration of Katie's phone on the end table woke Pandora. She grumbled and turned over, staring at the light on the screen. "Katie."

Katie didn't move.

Pandora growled and spoke louder. "Katie!"

Katie groaned, pulling the pillow off her head and slurring her words. "What. Fuck."

Pandora picked up the phone and tossed at her head. "You are being summoned."

Katie took a deep breath and picked up the phone, squinting at the screen, which bore a picture of Angie.

Knowing that Angie wouldn't interrupt her sleep without cause, she quickly answered. "Angie, what's wrong?"

Angie's voice was filled with worry. "There has been an incursion in DC. Juntto just left to catch a flight there."

Katie sat up in bed and clicked on the light. "What?"

Angie turned the volume up on the tv. "I'm watching it right now on the news. Katie, it looks really bad. There is a huge crack in the Washington Monument, and demons everywhere."

Katie looked at Pandora. "The pencil? They got to the pencil?"

Angie sighed. "Really? You call it the pencil too? What are we, twelve years old?"

Katie shook her head, trying to wrap her mind around what was going on. "So, okay. Incursion in the nation's capital. You are saying they are all over the Mall? Like, how all over it?"

Angie watched the scene unfolding. "They are running all over, crashing into the buildings and attacking cars. I mean, holy shit, they are fucking destroying whatever they can. Also, they used an EMP demon and took out the electricity around there."

Katie rubbed her face. "And? I mean, are they going nuts anywhere else? Brushwood hasn't called me. Maybe we should just wait and see what happens."

There was a pause, and Angie's voice started to shake. "It looks like they're in the neighborhoods, too. Spreading through the city. North East, The Navy Yard, Anacostia, and…Adams Morgan too."

Katie shook her head. "Yeah. We can't wait for that. We

can't just let this continue. I'll call you back, okay? Try not to worry."

Angie groaned. "Doing my best."

Katie hung up and looked at Pandora, who had gone back to sleep. She stood up and walked over, shaking her. Pandora snorted and squinted right and left. "What? *What?* Are we fucking or fighting?"

Katie chuckled, pulling on her clothes. "Fighting. And this looks like a good one."

Pandora yawned, sitting up and tucking her tits back into her tank top. "Fine. I can do that before breakfast. But after…"

Katie put her guns in the holsters. "I know."

Pandora leapt out of the bed and threw on her clothes. Katie looked at her and nodded, opening a portal. "Time to kick ass."

Katie and Pandora walked out of the portal into an alternate dimension. Katie grimaced, and Pandora gasped excitedly. The city was absolutely spotless, the buildings gleaming brightly in the light. However, all around them were beautiful, perfect, *naked* people. Katie pulled her hands close to her so as not to brush against anyone.

A man with perfect blond hair, a chiseled body, and long legs walked over to Pandora. "Hello. I couldn't help but notice you. Absolutely breathtaking! Could I possibly take you to dinner and then to bed?"

Pandora blinked at him for a moment and turned

quickly to Katie, grabbing her wrists. "We can stay for just a couple of weeks, right?"

Katie laughed, opening a portal. "Sorry, darlin'. We've got work to do."

Pandora pouted and waved at the guy. "I'll remember you!"

Katie stepped through the portal, with Pandora stomping grumpily behind her. "They have this under control. I don't know why…"

Katie pushed Pandora out of the way and jumped to the side as a rhino blew between them, running at full speed with his head down and his horn pointed straight ahead. It skidded to a stop and turned, its eyes glowing bright red. Immediately it charged back toward them as fast as its huge body could carry it.

Pandora lifted her eyebrows. "Okay, maybe I overestimated their control of the situation."

Katie pulled her gun and raised it, pointing the barrel at the rhino's head. She pulled the trigger and watched the bullet slam through the scales and into its skull. The rhino's pumping legs slowed way down, and its head sank. Finally, it toppled to the ground, sliding all the way to Pandora's and Katie's feet before bursting into ash.

Katie looked at Pandora, and she glared back. "I guess we found the right place. Better take these bitches out before the military does so they can't come back at us again."

Pandora nodded. "Probably a good idea."

She stepped to the side and curled her hands into fists, her body growing taller until she was twelve feet. Katie looked up at her and nodded. "You're getting pretty good at that."

Pandora smiled. "Thanks."

She took off at a run, heading straight for one of the large demons standing in the middle of the Reflecting Pool. As she grew close, she reared her fist back, slamming it into the demon's chin and knocking him into the water hard. Katie chuckled and flared her wings wide behind her. She looked around and pulled her other pistol, now having one in each hand. She beat her wings hard, soaring up in the air as a demon raced toward her.

She flipped over in midair and pointed her guns down, blasting the demon. It roared loudly, swinging its arms, but she was high enough that it couldn't reach her. She laughed, hanging upside down as it stopped and stared up at her. She aimed the gun in her right hand between its eyes, pulling the trigger again. The bullet hit the demon and sped through the skull, lodging in its brain. It looked at her, confused for a moment before falling. Its body turned to ash as it landed.

Pandora picked up the large demon she'd dropped and slammed it down again, stabbing her sword through its neck. As she did, she felt a blast of heat above her. She dove out of the Reflecting Pool and watched as a portal opened above the pool, vomiting demons out of it hand over fist. There were hundreds; thousands even, of all sizes and shapes.

Pandora looked at Katie. "Uh oh. This shit just got real."

While all hell broke loose on DC, Sonora, Texas found itself still in the danger zone. Deep in the woods, inside the dark cave off the hiking path, the walls vibrated wildly. In the darkness, two eyes opened, their bright green lighting up the cave. A creature of smoke and tentacles slowly began to creep from the recesses. As his body writhed beneath the moonlight, Kabbus became a reality. His body was rotund and sloppy, and he slithered along on dozens of tentacles surrounded by black smoke.

The shadow on the cave disappeared as he crawled into the forest, following the hikers' trail.

5

Katie and Pandora wasted no time going to town on the demons infesting Washington. They stood in the middle of the Mall on either side of the Reflecting Pool, blasting and slicing every demon they could get their hands on as they fell from the portal in the sky.

Katie moved to the side, glancing at Pandora as one of the falling demons hit the ground running. It screeched and screamed loudly as it sprinted across the lawn. Pandora, still twelve feet tall, reached down and grabbed the demon by the head. She stepped back, kicked hard, and punted it up and over the Washington Monument. They heard the demon screaming as it disappeared.

Katie nodded her head. "That was a damn good kick. Maybe you should talk to someone about joining the football team."

Pandora shrugged. "I would probably grab too many asses and they would kick me off. Besides, I don't understand the obsession. Men in spandex never did it for me, even if they did have really nice asses. I have a really nice ass, and this is the most spandex I have ever worn."

Katie shrugged. "Looks good on you."

Pandora struck an exaggerated pose. "Likewise, sister."

They both laughed, taking down several charging demons as they did. Pandora looked up at the monument and tilted her head to the side. "Still looks like a dick. Even more so with the crack up through the top. I wonder…if I rub it, will it give me a surprise?"

Katie laughed as she pulled the head off a small demon. "What do you think Congress uses to fuck us?"

Pandora giggled, shaking her huge finger at Katie. "I like you sometimes, you know that? Sometimes you can be a huge pain in my ass, but sometimes I really like you."

Katie raised an eyebrow. "Sometimes, like now, you have a really *huge* ass."

Pandora looked back at her ass. "Does this size make my ass look big?"

Katie shrugged, smiling. Above them, they could hear a plane. They both looked up as someone jumped, growing bigger as he approached the ground. A parachute exploded from his pack, yanking him upward. It was Juntto, and he quickly became annoyed with the parachute. He grew to full size and reached back, tearing the strings off.

He fell flat, belly down, pulling his machine gun around. His spear was strapped to his back. He started blasting the demons, careful not to hit Pandora or Katie. He lit their world up, creating a trail of bullet holes from the base of the Monument through the Reflecting Pool. Demons in all directions screeched and screamed, bursting into dust.

Pandora and Katie joined in as he plummeted toward the grass. Katie flipped backward, pumping her wings to take her higher in the air. She bit her lip as she fired, aiming for anything not caught up in the hailstorm of bullets falling from the sky.

Pandora pulled out her sword, now large enough to accommodate her twelve-foot stature, and swung low, taking the heads off half a dozen demons in one swoop. She slashed again in the other direction, clearing a path in front of her. The demons kept coming, wailing in high-pitched tones that scraped at Katie's ears. She winced, reloading her weapons and firing again for no other reason than to shut them the fuck up.

Pandora looked at Katie. "That sound is so fucking annoying."

Katie nodded as one of her bullets struck a demon in the head. "You're telling me. It's like screaming babies."

Pandora wrinkled her nose. "That's fucking gross. No one likes screaming babies."

Juntto flipped, putting his feet down as he slammed into the ground. His body created a crater in the lawn, and dirt and grass blew up all around him as he stood up, nodding at Pandora and Katie. Pandora rolled her eyes. "Talk about making a cocky entrance. For fuck's sake!"

Juntto grinned and pulled his spear from his back, surging forward as he jammed the blade through several demons at a time. He lifted it and snarled, trying to shake the demons' bodies off. It looked like a giant shish kabob. Finally, they burst into dust and he continued fucking up demons right and left. Ash, dust, and grass blew around the

Mall, and the ground shook as the three battled the demons to the death. Their demons' death.

Katie slashed a demon's throat with her dagger and took flight, heading straight for Pandora. She hovered next to her head, waiting for her to finish another huge blow with her sword. Pandora breathed heavily and glanced at Katie. "This is getting interesting. Where is the backup?"

Katie eyed the abandoned cop cars. "Either hightailing it the hell out of here or in the demon's bellies. Who knows, at this point?"

Pandora rolled her eyes. "Capitol police. They are supposed to be tough."

Katie shrugged. "In their defense, they are trained to take down criminals, not demons. But that's not why I'm hovering. You think we can close that portal with our angel powers? It is never going to stop raining flaming ballsacks if we don't."

Pandora looked over and shrugged. "Shit, let's give it a fuckin' whirl."

Katie nodded. "We have to get a little closer. It's too high to really see the formation from here."

Pandora smiled. "Not a problem. Hey, frost giant!"

Juntto slammed his fist down, crushing a demon, and looked at Pandora. She grinned at him. "Clear us a path, will ya? We gotta get closer to the portal!"

Juntto smiled and nodded happily before pulling out his gun and turning toward the demons that were blocking their path. He opened fire, moving his gun upward as he mowed down the demons. One demon was huge, so Juntto paused, tearing the beast to shreds with his special bullets. He let off the trigger and grinned.

Pandora nodded. "Good work, buddy."

Pandora and Katie flew forward while looking up at the portal. Katie pointed, making an oval with her hands. "You see the edges? They are shimmering."

Pandora nodded. "Yep. Focus on that. Remember, it's not much different than opening; just reverse it."

Katie nodded. "I got it. Use my powers to imagine closing it. It's going to take both of us, though."

Pandora beat her wings, going higher in the air. As she did, she shrank her body back down to Katie's size. Reaching out, Pandora smiled. Katie smiled back, her eyes flashing bright blue as she clasped Pandora's hand. They both shuddered, their chests pushing forward and light rippling around them. They focused, the vibrations of their angel magic rippling from one chest to the other, connecting them and their powers. Their light shone brighter and brighter and Katie clamped her eyes closed, imagining grasping the edges of the portal.

They both screamed as the portal shrank before snapping shut, spraying the lawn with sparks. Pandora and Katie let go, hanging from their wings, their magic keeping them in the air. They both breathed heavily after the light dissipated and they saw nothing but clear night skies where the portal had been.

Juntto cheered, pumping his fist. The demons left on the ground all stopped and looked at each other, completely stunned and shocked. They hadn't even had a chance to try to make it back through. The ones that had fanned out to the neighborhoods started coming back to the Mall to regroup with their fellows and Juntto chuckled, pulling his spear from his back. The special metal shone brightly under the moon, and he let out a battle cry as he charged toward them, ready to finish the mission.

Katie and Pandora were exhausted after cleaning out the remaining demons; they needed some energy to pick them up. They dragged themselves down nine city blocks on 18th Street, took a right on K for two blocks, turned left on N Street NW for another six blocks, then headed down New Hampshire, across Dupont Circle, and a half a block down Connecticut Avenue. When they finally saw the sign for Krispy Kreme, Pandora let out a muffled shriek.

She glared at Katie. "I told you we should have taken a cab."

Katie shrugged. "And miss the beauty of Washington DC? Pfft. You're fine."

They walked through the door, and Pandora groaned. "Great. It looks like it was affected by the EMP all the way out here."

The girl behind the counter smiled and waved. "Yeah, we're waiting for the power to come back on. Everything is kind of at a standstill. If you don't mind eating by candlelight, though…"

She pointed to the seating, where they had lit tea lights at every table. Pandora shrugged. "Well, shit, it's like a dream come true. A romantic date at Krispy Kreme. I'm telling you, if more men did this, they would be snagging bitches right and left."

Katie shook her head, walking up to the counter. "But

then they would have stage-five clingers. No man gets out of a date like that unscathed."

Pandora nodded. "You are too right, my friend."

They looked down at the showcase and wrinkled their noses. The girl behind the counter sighed. "Yeah, sorry about that. We don't get many people in this late, so we were just getting ready to start the new batch of donuts when the power went out. They are about a day old, but I won't charge you for them."

Katie smiled kindly. "Not your fault. We'll take four of the chocolate glazed."

That sat down at one of the tables by the window and Katie pushed two donuts across to Pandora, who sneered. "Just two? That's a total cock tease."

Katie shrugged. "Hey, it's something right now."

Just then a Humvee pulled up out front and Katie and Pandora watched, exhausted, as General Brushwood stepped out, nodding at them through the glass. He walked inside, taking off his hat and putting it under his arm. "I figured I would find you two at the closest Krispy Kreme. It's very romantic in here."

Pandora scoffed. "Don't get all sentimental on us, General. What are you doing here, anyway?"

He rolled his eyes. "Politics. I gotta make sure that the powers that be are all okay."

Katie smiled. "And?"

The general shrugged. "Well, the first thing I did was call Timothy. You know, he usually has the answers for all of this."

Katie laughed. "He did, didn't he?"

Brushwood smirked. "Of course he did. He went ahead

and sent some general directions over for how to handle the initial electrical issues, and he's currently writing up a plan for the more secretive locations and places that store sensitive data to get up and running. He is in contact with all of them at this point. Much easier than going through me."

Pandora shook her head. "It just baffles me that humans rely so heavily on these technologies but have no way to prevent the very weapons they create. I mean, they didn't create a demon, but they have EMPs. I don't know, I guess this was all a bit of a surprise."

The general sat down. "You're telling me! But my question is, why now? We went all this time with no incursions or demon attacks. So why now, out of the blue?"

Katie shook her head, wiping her mouth. "That's a really good question. It took me by surprise too, but it could very well have something to do with the remaining Leviathans. They are looking for a way in at any cost, and the Leviathans, if they can control them, could be it."

He sat back. "But they've been here this whole time. It's not like they just dropped in now."

Pandora swallowed her second donut. "Yeah, but right now, they are starting to wake up. I'm pretty sure it's got something to do with all the demonic energy coursing through this dimension. That has a profound effect on those things."

The general rubbed his face. "The big problem is, they are all so different. Even Doctor Thorough is struggling. He hasn't been able to track the last few Leviathans. They are an enigma to him. We are trying to work with things we know nothing about."

Pandora nodded. "That are not of this world."

Brushwood sighed. "Exactly. From what the doctor tells me, they apparently all have had different genetic structures, and he assumes the remaining ones do as well. In order to track them, we would have to have some idea of what they are."

Pandora shook her head. "I can't help you there."

He nodded and stood up. "Well, I figured that. Either way, I would like you two to be on standby with Juntto. I don't want to find us having a repeat with only him here trying to take them out. That could be the end of him, and of the city."

Kabbus made little sound as he moved through the woods to the edge of the forest. His tentacles writhed wildly as he peered around. Over the hill, he could see a sea of lights belonging to the closest town. He moved forward, smoke enveloping the world around him.

Down in the town, the people were either in bed or getting ready for it. In a small house on the edge of town, a mother squatted between two double beds, holding each of her twin girls' hands. "It's time for sleep. You have a big day tomorrow, so we can't be up all night. I read you a story; actually two, because you are sneaky."

The girls both pulled their blankets up. The mother rubbed her hand over one girl's forehead and then the other's. "It's the middle of the night, girls. It's time to shut your eyes."

One of the little girls reached out and grabbed her mother's hand, glancing at her sister. "But we're scared."

Her mother tilted her head. "Why? It's the same old house, the same old room, and the same old moon you've always had."

The other sister shook her head. "We've been having terrible nightmares. The same ones."

Her mother sighed. "Now, that is just not possible. You are two different people. You must have told each other about your dreams, and now they are frightening you. They are just nightmares. They aren't real."

The first little girl shook her head, tears in her eyes. She clutched her mother's hands tightly. "But these dreams are so *real*, and we had them at the same time."

The other sister nodded wildly. "It's true. There is a monster, and it's trying to poke out our eyes."

The first sister shivered. "It *does* poke out our eyes, Mom."

The mother stood up, leaning over and kissing both of the girls on the forehead. She pulled the blankets up to their chins and shook her head. "That is just nonsense. There are no monsters. Now, I'm going to my room. You two shut your eyes and go to sleep."

The girls tried to argue, but their mother shut off the light and closed the door behind her, shaking her head. She walked to her bedroom and flipped off the light, climbing back into her bed. She sighed and turned on her side, watching for a moment to make sure the girls didn't turn the lights back on. Slowly her eyes closed, sleep overtaking her body.

Out of nowhere screams erupted, echoing through the

house and through her head. The mother gasped, sitting straight up in the bed and clutching the covers to her chest. She blinked, looking in the doorway. Standing there were her two daughters, shadows shrouding their bodies.

The mother let out a sigh and turned on the light. "You two need to…"

She stared at them in shock as their eyes lit up. The eye sockets were empty and bloody. She covered her mouth, muffling a scream, and jumped from the bed. The girls left, slamming the door behind them and running down the hall.

The mother crept to the door and slowly turned the knob, her heart racing as she creaked it open. She slapped her hand against the wall and flipped on the hall light, but there was no one there. The sound of her daughters giggling faintly wafted from their bedroom. She clutched the front of her nightgown and swallowed hard, carefully creeping down the hall.

She collected herself and threw open the door, flicking on the light. The girls were there, fast asleep in their beds. She walked over to them and looked down; there was nothing wrong with their eyes.

Outside their home, slinking past the houses in the neighborhood, crept Kabbus. As he passed each home, the lights would suddenly flicker on and screaming would erupt. People all over the small sleepy town were awakening from nightmares that seemed all too real.

6

———————

Korbin walked along the wall of the fort, examining the construction completed the day before. The soldiers and workers were just getting up and heading to chow, not having to report for another hour or so. Korbin couldn't rest, though. He had woken several times through the night, a fearful feeling in his chest but with no memory of the dream he was shooting awake from. By four, he had gotten up and slowly made his way to the site.

Someone walked up behind Korbin and put his hand on his shoulder. Korbin jumped, turning around and grabbing his chest. "Soldier, you scared me."

The soldier nodded. "Apologies, sir. I came to bring you news of the incursion."

Korbin tilted his head to the side. "What incursion?"

The soldier stared at him for a moment. "Demons attacked Washington, DC. They did a lot of damage, but few people were killed. Katie, Juntto, and Pandora were there to rectify the situation. Either way, it looks like the demons are active again."

Korbin sighed and nodded. "Thank you."

The soldier left and Korbin jumped in the Jeep, heading back to the apartments. Calvin was up and getting ready for the day. "Why are you here so early, and why do you look like you saw a ghost?"

Korbin sat down at the table and Calvin plopped into a chair across from him. "There was an incursion in DC. Only a few lives lost, lots of damage, EMP from what I just heard, but the crew took care of them."

Calvin rubbed his face. "That means they are back in action."

Korbin nodded. "Romania isn't ready for us. They don't have the money for the whole thing yet. We need to figure out where to go instead."

Calvin shook his head. "Right. There is no time to waste waiting for a country to be ready. We need to go where we can knock the fort out and keep moving. Russia and Brazil are two options, right?"

Korbin thought about it for a moment. "Yeah. Either can be ready within forty-eight hours for us to start their forts. Personally, I am leaning toward Brazil."

Calvin agreed. "They are smaller and need the protection more than Russia. Then we can roll to Romania and back to wherever we should go next in Russia."

Korbin sighed. "Yeah. They don't have much in South America. It would be a good idea to have a fort down there and a team of Damned to help them any way they can."

Korbin leaned back in the chair and tilted his head back, looking at the ceiling. Calvin stared at him for a moment, taking in his appearance for the first time since he had gotten there. He couldn't help but notice just how exhausted Korbin looked. He had bags under his eyes, and they no longer shimmered with determination when he talked about things.

Calvin pursed his lips and tapped his fingers on the table. "There is no hiding it, dude—you look absolutely exhausted. Don't try to deny it. You have been going nonstop for months now. You are the only one out of all of us who has not taken a break, except maybe Katie, but she has superpowers. On top of that, you haven't seen your wife for a really long time, and I now know from experience that that can weigh on you more than anything else."

Korbin chuckled. "It's funny how when you are single, you can keep going like nothing in the world could stop you. Become one with another person, and it's almost like when you are away from them, you only have half of yourself."

Calvin smiled, looking down at the table. "It *is* funny how that works. I feel that way constantly. I feel recharged and whole when she is with me, then I go somewhere alone, and it's almost instantaneous that I no longer feel like I can take care of my own head. Personally—and I know you might want to fight me on this—I think you need to take a break."

Korbin looked out the window at the fort and wrinkled his forehead. Before he could say anything against it, Calvin put up his hands. "I know you will say you can't. I know you; that is your nature. But think about it this way: you can only keep going like this for a short time. What if you are like this and we have an incursion? Can you imagine fighting for your life right now when you can barely open your eyes?"

Korbin looked at him, then his eyes shifted down to the table. "I won't argue about being exhausted. I can't. It's written all over everything I am doing right now. But we are in the middle of a build…"

Calvin smiled. "I know, and I'm not saying abandon it. The Paris fort is going to be up and running very soon, and I promise you, they have this under control. They laid the last stone last night. It's all cleanup and setup, and they have been trained on that. Before we leave and jump head-first into the fort in Brazil, why not take some R&R? I know for damn sure Stephanie would love to see you. You both need a reminder of what the hell we are fighting for."

Korbin let out a long deep breath and put his hands on the table. "I think it's the best damn idea you've ever had, and even though I want to fight you on it, I don't think I physically have it in me."

Calvin laughed. "So *that* is the secret to getting what I want! Just wear you the hell out."

Katie put down the black card. "Thanks to the sharing economy, I can now make money renting out my… Jack, you go first."

Jack, one of the Krispy Kreme employees, bit the side of his mouth, looking down at his cards. He pulled one from the deck and set it down. "Thanks to the sharing economy, I can now make money renting out my…foreskin."

Pandora and Katie grimaced. Katie shook her head. "I will not be renting your foreskin."

Pandora laughed, pulling out a card and laying it down.

"Thanks to the sharing economy, I can now make money renting out my…anal beads."

Katie wrinkled her nose. "Also not very hygienic."

Jack laughed loudly, shaking his head. "What you got?"

Katie snickered and laid down a card. "Thanks to the sharing economy, I can now make money renting out my…inner demon."

Pandora gasped. "How dare you! *I* am the pimp in this relationship!"

Katie shook her head. "Not when I gots to pay the bills, bitch. Ante up, or you're getting the pimp hand."

Everyone laughed, looking at the cards on the table. Katie took a deep breath as Juntto walked in the door. "Hey there, Frosty. We were wondering when you were going to show."

He shrank and sat down in a chair, nodding at Jack, who was eyeing him fearfully. "Had to chase a demon off the lawn of the White House. Wrestled him down and speared him as the Secret Service came out."

Pandora snickered. "You can rent me to *them*."

Katie rolled her eyes. "Well, no lights on yet, but we have old donuts, candlelight, and Cards Against Humanity. Right now, we are voting on who has the best thing to rent out. Foreskin, Anal Beads, or My Inner Demon."

Juntto shook his head. "I don't understand foreskin. We are not born with a hood for our warriors. We come out swinging."

Jack looked at his watch and sighed. "At least I only have another hour of my shift. Not sure if the next people will show up, though. I doubt the Metro is running, and you won't find many Krispy Kreme employees hoofing or biking it to work."

Katie groaned, leaning back. "It is taking forever to get these lights back on, but I guess it should. That EMP did some real damage to your systems."

Pandora looked at the conveyer belt. "Krispy Kreme should have generators. Gas-powered ones. How are we supposed to live in a world without Hot and Ready? It is inhumane of the company to think we can."

Jack chuckled. "You could always rent out your anal beads and go get us one."

Pandora stood up, reaching into her pocket. Katie put out her hand and shook her head. "Please, please. For all the holiness in the world, don't tell me you have anal beads in your pocket?"

Pandora laughed. "No, but I've carried worse things."

Katie grimaced as she reached into her bag, pulling out her vibrating phone. She held it to her ear, staring Pandora down. "Hey there, Calvin. You always call at the right time. You kept us from hearing about things worse than anal beads that Pandora might have in her pocket."

Calvin laughed. "Oh, lord, I want to be a fly on the wall for that conversation. I can only imagine what kind of weird-ass shit she keeps in there. Freak."

Pandora yelled, "I can hear you, black man. Watch it, or I'll come for you."

Calvin chuckled. "I think I've had enough people-demons coming for me lately, and I don't mean that in an exciting way."

Katie smiled. "So, what's up? You calling to keep me company in the blackout?"

Calvin groaned. "I heard about that. You guys okay?"

Katie glanced around at everyone. "Oh, yeah. Me, Juntto, Pandora, and Jack—we're just chilling."

Calvin paused. "'Jack?'"

Katie shook her head. "Just a friend. What's up?"

Calvin took a deep breath. "Korbin and I are heading back to the base. Well, me, Korbin, and everyone else who belongs there. We really need some rest, and Korbin needs to see Stephanie before she starts looking for a replacement."

Katie laughed. "She would never. Now, coming over there and dragging him back by his balls, maybe. Everyone knows Korbin is not replaceable."

Calvin smiled. "True. I just wanted to let you know what's up."

Katie glanced at Pandora, who looked hopeful. "Yeah, no. That sounds awesome. Pandora and I are on call, but since we can travel by chimney flue, we'll jump on the plane with you guys in New York. Just make sure the pilot touches down there and we'll join you."

Calvin agreed. "Sounds good. I know Brock will be happy to see ya."

Katie blushed. "Yeah, well, I think Timothy will be even happier."

Calvin laughed, and they hung up. Katie hadn't even thought of reuniting until that moment, and she glanced at Pandora to see if she'd noticed. Of course, she had; the angel-demon was scowling at her from across the table. Katie rolled her eyes and looked at Juntto.

He was still staring down at the cards with a look of disgust on his face. "I think I would go with inner demon.

That might be more useful than someone's foreskin or anal beads."

Pandora scoffed. "You think that, but you've never been treated to my anal beads."

Juntto grimaced. "And I never will. Unless they pay the bills, answer the phone, and do paperwork, I would never even consider it."

Katie burst out laughing and grabbed Juntto's arm. "Sorry, Jack. I wish we could say we aren't always like this, but we are."

He shrugged. "You're not much different than my friends."

Pandora nodded. "They sound like good people."

Katie looked at Juntto. "We're going to head to the base."

Juntto stretched his arms. "I'll stay on this side of the country just in case."

Katie stood up. "Good. You need me, call me. We'll hop a portal and roll to you."

Korbin and Calvin entered the plane, putting their bags in the overhead compartments. They took seats across from each other, letting out simultaneous sighs of relief as they looked out the windows at Paris. Korbin had talked to the government, and they were more than comfortable with them leaving. He didn't need to be told twice. They were only in the plane for a few minutes before they latched it up and headed out, taking off smoothly.

They sat silently watching out the window as they

climbed. The stewardess came over, bringing a bottle of bourbon and two glasses. "I was told by Katie that the two of you might need this."

They laughed and thanked her. Korbin opened it and poured them each a glass. He lifted his up in the air and tapped Calvin's. "This is going to be a long flight, but at least we have bourbon to pass the time."

Calvin chuckled, clinking back. "Hell, yeah, we do. It's been a while since we've been able to relax."

Korbin took a sip and laughed. "I think that's why I love flying so much. No matter what is going down on the surface, there is nothing we can do until the plane touches down. It's pretty much forcing us to take a breather and relax."

Calvin nodded. "Amen to that. I don't know how many times I wished the plane ride was a little longer. Usually when I'm headed to an assignment, though, not heading home."

They sat there quietly for a moment, and then Calvin glanced at Korbin. He wanted to have a heart-to-heart and had been waiting for the right time. He couldn't really think of a better one. "I want you to know something, Korbin. I really believe in what you and the general are doing—putting forts all over the world, protecting all these people, and giving them some sort of chance for survival. It's really selfless of you guys."

Korbin smiled. "We are fighting for all of humanity, not just our own lives."

Calvin grinned, nodding his head. "I agree, but I do have a concern. As much as I have always loved putting the rest of the world before me, I do have to start thinking about the people I've brought into my life. I have a baby on the way, and although I've known it this whole time, it really didn't hit me until I saw that little belly on my wife. There is a child in there who will depend on me, at least partially, for its life and everything that comes with it."

Korbin let out a long, deep breath. "I know, man. I want you to be honest. What do you want to do?"

Calvin looked out the window and back at Korbin. "Honestly? I want to stay at the base with my wife. I want to be there for her and for this baby. At the same time, though, I don't want to leave you hanging or cause anyone to be unsafe."

Korbin reached across and squeezed Calvin's shoulder. "Trust me…if anyone understands, it's me. I might not have any kids, but I have a wife who I used to have a normal life with. If Katie hadn't done what she did, I would have never pulled the plug, and that would have been a huge mistake. Let's get back, and we can figure it all out there. We'll work something out."

The guys sat there for a while talking about nothing, really; just shooting the shit. After a few more bourbons, though, both of them could feel their eyes closing. They pulled the blankets out and curled up, quickly falling asleep. Paris had been amazing, but Korbin and Calvin were absolutely exhausted.

The two guys slept for a really long time, the flight attendant coming through and closing all the blinds. The lights in the cabin were dimmed, and the only sound was the humming of the engines as they soared toward home.

"Let's get drunk, bitches!" Pandora's voice rang out.

Korbin and Calvin sat bolt upright, wiping the drool

from their chins and looking around in a daze. Calvin looked out the window in shock. "Holy shit, we just slept from a little ways outside Paris to New York City."

Katie stepped into the cabin and smiled. "Then you obviously needed the sleep. I feel you there. Unfortunately, blackouts and politics refuse to let me sleep."

Calvin and Korbin stood up to greet them. Katie hugged them both, Pandora following behind her. Pandora gave Korbin a quick hug and a nod, then turned to Calvin, pulling him in. She hugged him tightly, hanging on for just a little too long.

Calvin glanced at Katie, straining as Pandora squeezed him. "I'm a married man. Just a reminder."

Pandora scoffed, leaning back and looking him up and down. "You're packing dong enough for a couple of sister-wives. We can head out to Utah and hook it up. Then your wife would never be lonely."

Calvin laughed. "I don't think she would be down for that, and I am not crazy enough to take on two women. I am good with just one. I don't know about you being out of Katie as much as you are."

Pandora sneered. "Oh, because I'm a unique individual with agency and shit? Why do strong women intimidate you, Calvin? Check your privilege."

Calvin blinked at her. "You just groped and harassed *me.*"

Pandora patted Calvin's ass as she scooted past him. "You're right. Sorry, sweetheart."

Calvin shook his head and let out a deep sigh of frustration. "That's not... I mean, I guess it's a start."

7

Brock stood in front of a group of soldiers who were smoking. "Does it look like taking a break right now is an option? Those fucking crates are not going to move themselves, so unless you want me to use your faces to move them, I suggest you get your asses moving. *NOW!*"

The soldiers threw down their cigarettes and took off in all directions, picking up anything they found in their way. Brock found Turner laying into a couple of newbies. "You are on my base, motherfuckers. We are not playing around. This place better look like it just got cleaned by the mouth of a fucking virgin by the time you are done. And if you ever open your eye holes that wide at me again, I'll make sure you are seeing nothing but my fist coming at your skull. MOVE!"

The newbies ran off, looking like they were about to piss their pants. Turner turned to Brock and grinned from ear to ear. "Sometimes you got to scare them into doing shit. It's the only way."

Brock chuckled, putting his hands on his hips and

looking around the base. "I know this is all a process, and I know that we have been doing a hell of a job out here, but I want this place in tip-top shape for when Korbin gets here. Not only is he a hardass when it comes to stuff like this, but he deserves to come back to a little organization, peace, and quiet."

Turner patted him hard on the back. "Shit, brother, you don't have to tell me that. He is a veteran. He is a badass who will be doing this shit until he dies. He deserves top-notch organization when he gets here."

Brock nodded. "Damn right he does, and we are going to make sure that when he steps off that plane, he doesn't side-eye anything out here. If I were him, and hopefully one day I will be, I would expect the same out of the people I work with and who work for me."

Turner glanced at a group of soldiers who were moving slowly. "I'm going to go bust their asses."

Brock laughed. "All right, man. I'm gonna go check on Stephanie; see what she's up to."

Turner took off in one direction as Brock slowly began to walk toward the main barracks. The wind was whipping pretty strongly that day, but they had put up barriers to try to keep the sand blow low. They seemed to be working pretty well. As he approached the building, he found Stephanie on her knees in front of her little desert garden. She was smoothing the beds down and watering them, and admiring the tiny little sprouts poking up.

Brock came up next to her. "Those are growing fast. Glad we put in the raised beds. They wouldn't have been the same in the greenhouse."

Stephanie smiled. "Just hope they make it."

Brock looked around. "Can I do anything for you?"

Stephanie chuckled, leaning back on her heels. "Not unless you can speed up time and get the plane here a little faster."

While everyone else worked hard, Eddie had slipped away to try to get some target practice in. He had put his team to work cleaning up the armory and polishing the gear. With Coco in him now, he figured he could get some work done on his shooting. The little guy was kind of annoying, but in the back of Eddie's mind, he knew it was mostly because when they argued, the little demon was usually right. Nonetheless, he helped Eddie aim and gave him a lot more strength then he'd expected.

Eddie laid down in the sand with his rifle, propping it on the stand. With no walls on the range, he had to use his stand, not usually liking it because it tended to wobble. He put his eye to the scope and looked through, aiming at the target. Coco stayed quiet, letting him concentrate. Eddie took a deep breath and slowly breathed out as he squeezed the trigger.

He took recoil into his shoulder and lifted his head, looking down the range. He had completely missed the target. The bullet had sped past and lodged in one of the wooden beams that held up the shelter from the sand. Eddie growled and sat up, shaking his head. "That's fucking terrible. I can't shoot the target even *without* the sand blowing in my fucking face."

Coco cleared his throat. *Now, I know you aren't big on*

people telling you anything, but I can help. That's what I'm here for. I could fix your aim, but that would be dumb. If you can do it on your own, then I come in and fix any small shifts you might need. That way we are working together on this and not taking the heavy.

Eddie clenched his teeth. *All right. What, in your opinion, is my problem? I assume it has something to do with the stand.*

Coco flinched. *I wouldn't say that. I would say it's more due to the fact that you are aiming high left.*

Eddie looked at the gun and then at the target, shaking his head. *Bullshit. My aim is dead on. I got it in the crosshairs, then, when I pull the trigger, it is completely off.*

Coco groaned. *Okay, so that time may have been a fluke. But the rest of the time, when you hit the target, you aren't dead on. You aren't hitting the bullseye. You know just as well as I do that that can mean taking down a demon or having it take you down.*

Eddie huffed, laid down again, and put his eye to the scope, moving the gun down and to the right. *Fine.*

He let out a deep breath and pulled the trigger. When he looked up, his face went flat. He had hit the target right in the bullseye. Eddie sat up and pulled his ball cap off, wiping his forehead. *All right, I guess you were right. I'm sorry for doubting you.*

Coco didn't make a big deal about it. *Hey, I understand. You don't have much faith in me since I'm a demon. It's not like I haven't experienced it before. In here I can talk better; get my words out better. Out there, I came off as a cute little demon with a small vocabulary. People treated me like I was an idiot.*

Eddie shrugged. *I guess that sucks. I can kind of relate since*

I am not the most intelligent person. I make up for it with brawn and tactics.

Coco chuckled. *You are a badass. You can say it.*

Eddie smiled. *So, tell me about you, Coco. I know you're a demon, but I have come to understand that demons have their own personalities, likes and dislikes, and ways of handling the world. Much like humans, but we tend to have a moral compass and compassion.*

Coco laughed. *True. Humans are fragile-hearted creatures, to say the least. Let's see. I'm pretty simple. My favorite food is burgers. I like all burgers, especially with melty cheese, mushrooms, mayo, and a fried egg. Mmm, delicious. Makes me want one right now.*

Eddie rubbed his stomach. *And apparently, that makes me want one too. When the day is over, we'll get a burger if we can.*

Coco was excited by that prospect and kept talking. *Let's see, what else? Oh, I like movies and shows, too. I like that show Deadwood. You know, the one where they curse all the time and the scenery never changes? That's a good one. And my other favorite is Paw Patrol. They never cuss in that one.*

Eddie furrowed his brow. *Uh... Paw Patrol? The kids' show?*

Coco cackled. *Mmhmm. I like puppies, especially when they are super furry and they run up and lick you in the face. I was stuck in a kid one time, not meaning to be. Well, he watched a lot of shows like that. He also had a puppy, Howie. He was a husky, a baby one. I miss him.*

Eddie was curious. *What happened to the kid?*

Coco sighed. *There was some Damned priest who exorcised me and sent me back to hell. I came back, but the kid is grown up now. Oh! You know what you should get? You should get a* Paw Patrol *tattoo on your arm. That would be amazing!*

Eddie chuckled. *Uh, we might have to discuss that one. That might fuck me up with the other guys.*

Coco went quiet for a minute. *Eddie, I have something to tell you. Something that I've been holding back, but now I know I can't wait. It's really important.*

Timothy sighed as he put his feet up on the desk. He sneered, leaning forward and rubbing a scuff from the top of his shoe. "Three-hundred-dollar loafers and I can't keep them clean. You would think I was one of those soldiers running all around the base."

Sean smirked, rolling his chair across the dungeon and typing something into the computer. "You should just walk around in those little hospital booties. Then you wouldn't have to worry about it."

Timothy gasped, putting his feet down. "I would rather die. Are you seeing anything on those stats over there?"

Sean looked at the screen, squinting as he moved the picture over. "No, nothing. I thought for sure it was revving back up again."

Timothy shook his head. "I just don't get what is going on. No incursions forever, then one huge one in Washington DC, then nothing again. Incursions are becoming more rare than regular. That alone gives me cause to worry."

Sean smirked. "You worry about everything, so I wouldn't go calling the National Guard yet. It does suck;

not on a deadly scale, of course. But when they are rare, you have no idea when to expect them. At least before, we knew it could be any moment. We were on our game all the time."

Timothy shrugged. "There is obviously something going on, but without a telescope allowing us to observe hell, I don't think we'll actually figure it out. Not that I want to look down there. Too hot for me. I don't do well with sweat."

Sean laughed. "Yet you live and work in the desert."

Timothy pursed his lips. "It didn't start out as my damn choice, but after I got here and became family, well… I didn't really have a choice, now, did I?"

Sean looked at him with a smile. "No, I guess not. I am feeling that whole thing as we speak. Wasn't my choice to be Damned or wheelchair bound and stuck in the dust, but now that I have a family, I don't think I could let it go."

The phone rang and Timothy winked at Sean, putting it to his ear. "Timothy here."

Doctor Thorough was nervous as always. "Timothy, glad you answered. I have been buried in my paperwork and research for days. One minute I think I have an answer, the next I am thrown off the rails again."

Timothy sat there staring at his nails, waiting for the doctor to calm down and get to the point. It had become a regular occurrence. When he finally took a deep breath, Timothy cleared his throat. "And how can I help you on this, doc? You need stats from me?"

He sighed. "No, I need a second set of eyes. Third, really, after Alice. I want to send my stats over to you and see if you can make heads or tail of them."

Timothy sat up, surprised. "Oh. Okay, well, I can give it my best shot. Why don't you start by telling me exactly what we are talking about here? Stats for what?"

The doctor took a long, deep breath. "Well, since the Leviathans have been coming forth, I have managed to extract specimens from them to study. I have some from Juntto, Teyollucuani, and Tiamat. I used those specimens to start collecting data and information about the different Leviathans. We ran a multitude of tests, compounded the results, and compared the three of them to find any similarities, although that turned out to be rare. At this point, I feel like there are no more observations I can take from these three samples. I have exhausted my resources."

Timothy raised an eyebrow. "What about Baylahn?"

The doctor groaned. "If only they could have brought something back. They were unable to get a sample from inside. The sub, having been docked within the belly of the beast, most likely would have brought back miniscule samples, but that was destroyed. Unfortunately, we didn't get anything from him."

Timothy pouted. "That's a shame."

The doctor scoffed. "You're telling me! That was one of the strangest Leviathans I have seen so far. No to mention the fact that from the stories they told, he holds another civilization within him. Of course, that could have also been some sort of hallucination from the chemicals within him, but we will never know. Getting a sample now would be too risky, and the Leviathan is constantly circling, with no real indication of changing that. I suppose we have time."

Timothy listened to him closely, glancing at Sean, who

chuckled since he had gotten stuck one time on a call with Thorough. The doctor had a tendency to veer off-track in his monologue, and it was more than a little frustrating. Nonetheless, his work was necessary, if only Timothy could figure out what its purpose was.

He cleared his throat, slightly cutting the doctor off. "I'm sorry. So you have samples of the Leviathans, and you would like me to take a look at them. You know I am not a scientist, right? I don't think I will be making any new discoveries."

Doctor Thorough put himself back on track. "Oh, no. No, I don't need you to look at it for that. We are trying to figure out a way to track the Leviathans. To pinpoint exactly where the remaining ones are."

Timothy tilted his head back. "Ohhhh. Okay, I get it. Right. So you want me to use my system knowledge to see if there is something in your results that will help us create a tracking system?"

The doctor let out a puff of air. "Precisely. They're still on Earth somewhere; we know this. Or at least, we are being told this. I guess we really have no perfect way of telling. Either way, we need a way to find them before they wake up on their own."

***

Stephanie crossed her arms over her chest and bobbed up and down on her tiptoes. The wind blew wildly and she put her hand up, blocking the sand from blowing into her eyes. She had been standing there since the radar had picked up the signal from the incoming plane. She was more than excited to see Korbin again.

The plane touched down, bouncing on the landing gear as it slowed. Eddie came up next to her, his eyes narrowed, hands clenched tightly together. Stephanie glanced at him, frowning at his worried look. "What's the matter? They're finally home."

Eddie took a deep breath and forced a small smile, eyeing Stephanie. "No, yeah, that's really exciting. I am stoked for you. Uh, nothing is wrong. I just need to talk to Calvin as soon as I can."

Stephanie nodded, giving him a side-eye. "Okay. You sure you're okay? I'm not used to you looking so…serious and determined."

Eddie forced another smile and relaxed his shoulders. "Yep. Just need to talk with Calvin. Nothing to worry about."

Brock stepped up behind them and put his hands on their shoulders. "The team is back together again. How about that?"

The plane came to a stop and they stepped closer, waiting for the side door to open. When it did, they all smiled, waving as the steps were brought over and Korbin emerged. He walked quickly down the steps as Stephanie took off across the runway. Meeting in the middle, she leapt into his arms, pressing her lips to his and not letting go.

Brock chuckled as he watched them, and looked up as Katie came down the stairs, her eyes trained on him. He smirked and went forward, not sure what to expect. She walked straight up to him, dropped her bag on the ground, and wrapped her arms around his neck, laying a huge kiss on his lips.

As Calvin emerged, he looked around, shaking his head with a laugh. He had to admit he wished his wife was there to greet him, but he'd had more time with her recently than any of them had so he couldn't be too disappointed. As he reached the bottom step, Eddie jogged toward him, nodding.

Calvin lifted his eyebrow, leaning back just a bit. "You're not gonna kiss me, right?"

Eddie chuckled, shaking his head. "No, but can we talk? It's very important."

Calvin and Eddie walked away as Pandora stepped into the doorway, putting her arms out, waiting for her welcome. As she looked around, she walked down the steps, pouting at all the couples locked together on the runway. She stopped at the bottom and dropped her bag.

Stomping her foot, she leaned her head back in agony. "Don't I get somebody?"

She looked around, then thrust her arm out and pointed at a random worker on the airfield. "You. Come here. Give me a hug, and make it a good one."

The worker glanced around and strode forward, putting his arms out. Pandora stopped him for a moment. "And tell me how much you missed me."

The guy looked at her, slightly confused. "I don't really know you."

Pandora grabbed him, yanking him in and hugging him tightly. "Say it anyway, butt-munch. And be sweet about it."

He hugged her tightly. "I missed you, Pandora."

She sighed and laid her head on his shoulder with a smile.

8

Calvin opened the door to his old room and stepped to the side, letting Eddie walk through in front of him. He didn't like how nervous Eddie was; it reminded him of when he was told that his wife had been infected by a demon. They went over to a small table with chairs and sat down.

Calvin looked at Eddie, who was clenching his hands tightly in front of him. "What's going on, dude? You look like you are about to drop some seriously bad news on me. I think you should take a deep breath first, okay?"

Eddie nodded, breathing in deeply and slowly letting it out. His shoulders relaxed a bit. "So, you know that Coco, my demon, is also the same one that infected Sofia."

Calvin nodded, leaning back and crossing his legs. "I do. It was my idea to hold onto him and give him to one of you guys. He seemed smart enough and easy to control. Are you having a problem with him? I'm sure Pandora could sort that out."

Eddie shook his head. "No, no. He's doing fine."

Coco chimed in. *Before you start, please tell Calvin how sorry I am for infecting Sofia. I was following orders, but had I realized she had a little human in her, I would have definitely not done it.*

Eddie nodded, putting his finger up to Calvin. "Coco wants you to know he's very sorry for infecting your wife. He was only following orders. He also said that had he known she was pregnant he would have never done it."

Calvin smiled. "I appreciate that. I understand what it's like to follow orders you don't necessarily want to follow. We will start clean and fresh, or at least you and I will. I can't speak for Sofia."

Coco sighed. *That's good. Real good. Okay, tell him the rest.*

Eddie bit the inside of his cheek and bore down, mustering his bravery. "Okay, so he told me something a little while ago about that whole situation. Something that will shed serious light on why all of that went down, including the shooting."

Calvin sat forward, interested. "Go on."

Eddie sniffled. "He said that he was personally told by Lucifer to track down Sofia and hurt her. After that, he was supposed to do the same to you—hurt you or kill you."

Calvin furrowed his brow. "What? Why me? Is it because I'm part of Katie's Killers?"

Eddie shook his head. "No. It's because, during the incursion at the last fort, you threw a dagger and hit Mania. Mania is his right hand."

Calvin leaned back in the chair, his mouth open and his eyes fixed in the distance. He was absolutely shocked by this revelation. He'd known there had to be someone behind it. He'd known there had to be some specific reason that they had targeted him and his wife specifically, but this? This had not even been on his radar. He barely remembered the woman from the battle. In fact, until that moment, he had all but forgotten about her, figuring she was a minion of the group who was trying to assert her power over Earth. He had never imagined she was the right hand of Lucifer.

Calvin licked his lips and leaned forward, putting his palms together. "So, you are telling me that I have been marked by the devil?"

Eddie nodded. "I suppose so. That would make sense."

Calvin blinked. "And Sofia?"

Eddie asked Coco, then shook his head. "Not specifically. He sent us after her because she is *your* right hand, and her death or injury would make it an eye for an eye for Lucifer, which is all he really needs to be satisfied. So far, they have not been satisfied, because every attempt on her life and health has failed or been headed off by you and Katie. He still has not gotten his revenge like he hoped."

Calvin stood up, running his hands over his head and pacing back and forth. Eddie sat still, watching him running the entire situation through his head. He held tightly to the arms of the chair, very nervous about how Calvin was going to react.

Calvin turned to Eddie and chuckled, then started to continue pacing, but stopped. He pressed his lips together and pointed at Eddie before erupting in laughter. Eddie pulled back. "Are you losing your mind or are you just coping right now?"

Calvin shook his head. "I tell you what. That is…actually kind of cool. The motherfucker knows my name. Of all the idiots and imbeciles on this planet, Lucifer has taken the time to find out my name because of a little scratch on his fucking girlfriend's arm. This is wild."

Eddie lifted an eyebrow. "I have to admit, this is not at all how I expected you to react. In fact, I was waiting for some sort of bodily harm to be pushed through me to Coco."

Calvin looked down at Eddie and softened his face. "It's not either of your faults. I am the one who slashed his girlfriend. Trust me, it's definitely an issue, but I'm just glad that it all finally fucking makes sense. I wonder if any of the latest happenings have anything to do with it."

Eddie listened to Coco for a moment. "He says maybe, but it's probably a combination of things."

Calvin slapped Eddie on the shoulder, still chuckling. "What do you know? I'm a celebrity in hell."

***

Pandora walked down the steps, running her hands along the walls. Everyone was in cuddle mode, and to be quite frank, it was nauseating her. She might have forced a soldier to hug her, but she was not down with the whole monogamy thing. That had never been her thing. So here she was, wandering around the building looking for something to do.

She turned the corner into the dungeon and leaned against the doorway, smiling and waiting for Sean and Timothy to notice her. After a few moments, she cleared her throat. The guys turned to the door and grinned broadly. Timothy put his arms out and walked over, kissing Pandora on each cheek. "You have arrived. Sister, it has been far too long."

Pandora grinned. "I know, right? And I am not cramped up inside someone else's body. I was getting pretty tired of staring at her kidneys."

Timothy smacked his lips. "Well, let me just tell you, you look fucking fabulous out here all on your own. You don't need someone else to carry you, girl, because you are walking that catwalk with some fierce shit going on. Big tits, tiny waist, curvy hips—you have all of it, and more."

Pandora clapped her hands. "I should come down here more often."

She tousled Sean's hair as she walked past him, peering at the large monitor in front of her. "I thought that there were usually a ton of dots rolling across this thing. I don't see any."

Sean shook his head. "No incursions on the radar right now. They just don't seem to be coming."

Pandora pursed her lips. "So, what are you guys working on then, because I know I would be bored out of my motherfucking mind right now."

Timothy smiled. "Mmm, no, we have more than enough to focus on. Actually, I am glad you decided to stop by. You might be able to help us."

Pandora clapped excitedly. "Okay. With what?"

Sean turned his chair around. "We've been in constant conversation with Dr. Thorough and Alice in Colorado. We're trying to figure out how to track down these remaining Leviathans. He has done a shit-ton of research on the others, minus Baylahn, and still has no idea how to even start figuring out a potential tracking system."

Timothy smiled. "That's right. But if we can learn more about the Leviathans and had some background on them, maybe that would help us tie the pieces together."

Pandora nodded. "Okay, I gotcha. You are basically looking for a little history lesson on these bitches, and because I have been around for quite a while and was a demon, you want me to fill you in."

Timothy smiled. "Exactly."

Pandora wrung her hands, tilting her head from side to side. "Okay. Let's see, where do I start? Well, they're the Seven Monsters of Time. This includes old Juntto, the Frosty One."

Timothy pulled out a notebook and crossed his legs daintily, taking notes. "So why can't we pick them up on this radar?"

Pandora shook her head. "Because they aren't from hell. Hell is just another dimension, like the worlds that these Leviathans come from, but far more protected. Their energy is not demonic, no matter how bad it is, like the Spider Queen. They can feed off demonic energy, they can sense it, and even be pulled toward it, but that energy does not linger in their systems. Kind of like if you eat an apple, it goes through you, and your body takes what it needs and expels the rest. They do that too; it just doesn't leave a mess behind."

Timothy tapped his pen on his lips. "Okay, so if isn't demonic energy, then what energy is it? If we can pinpoint that, say on Juntto, we should be able to build an identical system using that energy instead. At least in theory."

Pandora pursed her lips. "No, that won't work. It's like a flu shot. It prevents some strains, but only the ones that have been identified. Every single one of the Leviathans is different species with different identifiers. None of them are the same, which was probably noted in Thorough's work with their samples."

Timothy sighed. "So, if they aren't demonic and none of them are connected, then why are they here sleeping?"

Pandora shrugged. "They didn't come here to specifically sleep, per se. They came here seeking to destroy or to take advantage of or rule over humans. Them sleeping was a punishment, sedating them until it could be figured out how to remove them. Imagine, even as an angel, trying to get Baylahn back to his dimension. That would not be an easy feat."

Sean narrowed his eyes. "So, they are sleeping because someone did that to them?"

Pandora nodded. "Exactly. The angels, and at one point, even the Almighty, came here and imprisoned them."

Sean was shocked. "The Almighty?"

Pandora smiled. "Mmhmm. He stays out of it most of the time and lets the angels fight for us, but in that situation, the angels were just not strong enough so he had to come down and help. It was one of the few times, but it was that or watch his humans die."

Timothy scribbled something. "Okay. So, finding out the locations should be easy. I mean, do you know where they are sleeping? You *have* been around, sweetie."

Pandora lifted an eyebrow. "I've seen a lot of shit in my time, but I promise you that I don't know everything. Even as an angel, that information isn't given to me freely. Why would I need it until something like this happened?"

Timothy sighed and leaned his head back, groaning.

"This is starting to look impossible. Where's Katie? She might have a couple of ideas."

Katie giggled as she pulled the covers up over Brock, smiling at him. All that could be seen were their intertwined feet sticking out from the bottom of the bed.

The day went by pretty quickly, especially for the couples, who couldn't seem to get enough of each other, but even angels and Damned had to come out for food, whether Pandora agreed or not. Everyone had gathered in the now-extended dining area. Katie was surprised at the food laid out buffet style in the back.

Brock smiled. "We have a lot of soldiers now. We didn't want it to look like a mess hall, so this is our compromise."

Katie shrugged. "If it works, go with it."

In the corner to the right, Stephanie smiled, reaching across the table and taking Korbin's hands. They had been away from each other long enough for no one to give them shit about keeping to themselves for a while. There might have been a ton of other people in the room, but the group had situated their table so it seemed as if they were on a date, lost in each other's presence.

Before they even got there, some of the guys had put thought into it. They had turned the chairs to face each other, and not be distracted by everyone else. Someone placed a small vase in the center of the table and put a single flower in it. When they arrived for dinner, one of the soldiers had shown them to their seats, pulling out the chair for Stephanie and telling them what was being offered that day. They insisted on getting their own food, but they highly appreciated the effort. Everyone knew that they had struggled with being apart.

Across the room, Eddie sat eating dinner with Calvin, Sean, Timothy, Brock, Katie, and Turner. Pandora sashayed in and took the seat across from him. He stared down at his food, and it was obvious to Pandora that he was in conversation with Coco. He still had some getting used to it to do, and hadn't remembered to try not to show the inner conversation going on to everyone on the outside.

After a couple of minutes, he looked up and tapped Pandora on the arm. She smiled and raised an eyebrow. "Oh, you've decided to join the living side of life for a moment?"

Eddie chuckled. "Yeah, sorry. Still getting back into the swing of things with this demon. We were talking about..."

Pandora raised both eyebrows. "Yes? The suspense is killing me."

Eddie shook his head. "That's not important, really. I do have a question, though. I would like your opinion on something."

Pandora grinned. "Okay. I am good at giving my opinion. What is it?"

Eddie leaned forward and lowered his voice. "Do you think I should get a tattoo of a cartoon dog?"

Pandora's face immediately fell, realizing how trivial it was. She rolled her eyes and waved her fork in the air.

"No. And stop taking advice from your demon. He's an idiot."

Calvin leaned back in his chair, sipping his hot coffee. He looked around at everyone and cleared his throat loud enough to catch their attention. "I want to get everyone's opinion on something. We have the three options for the next fort. One is to go to Romania, although we may be on hold until they're ready. We can head to Russia, where they *are* ready, or we can roll to South America and build a fort there for them."

Timothy looked at Sean, and they both nodded as they swallowed their food. Sean wiped his lips. "Definitely South America. Actually, the more, the better there."

Timothy nodded. "I have to agree. There needs to be much better protection in South America. I have felt since Day One that we don't do enough there."

Turner shrugged. "Yeah, but think about it. We want to protect them, but these forts have almost turned into targets. The demons look for them to attack. I feel like you're putting a bullseye on them. I thought the whole point was to protect the cities and countries in case of an invasion, not turn them into the next destination. Don't get me wrong; we need protections like these either way, but do you think putting them in places that already struggle to protect themselves is a wise choice? I mean, the demons go right for them."

Korbin stood up from the table and walked over, standing behind Turner. "I know that you have concerns about this. That has been one of my concerns from the beginning, but you have to look at it another way. That is the *idea*. We *want* the demons to come to us. We want them to feel like they have the upper hand, and when they arrive at the gates, they are met by a brick wall. We roll out Damned soldiers, special metal weapons, and of course, me."

Turner pursed his lips. "Okay, I see where you're going with this. Just because the fort is there doesn't mean they won't attack."

Korbin nodded. "In fact, we hope they do once everything is set up and everyone is trained, because the way we run those forts, they will only attack once. I promise you that."

Katie smiled, listening to Korbin be so proud and determined. Her phone rang and she pulled it out of her pocket, seeing Brushwood's number on the ID. She winked at Brock and stood up, walking out into the hallway. "Hey. I was wondering when I was going to hear from you. Do we have an incursion?"

Brushwood sighed. "No, this isn't an incursion. But something just crossed my desk that I'd like you to take a look at. It's some strange activity in Sonora, Texas. It might be nothing, but…"

9

Katie smiled at Brock as she and Pandora stepped through the portal. They walked straight out into Sonora, Texas, this time bypassing a random dimension in between. Pandora looked at her, impressed. "Wow, you're getting good at this."

Katie shrugged. "I really don't have control. Sometimes I roll into the right place, others I end up in Volcanoland smoldering to death as I jump through another portal. I think it might have to do with focusing in on the location hard this time."

Pandora nodded. "Truth. I was too."

They looked around the town. It was small and quaint; exactly what you would imagine a small Texas town to be like. To everyone else, it would feel chilly, but for them, having come from Paris and the desert winter, it felt pretty nice . Katie nodded toward the small police station down a block. "Let's start there. If there is something strange enough going on to catch the general's radar, they most likely heard about it first."

Pandora nodded, squishing her tits together and standing tall. Katie laughed. "We are going into the Mayberry Police Station, not the Firefighters of California. Focus your shit, dude."

Pandora sneered. "I *am* focusing, but that doesn't mean my shit has to be crooked."

Katie opened the door to the police station and they walked in, pausing to stare around the room. There was only one cop inside, and as soon as he saw Pandora and Katie, he jumped out of his chair and aimed his gun at them with shaking hands. "You stay where you are. *Stay right where you are.*"

Katie put her hands in the air, glancing at Pandora. "Sir, we are here to find out what's been going on in this town. We work with the military."

The cop, sweating, shook his head. "Don't bullshit me. I know who you are. You're the Borrelli twins. You're them criminals that killed that old lady. I put you away years ago. Now you've come back for me. You broke out of the state pen, and now you want revenge. Let me tell you something: you ain't going to find it here today. I was just doing my damn job."

Katie furrowed her brow and shook her head. "Sir, I think you're confused. My name is Katie. I'm here to help."

He shook his gun. "You ain't here to do nothing but kill me. I ain't stupid."

As Katie kept his attention, Pandora crept around, getting behind him. She knocked the gun from his hand and put her arm around his neck. "Shhhh, go to sleep now."

After the guy passed out, Pandora slowly lowered him

to the floor. "He was completely useless and obviously out of his mind. He could hurt someone."

Katie put her hands down and looked out the window. "Come on. This shit is weird. Let's do a fly-by around the town and see if we can see anything else."

Stepping out of the station, both Katie and Pandora took flight. They spread their wings wide and soared above the highest steeple. Gliding along, they glanced down every street, every backyard, and every patch of woods in town. It was strange. There were barely any people outside, and those who were hurried from one place to another as fast as they could, slamming their doors after them.

Katie glanced at Pandora and back down at the ground, where a mother and her two twin girls were out in the front yard, and they descended to the ground, folding their wings behind them. The mom looked up, recognizing them. "You're those angels that have been fighting the demons, aren't you?"

Katie smiled kindly, glancing down at the girls. "Yes, ma'am. We were sent out here because the military got a notice that strange things might be going on. No sign of demons that we know of. Have you seen any in recent days?"

She shook her head. The two girls giggled, putting their hands up like claws and roaring. "That's what they look like on television."

Katie grinned at them. "They sure do, but if you ever see one, you run and tell your mom or the closest adult. Okay?"

Both girls nodded. Pandora looked around. "The town seems so quiet. Is it normally this abandoned?"

The mother shook her head, pulling her apron up and wiping her hands on it. "No. Normally this town is lively. We've all known each other since we were kids. But lately, no one wants to come out. The whole damn town is terrified, but the sheriff ran off, so we got no answers."

Katie furrowed her brow. "What exactly is everyone so afraid of?"

The mother looked at her and then bent down, smiling at her girls. "Why don't you pull out the bikes and you can ride them up and down the driveway?"

The girls smiled and took off, both pausing and waving at Katie and Pandora. The angels waved back and turned to the mother. She cleared her throat and shook her head, her face going white. "This may sound nuts, I know, but I've been seeing things. So have my girls. The other night I woke up and they were standing in my doorway with no eyes. It was real as could be. I chased them to their bedroom but found the girls asleep in their beds just fine. Other people are seeing things, too. The only thing I could think was, maybe the water's poisoned."

Katie sighed and nodded. "Thank you. We'll definitely go check that out. If you need anything, look for us. We're going to do our best to figure out what is going on here."

The mother nodded and headed over to the girls, who were happily riding the bikes. Pandora jumped into Katie for a more private conversation. *I don't know for sure, but this sounds a hell of a lot like a Leviathan. The Nightmare.*

Calvin sat down on the edge of the bed and ran his fingers over the comforter. The last time he had been there Sofia had been with him, snuggled up in his arms after a very long and trying ordeal. Things didn't sound like they were going to get any less tense, but he didn't want to scare her. The last thing he needed was to put stress on the baby, and once Sofia knew he was marked by Lucifer, she would be beyond herself with fright.

He picked up his cell and dialed her number.

She answered after a couple of rings. "Well, hello there, handsome. I wasn't expecting a call until later."

Calvin smiled. "I know. Things changed pretty fast in Paris. We all needed a break, especially Korbin. But I just got back from the airfield at the base. I have a plane waiting for you."

Sofia chuckled. "You do? Well. Why don't you come out here?"

Calvin cleared his throat. "I think you should come to the base and be here where it's safe."

Sofia paused for a moment. "Safe? Why would you think that my home isn't safe? I just got the renovations done and the yard and the fence fixed. It looks like home. I have classes again, and doctor's appointments here."

Calvin smirked, remembering how stubborn she was… and insightful, too. She knew he was hiding something. "And all that can wait, except the doctor, but we've got more than our share of those here on the base. Just trust me on this, okay? It's nothing for you to get all kinds of worried about. I just want to know you are safe and secure by my side. I don't trust anyone as much as I do myself to keep you safe."

Sofia sighed. "Well, all right. If it means I can see your face, then I will do as you wish. But you owe me a steak dinner when I get there."

Calvin laughed. "Anything you want, baby. I'll let the pilot know you have to pack and you'll be on your way."

Sofia chuckled. "Always keeping me moving. I love you."

Calvin grinned. "I love you too."

He pressed End and looked down at the phone, smiling from ear to ear. It felt good to know he would see Sofia and his baby in just a few hours. He needed to know they were safe, and out there he didn't feel like they would be. Sticking his phone in his pocket, he grabbed his lightweight sweatshirt, throwing it on as he walked out of the room and down the hall. He took the steps quickly and opened the front door of the building, finding Brock, Stephanie, and Korbin standing there looking around.

Stephanie smiled. "About time you showed up. Is Sofia coming?"

Calvin nodded. "Yep. So what is this meeting for?"

Korbin uncrossed his arms. "We are discussing the state of the base."

They walked around together, going through the different areas of the base. As they passed, the soldiers would stop and stand at attention. Brock looked at the armory. "Joshua wanted to be here for this, but with the volume of orders, he can't even take a second away. In fact, I'm pretty sure he has been running the place around the clock recently to try to make up for the time he has lost and the materials he is lacking."

Korbin shook his head. "Looks like you've kept everything in tip-top shape, Brock."

Brock chuckled. "Not just me; everyone had been busting ass to do so, and all under the direction and leadership of your wife. She's been our rock. The base is strong. Really strong, especially with the protections we put in place in case of another EMP. As far as the armory, they're behind on special metal, but that was to be expected with the large orders for the forts. Like I said, though, they are moving forward, and I'm sure they will be caught up in no time."

Korbin shook Brock's hand. "You guys have all done a hell of a job."

Brock looked at him and Calvin. "How *is* everything going with the forts?"

Korbin smiled. "We're on our way with them. They are definitely coming along. It takes quite a bit of planning, but once we start building them and training the Damned and the regular soldiers, they seem to almost take care of themselves. Calvin here is going to be staying stateside for a while, though. He's got a wife and a baby on the way, and we all want to make sure that he is able to take care of his family. Things in his life are going to be changing big time real soon."

Calvin laughed. "Don't I know it. Diapers and tears and giggles and the whole thing."

Brock smirked. "What about the baby? That'll be a big change, too."

Calvin faked a laugh. "Ha-ha, very funny. You are hilarious. You just wait…one day you might be facing little humans too. You never know."

Korbin chuckled at the fearful face Brock pulled. "The thing is, though, I can't possibly design the bases and train the soldiers on my own. There is far too much that goes into it. Because we know we are targets, we have to get the work done as fast as we possibly can. That means training at the same time as building. Now, I had Pandora last time, but with Katie's schedule and such, I know I can't rely on that."

Brock rubbed his chin. "So you need someone to step in where Calvin leaves off. I'll definitely start looking for a replacement for you. There are plenty of well-trained men here, so there has to be one to fill the hole for you."

Calvin nodded. "I'll keep my eyes open too. We'll get you the help you need. You know I won't leave you high and dry."

The Alamo stood valiantly in the San Antonio sunlight, as groomed and well-kept as it had always been since becoming a museum and focal point in the city. Tourists from all over the world milled about the grounds and took pictures or stood out front waiting on their tour, pushing their families together for the shots. One family walked around the inside of the chapel, gawking at the history behind it.

Stan, the father, reached out and tapped his wife's arm. "I am going to go find a restroom. I'll meet up with you guys out front."

His wife leaned forward and kissed him on the cheek. "All right, we'll be here."

Stan walked through the building, following the touristy signs posted on stands around the place. Finally, he reached the bathroom, but when he pulled on the door handle, it didn't budge. He looked around, but there was no one to ask about it. Apparently, that bathroom was closed. He shoved his hands in his pockets and hurried across the street. Entering the restaurant, he shot straight back to the back, not noticing how quiet it was inside. He pulled on the bathroom door, but again it was locked.

Stan groaned, feeling an impending sense of panic in the pit of his stomach. He had always had stomach issues, and one of his biggest fears was being somewhere when an emergency struck and not being able to find a bathroom. He took a deep breath and gathered his composure, rushing out of the restroom and taking a right. Up about a block and a half was a real estate office. He burst through the door and looked at the reception desk, but no one was there.

Standing in the room, he searched around, finally finding the bathroom. He let out a sigh of relief and hurried over, turning the doorknob. His eyes widened as it stopped short. He jiggled the handle, but that bathroom was locked too. Stan swallowed hard, panic building in his chest. Tears pulled at the corners of his eyes. How could there not be a single bathroom in the city that was open? And where the hell was everyone?

He shook his head and hurried back out, reaching the end of his rope. As he stepped out onto the street, the panicked sensation faded. He stopped in his tracks and looked around, gripping the railing tightly. The entire street was in total chaos. Men, women, and children were running around, grabbing at their hair and faces and screaming at the top of their lungs. He walked down the steps and latched onto one man's arms, shaking him.

He screamed loudly, and Stan let go. His eyes were shut. In fact, *everyone's* eyes were shut. They were all experiencing living nightmares, and no one but him was coming out of it. Just then he heard a strange sound like tentacles slapping the pavement. He stepped back up to the top of the stairs and looked down the street as a mass of people took off, screaming and shouting and flailing their arms. That was when he saw it, and the terror really set in.

Slithering slowly around the corner, tentacles undulating and slapping the street hard, was Kabbus. His large and bulbous body rolled forward, a cloud of black vapor surging around him and flowing over everything in its path. Stan swallowed hard and shook his head, turning to see a police officer stumbling down the street.

He put out his hand and yelled, "Hey! Hey! Get some backup."

The cop shook his head, grabbing his gun out of the holster. He pushed through a group of screaming people and jogged forward, picking up his pace as he grew closer to the Leviathan. He stopped about fifteen feet away and raised his arm, pointing his weapon at the beast. His hand shook wildly but he kept his feet planted, trying to keep the thing from going any farther. "Stop where you are!"

Tears streamed down the cop's face as he faced the enemy; he was not sure what was real anymore. Kabbus came to a stop for a moment, turning his head toward the officer. As soon as he did, the man's knees buckled and he crumpled into a fetal position, dropping his gun. He grabbed his knees and pulled them to his chest, beginning to rock back and forth. His tears flowed harder, and he mumbled inaudibly as he rocked. As Stan watched, the guy clenched his eyes shut hard and fell into the same state as everyone else on the block.

Kabbus snarled, his features hard to make out in the blob that was his face. His skin held him together but offered no definition, creating little shape besides the tentacles wildly waving from the sides of his body. The mist floated effortlessly around him, and it seemed to suck the life out of every living thing it struck.

Stan gripped the rail as the beast slowly slithered toward the cop and the dark fog covered his body. Stan moved right and left, trying to see the officer, wanting to know if he was okay. Kabbus only paused for a moment before slithering past the officer and down the street. As the black mist lifted from the man, Stan put his hand over his mouth and shook his head.

The officer was still curled in a ball. His skin looked cold and gray, and his body seemed to be frozen in place. His face was a mask of horror, a memory Stan knew he would never be able to shake. Kabbus had gotten what he wanted. He had fed on the officer's fear.

10

Katie leaned against the tall metal rail, folding her arms over her chest. Pandora stood on the edge of the roof, looking out over the town of Sonora. The water tower was huge and tall, but the technician went straight to work. "So, you say someone thinks there is something wrong with the water?"

Katie nodded. "Yeah. Apparently, there is some sort of psychological event happening here in town, and we wanted to make sure it wasn't being induced chemically. You know, something in the water making people sick? Causing hallucinations and such."

The technician was bent over, taking samples and checking the contents. He stood up and leaned back, stretching his spine. He wore a white hard hat and a one-piece jumpsuit with Sonora Water and Sewer embroidered on the front, and his face was freshly shaven. He shook his head. "Now, that is some scary stuff. What kind of chemical do you reckon would cause something like that?"

Katie shrugged. "I have no idea, but that's what we're here to find out."

The technician nodded, glancing at Pandora and turning back to the water samples. He held up the container and shook his head. "Like I said, I was out here three days ago and everything was up to par. You can see here that there ain't even a drop of anything other than what's supposed to be in the supply. Now, you could check each individual pipeline, but if these incidences are going on all over town, I would say it's not the water."

Katie pursed her lips. "All right. Thank you for taking the time to come out here for us."

She went over to Pandora, who was still staring into space. "Not the water."

Pandora took a deep breath through her nose and nodded. "That doesn't surprise me in the least. Who would put something like that in a small-ass town's water supply?"

Katie shrugged, then reached into her pocket and pulled out her phone and glanced at the screen. "I don't know, but the general is calling. Maybe he's got something for us."

Katie pressed Answer. "General. Looks like it's not the water supply here in Sonora. You find anything out on your end?"

He swallowed nervously. "No, but it doesn't surprise me that it's not biological. I got a call. There is something going on in San Antonio now. I couldn't get a clear reading on what the hell it is, but they mentioned people going nuts and acting like that officer in Sonora did. We know it's not in the air or water, so that leaves few other major things that would make that many people in one place suffer the same thing. It's starting to get out of hand."

Katie closed her eyes for a moment. "I have to agree with you. I've never seen anything like this before. The only thing we can do at this point is head over there and check it out. Hopefully, they will be able to provide us a few more clues than Sonora has. Everyone here is shut up in their homes, most too scared to say anything."

The general breathed out heavily. "I have a bad feeling about this, Katie."

Katie narrowed her eyes and looked out across the town. "I do too, General. Just in case we are looking at a Leviathan causing all these problems, I think it's a good idea for you get hold of Timothy. See if he can get a reading on San Antonio with his equipment. We'll check back in when we have more info."

Timothy rubbed his stomach. "I think I'm starting to get hungry. I swear, winter comes and I can eat a bitch out of house and home."

Sean grinned. "Could have something to do with us constantly watching cooking shows. Every time they show something, I want to run out, buy it, cook it, and rub it all over myself."

Timothy sneered. "Well, that's gross, but to each, his own."

Sean chuckled, reaching over and picking up the phone as it rang. "This is Sean."

"Sean, it's Brushwood. Can you put Timothy on the phone?"

Sean nodded and handed the phone to Timothy, then turned and wheeled to the other side of the room to make sure all of the equipment was working well. Timothy glanced at the screen as he took the phone. "Hey, General. I just checked everything, and it's been pretty quiet. Whatcha need?"

The general wasted no time. "Timothy, I was instructed by Katie to call you and have you check something out. Right now, she is on her way from Sonora, Texas to San Antonio, where there has been a rash of unexplained events. Biological agents have been mostly ruled out, and there isn't really any further explanation for what is happening in those areas. I need you to take a look via satellite and let me know what you see. Demons? Attack? Something else? I am trying to protect Katie so she doesn't walk into a shitstorm."

Timothy pulled his chair up and rubbed his face, putting the general on speakerphone. He was not in the mindset just then for something like that, being hungry and all, but at that point, he had zero ability to give up. "I'm pulling both Sonora and San Antonio up on the screen. I will transfer the images to your computer so you can see them too. Let me know when you get the feed. Sonora is on the right, San Antonio the left."

The general flipped on the screen to his computer and opened the invitation from Timothy. The screen came up. "What are you seeing?"

Timothy narrowed his eyes, initiating a few programs that might help him detect any activity. He could see masses of people, smoke, and general chaos in San Antonio, but nothing else. "I…uh… There isn't any demonic energy there, General, but I have to say, there is definitely something going on in both places. Right now, more in San Antonio than Sonora, which makes me think whatever this is, it's moving."

Brushwood groaned. "I had a feeling you were going to say that. All right."

Timothy tapped the satellite feed to zoom in, but everything was blurry. "I'm going to keep monitoring this for you, okay? I'm not sure what is going on down there, but it's a good thing that you already sent Katie. She should be able to get to the bottom of it."

The general agreed. "Good thinking on keeping an eye out. I'll let you know if I get any more information."

Hanging up, Timothy narrowed his eyes and leaned closer to the screen. "What are you? Show your face."

He shook his head and sat back down, setting several different warning alarms just in case anything cooperated. "Hey, Sean?"

Sean leaned his head back. "Yeah?"

Timothy finished the settings and turned toward him. "Can you scoot up and get me some snacks and an iced tea? I'm going to be here a while."

Katie and Pandora stepped through the portal into an alternate dimension and Katie sighed, shrugging. "Guess it didn't work this time. Strange, since I've been to San Antonio before and had the whole picture in my mind."

She looked out at the pristine cityscape all around her. "Well, this is a beautiful… Hey, wait a minute."

She whirled and stared at Pandora, who snickered, staring at the naked men working construction. "I took a note from your playbook and thought really, really hard about the place, and we are here."

Katie rolled her eyes and opened another portal. "Good to know, but we're working."

***

Katie and Pandora stepped out onto the River Walk and the portal snapped shut behind them. There were shops and restaurants lining the place, and a shit-ton of people everywhere. At first, Katie didn't notice anything strange, so she took a moment to brush sand from the front of her blouse. However, Pandora reached over and tapped her shoulder.

Katie furrowed her brow and then followed Pandora's eyes. The place was in complete pandemonium. "What in the hell?"

Katie and Pandora moved quickly to the side as people came running through, screaming and yelling with their arms flying all over the place. Some pulled at their faces, others their hair, while others sat perfectly still on the ground, knees to chest, with terrified looks on their faces. It was the strangest thing Katie had ever seen. She didn't even know where to start.

She took a deep breath, trying to wrap her head around it. "Oh, this isn't right."

Pandora shook her head as she looked at the people in

amazement. "Nope. Something is really wrong here. Like really, *really* wrong. We have to do something, and we have to do it quickly."

Katie shook herself out of the shock and reached up, slapping her hands together. Her eyes glowed bright blue, and armor appeared on her body. Her sword sat comfortably in the sheath on her back. Pandora nodded and called her angelic powers as well.

Stepping forward, Katie pulled energy from her chest and down her arms, her eyes closed tightly. The light glimmered at the edge of her fingertips, and she let out a hard breath as she pushed it outward. A wave of light washed over the people in front of her. One by one they began to calm, but not all the way. They still seemed to be possessed by some sort of spell or something.

Katie stood perplexed, gazing at the people. She glanced back at Pandora, who had the same look on her face. "That usually works really well."

Pandora clicked her tongue. "We are up against some really strong shit, and I…"

Katie's eyes shifted from Pandora's face to behind her on the river. She tilted her head to the side and walked forward. "What the fuck is that?"

Pandora looked at her, eyebrows raised. "What?"

Katie pointed at the river. "That."

At that moment black fog came rolling down the river, riding the waves just inches above the peaks. It moved with the flow of the water like silk fluttering in the wind. Pandora lifted both eyebrows. "Never mind the fog of death, look at *that* shit!"

Suddenly a loud horn blew, and Katie gasped. In front

of her, floating down the river behind the fog, was a massive barge carrying Kabbus. He was huge and his tentacles were writhing around him, some dipping softly into the water as the craft pushed down the river. On top of the water, cold, gray bodies floated with him, all of their faces frozen in fear. Katie put her hand to her stomach, a sense of nausea taking her over. The scene was more horrific and terrifying than anything she had experienced up to that point, and she had literally rolled through fucking hell.

Pandora shook her head, taking a step back. "Holy fucking shit. I can't believe it. I mean, I can, but I don't want to."

Katie looked at her with confusion. "What is that?"

Pandora sniffed, pulling her sword from its sheath. "That is Kabbus. He is one of the most terrifying beings ever to come to Earth. I thought for sure he was buried so far down in the caves he would never wake up."

Katie pulled her sword out and held it in front of her. "I guess you were wrong."

Pandora turned, grabbing Katie by the shoulders. "All right, don't get too close. We need to stop him before he gets much farther."

Katie nodded, her wings sprouting from her back. They moved to the edge of the walkway and took flight, going straight up and then diving down and over him. Katie wrinkled her nose as she flew, making a pass by him in order to gauge the kind of fight she was getting herself into. His gray eyes shifted up toward them, but he didn't say a word.

Katie shook her head. "That's new. I'm not used to them

not talking. Well, except Baylahn, but we were inside of him."

Pandora grimaced. "Kabbus has no reason to speak. His magic and abilities speak for him."

Katie's lip twitched. "Talk about a creature right out of the mind of Stephen-fucking-King."

Pandora gripped her sword tightly. "Don't say that. His movies rarely ever end on a good note, and I for one am not getting taken out by some huge blobby octopus wannabe."

Katie gritted her teeth. "Neither am I. Let's make one more pass to make sure there isn't anything else hiding down there. Then we attack."

They soared downward, heading straight for Kabbus but leveling out just above his reach. His tentacles writhed and slapped the water, but it didn't look like they had much direction. Katie swerved as she flew over him, one of his tentacles missing her by mere inches. Water splashed on her face and she grimaced, spitting and wiping it off.

Katie flipped right-side up, her legs carefully positioned beneath her. "What's the strategy?"

Pandora scoffed. "With this sonofabitch, there really is no strategy. Try to kill him in any way you can. But if you notice, he's still alive, so whatever angels fought him before, they didn't kill him off."

Katie blinked. "That is not very reassuring, but then again, we aren't just *any* set of angels, now are we?"

Pandora smirked. "Hell, no, we aren't."

Both Katie and Pandora flew straight at him, lowering their swords and lunging. Pandora went to the right, pulling her sword back and smiling as she attempted to slice the beast across the neck. Before she could maneuver, though, one of his tentacles came up, slapping her hard in the stomach and sending her flying back to crash into a building.

Katie snapped her head around, watching Pandora's body smash the wall in as it hit. She pressed on, nerves fluttering in her chest. She raised the sword high over her head and attacked, swinging downward. As her arms moved, a tentacle writhed up from Kabbus' side and slammed hard into her stomach as well. All the air left her lungs and she soared back, slamming hard into a different brick building. The wall collapsed, and she landed hard in a pile of dust and bricks.

Katie groaned and pushed several bricks off her stomach, then sat up, reaching over and grabbing her sword. Blood dripped from the corner of her mouth and she coughed, watching plumes of dust billow around her. Screams from below caught her attention, and she pushed herself off the pile of bricks and stood. She sniffed, brushing debris and dirt off her shirt before sheathing her sword. Obviously, this beast was going to need a little more attention than they had just given it.

Katie stumbled out of the debris, looking for Pandora. "Pan? Where are you?"

The dust was thick and she waved her hand in the air, but there was no answer, and she couldn't see through the haze. She took a step forward and kicked a small stone with her foot. She watched as it bounced along the ground, clinking through the rubble before flying over the edge. Suddenly, her building began to shake. She put her arms out for balance and looked around as the building next to her went tumbling down. The screams of the people beneath it rang out but quickly stopped.

Katie looked across the river as another building began to crumble. Standing right beneath it, huddling together in fear, were a woman and man holding their two kids. Katie waved her arms wildly. "Watch out!"

She raced forward and dove off the edge of the building, heading straight for the people. Before she could reach the little girl's hand, her wings pulled her back, the building collapsing on top of the family right in front of her. She screamed, covering her mouth. "No!"

The sound of another building rattling forced her to look to her left. On the top of the building, standing on the balcony, was a little old man. He was trying to find a way out, but he couldn't. She gritted her teeth and flew up to him as fast as she could. As she grabbed the man's hand, the building collapsed and he hung from her grip, clinging for his life. "Hold on!"

One hand slipped, and she shook her head. *"Hold on!"*

He looked up at her with sad eyes as his other hand slipped and he fell, disappearing into the dust and debris below. She shook her head, tears welling in her eyes. "Why can't I save them? Why can't I save them?"

The water lapped gently along the River Walk as the barge moved slowly through. A low growl came from Kabbus' throat, and his mouth curved into an evil grin. All around him were chaos and screaming, but in the real world, the one he could see through his eyes, not a single building had fallen. The only lives taken were the ones he took with his own tentacles.

Along the street people screamed and yelled, falling to

their knees in terror. However, Katie was not one of them. She was not flying through debris, and she was not crying in the sky. There was no dead family, no deceased old man, or even any brick building lying in ruins. Everything was as it had been just ten minutes before when she had taken flight to fight him as he seeped along through the river, his tentacles whipping wildly.

In fact, she was doing nothing but lying on the ground, her face contorted in terror as she had a waking nightmare she couldn't snap herself out of.

11

Pandora coughed, waving her hand in front of her face. She couldn't tell if what was in front of her was fog or dust and debris from the violence going on at the River Walk. She narrowed her eyes, taking a careful step forward, seeing figures dancing like shadows in the pure white obstructing her view. She looked up at the sky, seeing nothing but a bright purple hue. "I must be in another dimension, but how in the hell did I get here?"

She scratched her head. "Holy shit, he actually slapped me back to another dimension. That bitch is hardcore!"

A light breeze blew around her, whipping her hair out behind her. The fog floated along with it, clearing the air. All around her was a beautiful glistening city, the windows spotless, the ground shimmering, and the air clear of all pollution. It was like being in the perfect place, with nothing out of the ordinary except for her. She turned around, finding groups of people smiling and laughing, their skin shimmering in the light. They were completely naked, but there wasn't a single bit of shame in it.

Then it dawned on her. This was the alternate dimension she had been to twice before, the one that she had tried hard to get Katie to stop in. "I've been here before. This is the place I truly believe was made for me."

She smiled widely, figuring she'd gotten the better end of the deal if she'd ended up there without any idea how to get back. She stepped forward, reaching out as the others reached for her. The light of the sun reflected off the person in front of her and she squinted, putting her hand up to cover her face. "Wait a minute…this…this isn't right."

A frown quickly replaced the grin on Pandora's face as she got her first good look at the men and women around her. She stepped forward, carefully placing her hand on the man's chest. It was hard, like plastic. It curved perfectly, creating pecs and a flat stomach, but there was nothing more than a small nick for his belly button. As her eyes dipped lower, she gasped, watching as his crotch curved under and around. It was completely smooth.

Pandora shook her head, pulling her hand back. "Wait, where is your dick? Where are your balls? Where is your fucking belly button?"

She freaked and turned, running straight into one of the women. Her smile was painted on and she could see the roots of where her hair attached to her head. Pandora stumbled back, taking a good look at the females coming toward her. They were all as smooth as Barbies. Their breasts curved around like small mountains with no bounce, no detail, and no nipples. Their crotches were smooth plastic, just a small indention in the center to show she was a woman.

Pandora took a deep breath and put up her hands, shaking her head. "No, no. I made a mistake. Seriously, I…"

As she pointed to herself, she felt her skin. It was harder than she remembered. She gasped and looked down at the plastic sheen on her breasts. "No. Oh, God. *No!*"

Instantly she began to tear at her clothes, pulling her shirt off and ripping down her pants. She was as smooth as a Barbie too, only she didn't even have the crease. Her crotch looked like a plastic pair of panties. She screamed, putting her hands over her eyes.

Katie came running up, grabbed her hard by the shoulders, and began to shake her. "Pandora, wake up. Snap out of it."

Pandora shook her head wildly, more panicked than before. "I've got no coochie! I've got no coochie! It's all plastic… It's all…"

Katie pulled her arm way back and slapped Pandora right across the face. Pandora gasped and grabbed her cheek, slowly looking up at Katie with angry eyes. "Bitch, are you out of your damned mind?"

Katie shook her hand, which was stinging from slapping Pandora that hard. She hadn't wanted to do it, but she didn't know how else to help her. And from the sound of it, she was in her own personal hell. "We both are out of our minds."

She turned, putting her arm out for Pandora to see. Pandora dropped her hand and blinked, then stepped forward and looked around. She was incredibly confused. The beautiful city, the clear crystalline skies, the plastic people—they were all gone. She wasn't in the alternate dimension anymore. She was back on the River Walk in

San Antonio with people screaming and wailing as they ran around her freaking out.

She sniffed, swearing she could still smell the warm plastic of her body. She looked down and began to grope herself, letting out a sigh of relief when she grabbed her crotch and found a soft mound instead of hard plastic.

Pandora spun to look at Katie. "I was in the other dimension, and there were thousands of beautiful naked people. But then I looked closer, and their bodies were made of plastic. They had no dicks, Katie. They had zero dicks."

Katie raised an eyebrow. "That sounds terrible!"

Pandora shook her head in disbelief. "But that wasn't the worst part about it. I ripped off all of my clothes, and I was made of plastic too. My crotch was a pressed piece of plastic in the shape of panties, and not even fucking cute ones."

Katie walked over to her, rubbing her head, and put her hand on Pandora's shoulder. "You're safe now, and so is your crotch. We were both having waking nightmares."

Pandora nodded, taking a really good look at Katie for the first time since she had come back from the dimension. Her eyes were dull, her face was dirty, and she looked absolutely terrified and exhausted. It had been a long time since Pandora had seen her in that kind of shape. Quickly she whirled, remembering that Kabbus had been on the barge. "Where is he?"

Katie shrugged. "I don't even know how long we've been in the nightmare. When I came to, he was gone, no sign of the barge on the river."

Pandora went over to Katie and they stared at the

water, no more trace of the Leviathan or the black fog that crept over the river haunting them. Both were on the verge of tears, and both were holding back, trying to be strong. Pandora gently grabbed Katie's arm, turning her toward her. "Come here."

Pandora put her arms out and Katie fell into them without a thought. They stood there in the crowd, hugging each other, not caring how long it took to break themselves free from the spell that still fogged their minds. Both of them felt the terror in their chests slowly begin to fade, and their heartbeats slowed.

Katie pulled back and looked at Pandora. "Thanks. I feel a little better."

Pandora nodded. "Me too. We need to help the others. We need to wake them from these nightmares."

Katie sighed. "I was thinking the same thing."

Timothy sat on the edge of his chair, biting his fingernails and watching the screens. Sean sat next to him in his wheelchair, slowly moving back and forth rhythmically, trying to calm his nerves. There was still no demon signal, no incursion, and no call from the general or Katie. From the satellite feed, though, they could tell that things were chaotic; nothing had changed. They were desperately trying to get any type of reading at all from San Antonio.

Sean slammed his fist on the wheelchair's armrest in frustration. "I just don't get what the fuck is going on."

Suddenly the phone began to ring loudly, making them

both jump. Timothy scrambled forward, grabbing the receiver and putting it to his ear. "Hello?"

He heard a sniffle and a sigh before Katie began to speak. "Timothy, it's me. Pandora is with me."

Timothy put his hand to his chest and sank back into the chair. "Oh, good God Almighty, girl. You are going to cause me to just drop dead right here in the dungeon one day."

Katie chuckled lightly, but he could hear the exhaustion in her voice. "I'm sorry. It's been wild."

Timothy shook his head. "What in the hell is going on over there? We aren't seeing demon readings, but we could tell there is complete chaos. Are you all right?"

Katie let out a deep breath of relief. "I am. I'm okay. I think. Physically, Pandora and I aren't hurt."

Timothy raised an eyebrow. "Uh oh. Not physically, but mentally?"

Katie shook her head. "We'll be okay. But there is definitely something wild going on in San Antonio, and I think this is what was affecting Sonora too."

Timothy furrowed his brow. "What is it if it's not a demon? I mean, we aren't really equipped for attacks by other countries. That kind of thing goes to the general."

Katie paused for a second since there was someone screaming in the background. Timothy listened closely, hearing Pandora speak, only her tone was soft and caring. "Is…is Pandora hugging someone?"

Katie growled in exhaustion. "That is a very long story. Yes, she is, but you would have to be here to know what the hell that means. Trust me, she isn't doing it just to *do* it."

Timothy shrugged. "I won't go signing her up for UNICEF, but it's weird."

Katie shifted the phone to muffle the noise. "It *is* weird, but what is going on is even crazier. We have another Leviathan. It has woken and has been slithering along, starting somewhere in Sonora and heading through San Antonio. The last I saw of it, it was on a barge heading down the river."

Timothy leaned back in his chair. "Good lord. And what is this one's name?"

Katie's breath picked up as she spoke his name. "Kabbus, and he doesn't even need to touch you to turn your mind upside down. If he gets close enough while you are defenseless and stuck in your own mind, he will feed off your fear and leave little human gray freaked-out statues behind."

Timothy shook his head, staring at the screen. "Oh, my God. This is not good. What do you need me to do?"

Katie looked out at the river. "He went down the river on a barge. I was hoping you could pick him up on the satellite and track him to find out where he is going. We need to be on top of this."

Timothy sat up straight. "Right. I'll do my best."

The barge blew its loud horn again as it pulled to the edge of the river, slamming into the side. Its large bottom hit the floor of the river and scraped along, the whine of the steel echoing across the land. Chunks of dirt fell into the water and trees tipped as the barge finally came to a stop. Kabbus snarled, his tentacles going wild, reaching for the shore and grasping the soil and stones along the edge.

The black fog cascaded down the side of the barge and out onto the grass as Kabbus slithered onto land, his whole body thumping onto the ground below. Without hesitation, he moved toward the highway in front of him, seeing no cars for miles. As he grew close, something shimmered in the air and his body shook. He came to an abrupt stop.

A portal sparked as it opened up in front of him. Beelzebub grunted as he pulled it open and stepped out, smiling at the large Leviathan in front of him. At his feet, small mews caught his attention and the demon whipped his head down to see sweet fluffy kittens running toward him, their fur flapping in the wind and their noses bright and pink. They reached his legs and jumped, more gathering by the second. His stomach churned as they gripped his scales, trying to climb into his arms. They were so cute and fluffy.

Beelzebub covered his mouth, gagging, and stepped back, kicking the kittens off of his legs. They rolled off, bouncing across the ground, and began to play. They pounced on each other, making the most adorable squeaking noises anyone had ever heard. Beelzebub gasped, beginning to freak out. "That's...that's disgusting. What... I can't look at them. They are just so...so...*cute*. Oh, fuck."

He stumbled back, falling to the ground as the portal closed behind him. He put up his arms as they charged toward him, jumping up on his legs and bouncing toward his face. He knew they had one mission, and one mission only: to lick him all over with their little sandpaper tongues as their squishy, furry paws tromped around on his face. It was the most torturous thing he could have ever imagined, even worse than being torn apart by Lucifer, and he knew exactly what *that* felt like.

Beelzebub shut his eyes and yelled, stopping for a moment and remembering who he stood in front of. "This isn't real. It's not real."

Struggling, he sat up and pulled himself to his feet. The kittens were still there, clinging to his body through his every movement. He cleared his throat and swallowed hard, forcing his hand forward and bowing low. The adorable kittens continued to stick to him as he moved. "Oh, Kabbus the horrific, Kabbus the terrible, Kabbus the Nightmare, spare me. I am not here to do you harm. In fact, I am here for the opposite. Do you not remember your friends, the demons? We come from a world that is beyond most humans' comprehension of a nightmare. We are on the same team. I am a fan of your powers."

Kabbus tilted his large head to the side, watching as Beelzebub did his best to stand still with the kittens still haunting his mind and clinging to his body. Beelzebub kept his eyes clenched shut, trying to drown out the sound of the kittens with his thoughts and reassurances. After a few moments, though, the sounds stopped, and he could no longer feel their tiny claws scratching his scales.

Very carefully, Beelzebub opened one eye and looked down at his body, the kittens having all disappeared from around him. Slowly he straightened, clearing his throat and relaxing his muscles. The kittens had been nothing more than a waking nightmare for Beelzebub, something he had not been looking forward to when he realized he was going to be dealing with the Nightmare Leviathan. Nonetheless, it was over for the time being, so he could now focus on why he'd come to meet Kabbus in the first place. He knew one thing, though: kittens would not be on his dinner menu anytime in the near future.

Kabbus stared at him with his gray eyes, and Beelzebub felt that if he'd had a soul, the Leviathan would be peering into it at that very moment. He cleared his throat and turned to the side, pointing out on the road. A loud beeping rang out and Kabbus turned as fast as he could, alarmed. His tentacles flailed wildly as he watched a huge semi backing up toward them.

Beelzebub put his hands out. "There is no need to be frightened. The eighteen-wheeler is here to help you. It will take ages for you to get around like this, and you are too valuable and powerful to be walking around on your own…tentacles."

Beelzebub looked over as two men, their eyes glowing bright red, jumped from the front cab of the truck and hurried to the back, opening the back doors and pulling out the ramp. They then stepped to each side and got down on one knee, lowering their heads in reverence. "You see, they work for me."

Kabbus stared at the vehicle curiously for several moments before shifting his gray eyes back to Beelzebub. The demon jumped slightly and lowered his head, knowing that looking straight into his eyes was reserved for special occasions. He did not want the kittens to come back. "My minions will keep you safe. The truck is lead-lined. The humans and angels shouldn't be able to find you.

It will block all signals searching for you from above or below."

Kabbus moved closer, leaning to the side and looking into the large bed. There was a frightened human chained to the back and several large pillows for Kabbus to lie on. His fog slithered up the ramp and hovered in front of the human. Beelzebub watched as her eyes went gray and she seized up, curling into a fetal position. Her face was frozen in fear, and her body no longer moved.

With a smile, Beelzebub bowed again. "This truck will take you to a base that is filled with people you can feed on. You will be able to eat as much as you desire, and when that runs out, there are billions more all over the planet. We can help you acquire them without the hassle you just went through in the city."

Kabbus breathed steadily as his tentacles relaxed, the energy from the human's fear surging through him. Beelzebub watched as he began to slither forward, moving up the ramp and into the back of the truck. His body covered the human and he turned around, folding his tentacles beneath him like a cat and lying down on the cushions.

The Damned quickly shut the doors.

12

A portal opened slowly in the center of the base. Carefully, Katie stepped through, Pandora clinging tightly to her arm. They were both shaken up very badly, worse than they had ever been after any battle. Katie and Pandora huddled next to each other for several moments, just staring around the base. Katie shook her head. "It's almost like I can't tell what is real and what isn't. I am terrified that what I am looking at is nothing more than a nightmare. I am waiting for the horror to begin."

Pandora gripped her tighter. "I know. That was the strangest and most horrifying thing that has ever happened to me. It all felt so real. It even smelled real, and I could hear the wind blowing in my mind."

Katie shivered. "This is something we don't know how to stop. And if we can't even be in our own right minds, it could attack us at any time and we would never know it. Those poor people; they died absolutely terrified."

Pandora sighed. "It's almost as if him killing them was a

gift—a stop to the horror that was circling through their minds. If it did stop. I *hope* it stopped for them in death."

Tears gathered in Katie's eyes and she put her arm over Pandora's shoulder. "I'm sure it did. Try not to think about it. Why don't you get inside?"

Pandora nodded. "Can I? I would feel much safer."

Katie let go of her. "Of course."

Pandora immediately dove into Katie and she toppled backward, catching herself. Her mind was weak, and so was her body. For a moment she didn't even know where to go, too afraid to even take a step forward since she feared it wouldn't be real. All she could do was stare down at her shaking hands and wait, hoping that at any moment she would snap out of it.

Across the sandy ground, Stephanie and Korbin walked outside, laughing about a movie they'd just watched. Stephanie glanced at Korbin as they walked out of the building. "From now on, every time a helicopter comes to rescue us, I'm screaming, 'Get to the choppa!'"

Korbin laughed and walked forward, running right into Stephanie's back. She had stopped, the smile fading from her lips. "Is that Katie?"

Korbin squinted. "It looks like it."

Stephanie shook her head and started to jog. "What happened to her?"

Both of them ran full speed to where she was, slowing down as they approached. Korbin walked forward and put his hands on her shoulders. She gasped, jumping in fright and looking up at him. He stared at her fearful face, feeling her body trembling. "Come here."

Korbin pulled her into a tight hug, looking at Stephanie

in concern. Whispering into her ear, Korbin tried to pull her out of it. "Katie, what happened? Pandora, are you in there?"

Katie's body began to shake harder, so he could tell that she was inside of Katie, and in about the same shape. Korbin looked at Stephanie. "Go get Brock. I'll carry her to her room."

Stephanie nodded and took off in the other direction, heading for the training area. Korbin leaned down and picked Katie up, cradling her in his arms. She laid her head on his shoulder and stared into the distance as they walked slowly across the sandy base toward the main barracks. When he reached the building, Calvin opened the door and paused, looking at Korbin and down at Katie.

Korbin gave him a concerned look and he stepped to the side, letting him carry her through and following them. They walked up the stairs and down the hall to her room. Calvin flipped on the lights and sat on the edge of the bed as Korbin laid her down. Immediately she curled into a ball and began to shiver.

Calvin grabbed her blanket, pulling it up and over her shoulders. He rubbed his hand over her hair, shaking his head. "What in the world could have done this to her?"

Korbin looked very concerned. "I have no idea."

Stephanie and Brock walked quickly into the room. As soon as Brock saw her, he slowed down, looking up at Korbin and then back at her. He sat on the edge of the bed and the rest of them left, closing the door behind them. Katie sat up and looked Brock in the eyes, tears finally escaping and cascading down her cheeks. She collapsed in his arms, sobbing.

Brock rubbed the back of her head. "What's wrong?"

She sniffed, shaking her head. "Let's just be together for a minute; just for a minute."

Calvin walked back outside, trying to shake his shock from seeing Katie like that. The plane carrying Sofia was landing on the runway in the far corner of the base. The last thing he wanted to do was freak her out. She needed to stay calm and cool while she was pregnant. They already had so many things going on that they couldn't control.

He picked up his pace and trotted toward the runway. The plane came to a stop and turned, facing the other direction. Calvin grabbed the set of stairs and rolled them up to the door as it opened. He put the brakes on and stood at the bottom, forcing a big smile as Sofia stepped into the doorway. She had several things in her hands, including two coffees and a box of what looked like pastries.

She carefully came down the steps, Calvin meeting her halfway and taking her things from her. She put her hands on his face and kissed him softly. Calvin grinned, looking down at her tummy. It had grown a lot, and he thought about his words before he said them. "Our baby is getting so strong. You look absolutely radiant."

Sofia grinned. "Your mother taught you well, my love. You always know exactly what to say."

When they got to the bottom, she took one of the coffees and sipped it. "Oh, do you have bacon?"

Calvin lifted an eyebrow. "If we don't, we'll make sure to get some."

Sofia let out a deep breath of relief. "Oh, good. Because I have been having the worst cravings lately. It started with bacon, and that has seriously not gone away. I had to portion myself out bacon for each day, or I would cook an entire package and eat the whole thing in ten minutes."

Calvin smiled. "Even non-pregnant people do that because, well, bacon is amazing."

Sofia giggled. "Then it started including apple fritters and Vietnamese coffee. I tried to make my own fritters, you know, to save money and so I didn't feel like such a hippo going in there every day, but that didn't work. So, I started blaming it on you, saying you requested them a dozen at a time."

Calvin laughed. "Okay. So, when I go back to San Diego, where am I not going?"

Sofia smiled. "I always get them from Rose Donuts. Of course, if I'm not in San Diego, I will have to make do and get them from wherever I can. I am not that picky, but I probably *will* complain."

Calvin juggled the coffee, looking at her with a grin. "Well, you have the right to complain about anything you want to. You are growing an entire human inside you right now. I would be blowing people up."

Sofia shrugged. "Sometimes I get testy, but it's mostly when I'm hungry…or horny. Then I'll snap at people for pretty much nothing. You will see my Mexican sass come out really fast. I remind myself of my *abuela*. She would be proud; I take no shit from anyone."

Calvin blinked, slightly worried. "I need to make sure to feed you, and I mean that both ways, no matter whether you are hungry or horny. We don't need the wild woman coming out in you."

Sofia looked at the box in his hands. "Well, I made sure to eat enough to at least be pleasant when I got here. I brought a box of apple fritters and two coffees. One is for you, of course. I am obviously trying to control my caffeine intake since I have a little bean in there. I love him, and I love my heritage, but what I don't need is a Mexican jumping bean. My stomach only stretches so damn far."

Calvin glanced down at the box and then at Sofia. "Just a warning. Pandora is partial to Krispy Kreme, but I'd keep these away from her just the same."

Sofia furrowed her brow. "I like Pandora a lot, but let me just tell you… Let that angel come up here and try to take my fritters and I'll… I don't know what I'll do, but it will hurt. *Se arranca el cabello por las raíces y la patea en la entrepierna, probablemente.*"

Calvin laughed as he pulled the door to the barracks open and let her walk in before him. "You are so adorable when you get mad and start speed-talking in Spanish."

Sofia laughed. "Until it is aimed at you. Then you won't think it's so funny *or* cute, for that matter."

They stopped in the center landing halfway up to let Sofia catch her breath. Calvin leaned over and kissed her forehead. "You are my wife. I am pretty sure there will be some point in the next sixty years that you will be that livid with me, and when it comes, I will take it in stride."

Sofia grinned. "You'd better."

They headed the rest of the way upstairs and into the dining hall, which was mostly empty. Sofia lowered herself into a chair and Calvin grabbed some napkins. Over coffee and fritters, Calvin knew it was the perfect time to talk to her. "So, I had a long conversation with Korbin on our way here from Paris."

Sofia nodded, chewing a huge bite of fritter. Calvin chuckled. "And we have worked it out so that I will be staying here at the base from now on."

Sofia swallowed hard and looked at him lovingly, tears forming in her eyes. "Damn hormones. I cry over every-thing. A bird looked at me the other day and I burst into tears."

Calvin reached out, smiling, and took her hands. "We are having a baby. A beautiful baby. I cannot wait to hold that sweet angel, and I want to be here for the rest of this pregnancy. I have left you alone for far too long, and it is not okay."

Sofia shrugged, smirking. "Gave me time to spend with all my other lovers."

Calvin laughed, shaking his head. "You are going to drive me crazy for the rest of my life. I am a very lucky man."

Sofia giggled. "Okay, so what are you going to do around here? Train? Go to incursions?"

Calvin took a deep breath and leaned back. "We haven't fully discussed that yet, but a new Leviathan has woken up. It is causing a lot of problems out in Texas right now. We are going to need to track this thing so that we can stop it. Apparently, Katie had a run in with it today, and let's just say, she's curled into a ball in Brock's lap right now."

Sofia stuck out her bottom lip. "Poor Katie. I have never seen her not be tough."

Calvin sighed. "Me either, which means this thing is rough."

Sofia bit the inside of her cheek and narrowed her eyes. "This actually is very interesting to me. I shifted my major in school and have been studying genetics."

Calvin was surprised. "Wow. That's amazing. I don't know why I am surprised, though. You are incredibly intelligent, and can do anything you put your mind to."

Sofia smiled. "I would actually love to help in whatever way that I can. This would be an excellent opportunity to get some lab time in, maybe gain some experience in the new world of genetics."

Calvin thought about it for a moment, wanting to make sure that whatever he put her into, she would be safe. He tapped his finger on his lips. "Actually, I think that would be an excellent idea. This world is new to all of us, so we don't have a lot of people who are capable of doing or assisting in the research. And I would love to see you get involved in this with us. You are already part of the family, and I know it drives you crazy having nothing to do out here."

Sofia rolled her eyes. "Boy, does it ever. Everyone else is work, work, work, and I'm over here bored out of my mind, being infected by demons, eating off other people's plates, and walking around in my nightgown."

Calvin laughed, shaking his head. "That has passed. No one even brings it up…much."

Sofia laughed. "Oh, well, I had two other beings in my body at once. I was not responsible for my actions. Anyways, who could I help with this stuff?"

Calvin thought about it for a second. "We got our top

minds working on it, but there was a doctor who helped Juntto. His name was Dr. Ozu. He's literally the closest thing we have to an expert on Leviathans or alien creatures in general."

Sofia bit her fritter and held it in the air, tapping it to Calvin's. "Sign me up, doc!"

Katie's room was completely silent; Pandora had huddled up inside her without a word. She lay in Brock's lap as he stroked her hair, leaning up against the headboard. She held her hands tightly together in front of her lips and stared out into the room, lost in her thought. Brock's attention and the caring of the others had warmed her on the inside, and she was beginning to feel better again. Still shaky, but better than she had been.

She lifted up out of Brock's lap and rolled her shoulders back, wiping the tears from her cheeks. Katie leaned her head back and took a deep breath through her nose, slowly letting it out of her mouth. When she opened her eyes, Brock was looking at her with a kind and caring face.

Katie smiled, shaking her head. "I'm sorry I folded like that."

Brock reached out and took her hand. "Are you *kidding* me? Do not ever apologize for being a living, breathing creature on this planet. You don't always have to be tough. I am here for you, no matter what."

Katie rubbed her hand over his and let out a deep breath. "I came face to face with the new Leviathan. He is probably the worst so far. He has this ability to mess with your mind. One minute I was soaring toward him with my sword at the ready, and the next, I was stuck in a nightmare. He made my worst nightmare come to life, at least in my head. It was like, no matter how hard I tried, I couldn't save anyone. They were all dying at my hands."

Katie's voice cracked, and Brock stroked her hand. "Shhhh. Just take a deep breath. One thing at a time. It wasn't real, and you are here with me now. Take your time."

Katie swallowed hard and nodded. She took a deep breath and continued, "I thought that buildings were falling down around me. I raced for this family, but just as I was about to pull the little girl out, the building fell on her. Then there was an old man, and I had him; I was holding on to him high up in the air, but his hand slipped and he fell. He fell into the dust and debris and I couldn't see him anymore."

Brock furrowed his brow. "That must have been an absolutely terrible dream."

Katie nodded. "It was. No matter how hard I tried, even with all the power I have in me, I couldn't save them. It was the worst thing I have ever felt or experienced in my life. I can't even imagine what the other people were seeing. And the people that died stuck in their dreams…"

Katie looked down at the bed, trying to push out the sick feeling in her belly. Brock reached over and put his finger under her chin, pushing it up. He leaned forward and pressed his lips to her cheek, pulling her hand into his lap. "Let me tell you something about yourself that you never think about. You have saved and helped many people on this planet since you became a Damned. Thousands and thousands, possibly millions of people, are alive because of the work you have done. You have eradicated a huge portion of the super-huge, super-dangerous demons. You have literally walked through hell to save people in this world. Some saw it directly, and others saw it indirectly."

Pandora cleared her throat. *I hate to be mushy and all, but the dude has a point.*

Katie smiled, putting her head back down. *Then you have to know it's true for you, too.*

Brock leaned back with a grin on his face. "All the bad stuff, all those fears? They are all just in your head. You may not think about them often, but they are always there. We all have them. Some are more personal, while others, like you, worry about not being able to save the world. In my opinion, that makes you one hell of a person, and absolutely earning those wings as an angel."

Katie grinned at him, feeling better just because of his words. He leaned in, lifting her chin. "Even without your wings, you are my sassy, bitchy angel."

Katie laughed loudly, and Brock kissed her lips.

13

It was a clear but brisk day in New York. All of the sidewalks were dry, but there were still large piles of snow from the shoveling and plowing on the roads. The temperatures had stayed in the low thirties and even gone down into the teens, and the wind chill factor was awful. It was one of the colder winters in New York, but that didn't stop the people from coming out and going about their normal routines. Angie had even been able to convince Juntto to get out from beneath the furry Hygge blanket and take a walk around the city with her.

Of course, it wouldn't be New York, or Juntto for that matter, if the conversation wasn't revolving around food. On this particular day, pizza was the topic of discussion. Angie held Juntto's hand, swinging it back and forth. He had morphed into a normal regular-looking guy with dark hair, a beard, and dimples.

Angie looked at the sign for a pizza place and nodded. "See? The New York Slice. That's what I'm talking about. I don't know how you can be a true pizza lover and not love that huge slice of pie. It's as big as your fucking head. Or mine, at least. Yours can get quite big."

Juntto gave Angie a deadpan stare. "Funny. But I have to disagree. I like to sit down in front of those really thick, big, and bulky pizzas. You know, the kind that weighs like ten pounds and you almost have to eat it with a fork?"

He snapped his fingers, looking up as he tried to remember the name for it. "It's uh…uh…oh! Chicago-style pizza! Thick crust, sauce piled on top, and cheese that goes right down to the dough. Throw a little sausage on that bad boy and you will have me forever."

Angie rolled her eyes. "But you live in New York. And what good is pizza if you can't pick it up in your hands and have the grease run down your wrists? One paper plate is never enough to hold the sucker. It just falls apart when you are trying to eat the thing. Might as well wrap a tissue around it."

Juntto shook his head. "But you can eat a large Chicago-style and not be hungry for three days! You eat the New York slice and boom, twenty minutes later you're in line for a hoagie. Chicago all the way!"

Angie leaned her head back and growled. "But it's not even pizza! It's a doughy cheese pie."

Juntto shrugged his shoulders. "Don't care how you classify it here in New York. The point of the matter is, it's fucking delicious down to the last melty, cheesy bite. In fact, I want one right now. But of course, we're in New York, so that does me no good."

Angie laughed and shook her head. "You are adorable. So, I've been thinking about some things."

Juntto glanced down with a raised eyebrow. "This isn't

one of those Dear John moments, is it? 'It's not you, it's me?'"

Angie chuckled. "No, not at all. This is about me and my future. When Katie found me and pulled me out of my situation, she gave me the chance to really prove to myself that I could do anything. I have been handling her day-to-day matters since before she even bought the condo. It's been fun and great, and I wouldn't give it up for anything in the world."

Juntto nodded. "So what's the issue?"

Angie shrugged. "There's no issue, exactly, but things have changed and evolved. With Katie out of pocket more often, I have a bit more free time. Actually, I would calculate it as a *lot* more free time."

Juntto sighed. "I would love more free time. Just wrap me up, stick a slice of Chicago-style pizza in my pie hole, and hand me the remote. Oh, and of course, I want you by my side."

Angie snorted. "Gee, thanks. I'm not complaining about the free time. I just ran out of hobbies to try. So, I was thinking about getting a side job. I mean, it's not for the money. Katie pays me a ton of money. In fact, I could retire right now and never need or want for anything. It's more about filling my time with things that fulfill me. Make me feel like I am being true to myself. Something I would really enjoy."

Juntto shook his head. "Okay. Like when my father wanted me to take over the family business, but instead I became a warrior? I enjoyed chopping heads off and winning battles to become the ultimate warrior of my country."

Angie lifted an eyebrow. "Uh…yeah, like that, only minus the killing people part."

Juntto rubbed his chin. "Hey, I know what you can do. I have seen these people on the internet. They do these live-stream cams. You could do one of those. They have all kinds of followers and they make money and they seem to love what they do. The way they dance and cheer and answer questions from their streaming chat, they seem to really enjoy it."

Angie stopped, causing Juntto to as well. Her mouth was open in complete shock. "Juntto! I can't believe that you would suggest that."

Juntto looked at her confused. "What? There is no shame in that."

Angie struggled to get through the shock. "What? I…you…"

She leaned in and whispered to him angrily. "I am not going to do amateur porn. I told you already that we aren't taping a damn thing."

Juntto put his head back and laughed. "No, no. I would never. You are mine to look at."

Angie opened her mouth to protest but just let it go. "What are you talking about then?"

Juntto waved his hand in the air, walking again. "You know. Like Twitch. YouTube. Beam. Those people make money, right?"

Angie's face lit up. "Ohhhh. Yeah, they do. And I could do what I love at the same time. I like that. I like that a lot."

Baal shivered, pulling his long coat with tails closed in front of him as he waited outside of Beelzebub's cave door. Usually, it was unlocked, but for some reason, it wasn't this time. It was quite a bit colder on the outer rings of hell where Beelzebub dwelt, but there were too many ears listening where Baal lived. At least, that was what Beelzebub's concern was.

After a few minutes and several knocks, he finally opened the door. He put his hand up, smiling and swishing his glass of bourbon around. He was wearing what looked like a silk smoking jacket as they sauntered through the dark hallways of his cave. When they entered his study, the fire was blazing, cutting the chill in the air. Baal finally felt warm.

Baal took off his jacket and hung it over the back of one of the chairs. "I honestly don't know how you deal with the low one-fifty outside. It's frigid."

Beelzebub shrugged. "I'm sure I won't be here forever."

Baal sat down, taking a glass of bourbon from Beelzebub. "It looks like a celebration again. What are we celebrating?"

Beelzebub turned dramatically, throwing his hands out. His bourbon splashed onto the floor and evaporated. "My readmission to the council, of course. It has been many centuries, but I have waited patiently. That patience has finally paid off. On top of that, my first order of business is going amazingly."

Baal sipped his drink, lifting an eyebrow. "Oh, yes? Which one would that be?"

Beelzebub chuckled, plopping down in the chair by the fire. "The Nightmare, Kabbus. Right now, he is free and sowing fear among the humans just like he was created to do. Of course, it took me speaking to him and having him moved to a better area, but after a few moments of groveling, he was more than happy to come along."

Baal raised his eyebrow as he watched Beelzebub's face. He was suspicious of the other demon's every move. He had thought he was suspicious before, but now it seemed that the plot was getting even thicker. He wasn't sure if he could even continue to associate with him if he kept striding cockily down that road.

Beelzebub waved his hand in the air. "You see, it takes two things to be successful in these missions. It takes finesse with the lesser creatures, and it takes the ability to grovel and not mean a word of it. Confidence in everything you do will sell it, even if you are lying through your damn teeth."

Baal nodded, faking a smile. He could see Beelzebub's wheels turning. The old schemer always had something up his sleeve, and there was no way he was done with the situation. He was too antsy to just let it go like that. "You know, I've noticed that you're awfully buddy-buddy with Lucifer these days."

Beelzebub's lips vibrated, and he spat all over the place. Baal narrowed his eyes, wiping a fleck off of his eyebrow. He gazed into his glass and put it to the side. "So, you aren't?"

Beelzebub leaned forward, looking into the fire. "In a way, I guess I am, but I know full well that no one stays in favor for very long. And in the end, those so-called friends end up as meat under his feet. No. Lucifer is, in a word, twat-struck. He's either pining over his lost wife Lilith or trying to please Mania by getting her a pair of grackles or some shit."

Baal smirked at the characterization of Lucifer as "twat-struck." Beelzebub did have a point. Over the centuries, Lucifer's mood had always ebbed and flowed with wherever he was with that one woman he'd decided to spend a few hundred years obsessing over and pining for. Yet the women never saw it; they were always fearful. Baal didn't blame them. Lucifer often lost his temper and killed someone, then later regretted it. Too late then.

Beelzebub took a deep breath and gulped his drink. "The point of the whole thing is, I am now back on the Council of Eight, and I would like to stay there. So if it takes sucking up and rubbing elbows for a bit, that's what I'll do."

Baal shrugged. "Actually, right now the Council is more like five, but I get your point."

Beelzebub rolled his eyes and looked at Baal. "Five, eight, who fucking cares? It could just be the two of us, and it would still be a position of power. That is what I wanted: the ability to wield that power in ways that I can see working out in the best interests of my closest comrades and me. Of course, right now that is you. I've got the power, and Lucifer is otherwise occupied."

Baal watched him, not replying. Then again, he had done that his whole life. When he saw someone spiraling, he tended to stay near but keep his mouth shut so as to not be implicated in their ludicrous plans. "You do have the power, that is true, but you have to be careful, or you could lose it. Though, looking around, I don't think I need to tell you that."

Beelzebub was too caught up in his head to hear what Baal was saying. He turned to the other demon and leaned his elbows on his thighs. "What we need to do, Baal, is plan ahead. That is the most important part. Always stay two steps ahead."

Baal smiled and picked up his drink, lifting it into the air. He smirked snidely. *You silly fool. I always* think *ahead. How do you think you got here in the first place?*

Beelzebub poured another glass and threw it back, stumbling around the room. Baal's smile faded, and he sighed. *Beelzebub, you are going to fuck yourself. Just wait and see.*

The sun was setting on the base, and training was over for the day. Most of the soldiers had already eaten and retired to their living quarters, knowing the next day would be full of more training and hard work. A small group of them stayed in the dining hall, playing poker for quarters and drinking a case of beer one of them had picked up in town.

Outside, you could see a bunch of fruit lined up on the fence, glowing in the evening light. Eddie had his tongue hanging slightly out of the corner of his mouth, and he was aiming at the orange. He had already taken down a watermelon. He was doing better with his aim since Coco had given him the pointers. He breathed in through his nose and slowly let the air out of his mouth before pulling the trigger. He lifted his head just as it hit the orange, exploding it from the center. Eddie smiled proudly, moving over so Sean could wheel up and take a shot.

Sean held the gun up, no longer needing Eddie's help with it. He went through the steps, lining the shot up, focusing, and then pulling the trigger. He looked up as the bullet grazed the side of a grapefruit and watched as it spun in wild circles before falling to the ground and bouncing through the sand.

Eddie slapped Sean hard on the shoulder. "It's all right, buddy. You can always get a good job in a grocery store. You can explain to old ladies how to peel a grapefruit."

Sean rolled his eyes. "At least I hit it without the assistance of a demon."

Eddie chuckled. "I am not ashamed in the least, and you shouldn't be either when I shoot that demon who is chasing you around the base in your wheelchair."

Sean leaned his head back and laughed. "Okay, so he helps you with your shots. That's great. Shouldn't you already be good with that? The rest of the guys are. The only way your demon would be fierce is if someone pulled it out of you and tossed it back in the pregnant woman. She straight scared the living shit out of about forty highly-trained military personnel, some black ops, and some Damned."

Eddie fake-laughed. "You keep at it. Wait until *you* get a demon. Watch it be a demon in a fucking wheelchair. In fact, I'm half-tempted to cut one's legs off and toss him inside you. The invalid leading the invalid."

Sean smiled. "I could probably still outrun you."

Eddie laughed, shaking his head. "I'd fucking roll this wheelchair right off a cliff, my friend. You better hope your demon has wings."

Sean smirked. "I'm pretty sure the one who saved your ass more than once did."

Eddie threw his head back. "Ohhhh, Sean's got jokes."

They laughed, slapping hands and looking out at the sunset. Eddie sat down next to him and let out a deep breath. Just then, Brock and Turner walked out onto the roof. Turner smacked Eddie in the back of the head and roughed up Sean's hair. "Aw, look, Brock. We interrupted the two lovebirds watching a warm and beautiful sunset together."

Brock laughed. "What you doing up here? Shooting shit? Let me have a go."

Brock and Turner took turns using Eddie's sniper rifle. They each shot a watermelon, and Turner hit two grapefruit. He turned to Brock, grinning. "Okay. I got two grapefruit. You gotta hit an orange or two to beat that."

Brock rolled his eyes. "This is a real waste of food. You know that, right? We are facing an apocalypse, and we are shooting fruit. Fast-forward two years, and we'll be kicking ourselves."

Turner looked at him seriously for a minute and then raised his leg. He stuck his tongue out of his mouth and made a loud, long fart noise. "You're a real waste of food."

Brock threw one of the leftover apples at him and shook his head. "I can see that the IQ level of my team is still in the lowest bracket."

Everyone laughed as Turner shined the apple on his sleeve and took a bite of it. They all took seats, looking around as the moon began to show in the sky. Sean reached over, slapping Brock in the chest. "Hey, how is Katie doing? I know she came back pretty fucked up from her last mission. I don't think I've ever seen her like that before, and I've been waiting until you resurfaced again to ask."

Brock sighed, leaning back on his hands. "She's resting right now. I finally got her to fall asleep. It took a while for her to feel comfortable with it. She was in really rough shape when she got back here. I was just glad she managed to get herself back before falling apart like that, but she's getting better by the minute. You know her; she's hard as nails. I bet by tomorrow she's back up and rocking out, ready to kick more fucking ass. But it's good that she let her human side rest and recover from things like that sometimes. Otherwise, she might just get too tired."

Sean chuckled, tilting his head to the side. "She is one of the toughest people I know."

Turner laughed. "Hell, yeah, she is. When she gets mad, I'm in a fetal position calling for my mommy."

Eddie smirked. "Shit, that happens when you fucking stub a damn toe."

Turner gave him the middle finger, and Brock shook his head. "Oh. Sean? Turner? You guys are missing demons. I know it's something that you had set up with Katie and Pandora, but they are both pretty fucked up. When they are up for it, we'll talk to Pandora."

They both nodded. Sean tapped his knee. "Hey, man, no stress. Tell them thanks, and to feel better. That's the biggest thing to focus on."

14

Katie leaned her elbow on the table and took a bite of the donut in front of her. The texture of the fresh dough and the sugar almost immediately warmed her chest, helping her to feel better. Stephanie sat beside her, glancing at her nervously from time to time as if she were going to shatter into a hundred pieces. On a normal basis that would have driven her mad, but it was nice to know she had such a strong support system in her family.

Sofia took a deep breath and rubbed her belly. "It's funny. I'm starving one minute, but after I eat two bites, I feel like I can't move. Then about ten minutes later I'm starving again because the kid has stopped resting his elbow on my stomach, closing it off."

Pandora giggled inside of Katie. *I think being able to control metabolism would be terrible for a pregnant woman. She would birth a 150-pound full-grown child from all the nutrients she would be giving it.*

Katie chuckled, glad to hear Pandora talking again. Katie looked more tired than she felt, but Pandora was feeling much better and eating her fair share of the donuts. Stephanie sighed and put her chin in her palm, leaning her elbow on the table. "What is it like having a baby in you? Is it like having a demon?"

Sofia laughed, then stopped to think about it for a moment. "Wow, I guess in a way, it is. But the baby doesn't do things on purpose, and I love it more than life. The demon did stomp on my bladder while it was in there and move around, making me feel very uncomfortable, but more in a weird fluttering-of-the-chest kind of manner."

Stephanie sat up and picked up her donut. "Yeah, I didn't think about us having disdain for the demons inside of us, at least at one point or another. I never had any kids. In my former life I was never set up for it, and then I had all the girls. After that I became Damned, and by the time we were blissfully unaware of ever having been Damned, we were afraid to try since I was a bit past my prime in that area."

Katie put her hand on Stephanie's shoulder and squeezed. "You have all of us, and I know the guys look to you as a mother figure. I know it's not the same, but…"

Sofia shook her head. "Please, by God, don't look at me all wistfully. It is not as magical as it might seem. There are things your body does and produces that I swear have been written into horror novels."

They all laughed. Katie smiled. "How far along are you?"

Sofia puffed out her cheeks. "Twenty-two weeks—almost to my third trimester. Even with all the shit that has gone down, it has really flown by. I feel like just yesterday I was strapping on a bikini to go for a dip in the ocean. No bikinis for this girl now. All I think about is food."

Stephanie glanced at the coffee. "So you can have caffeine?"

Sofia nodded. "Oh, yeah. They used to say no, but my doc said just don't overdo it and I'll be fine. I don't know how I would have functioned without Calvin around with no caffeine. I would have just been sleeping on the couch all the time."

Katie perked up. "What about wine? Did they change that rule?"

Sofia pouted. "Unfortunately, no. No wine. I miss wine. Oh! And soft cheese. Oh my God, I miss soft cheese. Spread on some homemade crackers. Mmm."

Stephanie furrowed her brow. "Why not soft cheese?"

Sofia shrugged, chewing her apple fritter. "Apparently it can carry listeria or something like that. All I know is that he said no and I sank into a deep depression. And you know what I really miss, out of everything?"

Katie chuckled. "Balance?"

Sofia smirked. "That too. But no. I desperately miss not having to pee every twenty minutes. I have never spent as much time in the bathroom as I do now."

Pandora grunted. *Hell, no. That whole situation sounds absolutely miserable. And God knows I would end up with some weird craving like sardines. Nope. Not this body. I'm all about what leads up to a pregnancy, but I'm never gonna even think about putting one of those tiny shitting meatsacks in my belly.*

Katie held back a laugh. *Maybe if you met the right guy. Might be all for it.*

Pandora spat as she belted out laughter. *Uh, honey? Let*

me just tell you about my romantic philosophy. There is never a Mr. Right. He does not exist in anything but fairytales and romance novels. What there is, though, is Mr. Right Now. There are plenty of those going around on a daily basis. And Mr. Right Now will never see me with a big, bloated belly unless I just left an Italian restaurant.

Katie let out a deep breath. *Yeah, but isn't it wild to think that while there is so much bad in the world, something like a baby can take all of that away in like two seconds? There is something about a baby that brings hope.*

Pandora scoffed. *Hope that it doesn't pee in your eye when you go to change its diaper.*

Katie chuckled. *I know you feel what I'm talking about, even if you try to act like a stone-cold bitch all the time. There is something inside of you that sees the beauty that is going on. The hope it brings that our species is stronger than Lucifer's hordes. I don't know. That's just my thought process on it.*

Pandora let out a long deep sigh. *I suppose you're right. After feeling that fear from Kabbus and sitting here listening to the stories about the beginning of a new life, I guess it does make you feel a little bit hopeful. How can something so beautiful ever be overshadowed by something so horrible as Kabbus? The answer is, it can't. Even if it just can't in our minds, that is a start.*

Katie was proud of Pandora. *See? And you never thought you could pull the demon from you. Here you are with angel blood, talking about the beauty and sanctity of a brand-new little baby. I'm proud of you.*

Pandora sniffed. *Don't get all mushy on me just yet. You never know; that thing could come out with horns and a tail.*

Katie smirked. *And...it's gone.*

Feeling better about everything, Pandora finally pulled herself out of Katie and walked around to sit next to Sofia. Stephanie smiled at Pandora. "Nice to see you up and around again. We've missed your snark."

Katie laughed. "Must be nice. Didn't stop in my head at all."

Pandora stuck her tongue out at Katie and waved her hands. "Well, give a sister a fucking donut and stop looking at me like I'm some homeless child."

Stephanie chuckled and passed the donuts to her. Pandora looked at Sofia. "Okay, let's get real here for a minute. Sofia, how big your boobs gonna get?"

Korbin held open the door to the armory as Stephanie ran across the yard, her coat pulled up on both sides of her face to block the wildly blowing wind that was throwing sand all over the place. She walked in and the door shut hard behind them. She shook the sand off of her and looked at Korbin with wide eyes. "Whoop, I tell you what! The winds have been wild this last month. We put up blockers, but on a day like this, there is no stopping that shit. We'll all become sand castles."

They looked up to see Joshua waving at them from his glass-fronted office's door. They hurried through the armory, smiling and waving at the girls as they passed. He held the door for them and shut it, which completely cut out all the noise from the machines, then sat down behind the desk. Korbin and Stephanie sat in the chairs.

Korbin looked out at the armory. "You guys are really working hard."

Joshua sighed. "Yeah, we are. We've taken up working at night, too."

Stephanie looked at him with concern. "Are you sleeping?"

Joshua smiled. "Yeah, although usually in this chair. But we have to pick up the pace, and that's why I called you guys here. Even with extending production hours, we are still struggling hard to keep up with the demand for bullets. Once the government got involved and the private sector learned about them, we went to max production. Add on the forts on top of that, and we are just not producing enough to meet the orders. We have private orders that have been on hold for three months because we have to get to the other ones first."

Stephanie furrowed her brow. "And right now, building a whole new armory would be hard to do and hard to manage."

Joshua nodded. "I know, and the government is ever-growing, which means their orders are coming in faster and larger. As of right now, given the status of our warehouse, it looks like we are going to have to short the forts a few shipments in order to make sure other governments get enough. Hopefully, those governments are sharing with the forts, but they have to be armed too."

Korbin leaned back in the chair and rubbed his chin, looking out at the manufacturing floor. He groaned, tilting his head to one side. "Obviously I'm not thrilled about that. It's bad to build a fort and not arm it, especially since they seem to be the favorite targets for incursions. At the same time, the governments are the ones footing the bills for these things, and they can't be without either. It's a no-win situation right now."

Joshua sat forward, clasping his hands together nervously. "I knew you would be upset, but I am literally pushing these machines to their max, not to mention the people that work here."

Korbin put up his hand. "No, I know that, Joshua. You are doing a fantastic job. I can't fault you if we don't have the machine power, resources, or staff to handle the load we have put on our shoulders."

Just then there was a knock on the door and a soldier, uniform perfectly pressed, her makeup done just right for uniform standards, opened the door. "Sorry to interrupt."

Joshua waved her in. "It's okay, Wanda. What's up?"

She walked over next to him and held a clipboard in front of him. "The shipment for DC is ready to go out."

Joshua nodded. "Thanks. I'll sign off on everything after the meeting."

Wanda touched his shoulder and smiled. "Thanks, baby."

Immediately Stephanie and Korbin sat up straighter in their chairs. They glanced at each other and up at Wanda, giving her a smile as she left the room. They then looked across the desk at Joshua, who seemed to be completely oblivious to anything that was going on. Stephanie pursed her lips and went to speak, but Korbin reached over and patted her hand, giving a quick, discreet shake of his head.

Joshua let out a deep breath, tossing his notes on the desk. "Yeah, so that's where we're at right now."

Korbin nodded, glancing at Stephanie. "Honey, could

you give me just a couple of minutes to talk to Joshua alone?"

Stephanie cleared her throat nervously and stood up. "Of course. I have some work to do with the trainees, and I want to check up on the guys."

She walked around the desk and gave Joshua a hard hug. "Don't be stressed. You are literally doing everything you can, and you are doing a fantastic job at it. We can't just make this stuff appear out of thin air."

Joshua patted her back. "Thanks, Stephanie."

She turned back around, winked at Korbin, and left the office. Korbin sat there for several moments, waiting for the door to shut and the noise to cease. When it had, he looked at Joshua and tilted his head to the side. "So, uh… anything new, Joshua?"

Joshua furrowed his brow and looked at Korbin, slightly confused. "No. I mean, with the amount of time we are spending here at the facility, the only thing new would be the upgrade in coffee blend we ordered, but only because we had bought up all of the other kind from the supplier."

Korbin blinked at him for a moment and pointed to Wanda, who was standing outside checking paperwork. Joshua shook his head confused. "Her?"

Korbin nodded. "Yes, her. Wanda."

Joshua scratched the top of his head. "What about her?"

Korbin leaned back nonchalantly, waving his hand. "You two…friends?"

Joshua shrugged, putting a file in the drawer. "I guess."

Korbin slapped his hand to his head and sat up, staring at him. "I'm really trying to not make you feel weird here."

Joshua just gave him a confused look.

Korbin rolled his eyes and motioned to Wanda. "You know she's totally into you, right?"

Joshua let out a long deep breath and his shoulders slumped. "Yes, of course I know she's into me. I've known that since we first met. She isn't really the type of girl to hold those kinds of things back."

Korbin smiled. "So, what are you gonna do about it?"

Joshua grumped. "That's the problem. I have no idea what to do about it. You have to know that girls being interested in me was not something that EVER happened before I came here. Even after this long, she's the first one who has actually made it known."

Korbin nodded. "I get it. You are nervous. This is new to you. It's new to everyone at some point, but we as a species have made it work."

Joshua shook his head, rubbing his face. "I wish it was still caveman times, when grunting was acceptable and clubbing was the way to get your woman, and I don't mean dance clubs. We work together, and you and I might be blatantly misreading her. There are far too many variables that could cause this whole thing to blow up right in my face. So, like I do with all things that make me slightly uncomfortable, I am going to stay out of it and act like nothing is going on."

Korbin put his palms on the desk and looked at him seriously. "No, buddy. That's not the answer here. You live in the same world as me, right? We watch people die left and right. Men, women, children, lovers, families, couples—this war does not care who it kills. It is not picky. No one gets left out. So, when something happens that is good, we need to hold on to it with everything we've got."

Joshua looked at her and back at Korbin. "So, you're saying I should ask her out? Or talk to her about it?"

Korbin smiled. "What I'm saying is, if and when you find something that's good, you go after it with everything you've got. Because there are very few good things left in the world. If it's not her, fine, but don't miss out on something you want because you are scared of the outcome. I almost did that, and I am telling you right now, my life is better because I took a chance."

The eighteen-wheeler bounced along the curvy road as the driver sped toward their destination. Kabbus was still in the back, lounging on the large pillows the Damned had set up for him. The space was cramped, though, and he barely fit inside without bulging the sides of the semi. It was also completely dark back there, no lights set up for the Nightmare. His gray eyes were the only things that were somewhat visible in the cloak of darkness.

They hit another bump, and Kabbus shifted to the right. His body shivered and he squirmed, trying to get himself in a better position. The frustration was building inside of him and his tentacles began to wave and flail, slamming into the floor of the truck. Up front, the two Damned drivers were trying to make it through Colorado as fast as they could. The loud thump caught both of their attention, and they looked at each other with concern. They hadn't really been told anything about the Leviathan, and they were starting to get nervous from all the thumping and the swaying coming from the back of the truck.

The driver shook his head. "I won't lie. I can't help but be a little fucking worried about whatever monster it is that we have cramped up in the back of this semi. He's definitely not making it easy to drive this fucking big-ass thing."

The other driver pursed his lips. "Did they tell you what it is? Do you know?"

He shook his head. "No. I have no idea what that thing is. The only thing Beelzebub told me was that it is a night-mare, whatever the fuck that's supposed to mean."

The other guy scoffed. "You got that shit right…"

The driver sighed and looked at the sign they were passing. "Hey, there's a place called Glazed and Confused. We could get a dozen donuts and a few joints for the road. Wouldn't take us too long."

The other guy shook his head. "Fuck that. Let's get this thing where it needs to go. I'm a little freaked out, for real."

The driver nodded. "Me too."

The other guy slapped him on the shoulder, their eyes glowing brightly. "Let's just get this over with."

In the back, Kabbus began to calm, his tentacles slowly dropping down next to his large body. He could sense the fear from the guys up front, and he more than liked it…

15

Katie stood on the edge of the helipad, her hand up to block the sand. She watched as the helo slowly descended. It touched down and the engine was turned off, the blades very slowly coming to a stop. When the doors opened, Katie walked forward, giving Doctor Ozu a hand down out of the chopper. She took his bag, and the two of them hurried from underneath the still whirling blades.

Katie shook the doctor's hand. "It's so good to have you here with us. We've got the whole crew here with us on this one, and there is a lot happening. The only two who aren't here are Juntto and Angie, but we can get them here if you need them. They are manning the house in New York."

The doctor smiled. "It's an exciting and frightening time right now, but beyond the Leviathan stuff, I will want to do some general medical exams. As far as Juntto is concerned, as long as he is doing well, I don't think I'll need to see him. I have taken more than enough samples from him. The general told me that he is on call right now, ready to move if anything happens."

Katie nodded. "He is. Juntto is one of our biggest assets in the fight against the Leviathan. He is huge, and not of this world. He has an understanding that we just don't have of these creatures. And the tracking system you will be working on? That will be with our tech guys, Timothy and Sean. Timothy is the lead. Sean is an injured vet, not Damned anymore, and has been working with Timothy to learn everything. He isn't as knowledgeable, but he is definitely getting there."

The doctor gave a thumbs-up. "I've heard about both of them. I am very anxious to meet them and pick their brains on this tracking system. First, though, I think it is important that I take some time to examine Sofia."

Katie took a deep breath. "Absolutely. She has been waiting for you to get here. She's been feeling just fine. The baby is moving, her appetite is good, and there haven't been any outward signs that would worry us."

The doctor looked at the base. "That's good. That's really good. I hope everything on the inside matches the outside. She was infected by a demon early in her pregnancy. We have never had a chance to see what the possible side-effects are on the mother and child. I believe I've heard stories about infected pregnant women, but usually they die pretty quickly after infection. The body—its natural reaction—is to fight off foreign objects, and it works double-time in pregnant women. I'm sure she's going to be just fine, but I want to do an exam, talk to her, and listen to the baby just to make sure."

Sofia sat up on the cold metal table in a hospital gown with her bare feet swaying back and forth. Dr. Ozu was taking notes in his file and printing out the pictures from the sonogram. He turned with a smile and handed them to her. "Is this your first sono?"

Sofia shook her head. "No, but it's been a while. The baby was just a bean the last time I saw it. I can't believe how quickly they grow."

Dr. Ozu nodded. "I know. The human—and not human—body is an amazing thing."

He opened the file and scanned through his notes. "So, your bloodwork looks great, your levels are in perfect ranges, and you show no signs of high blood pressure, cholesterol, or elevated sugar. The sonogram was perfect too. The heartbeat was healthy and strong, there is ample movement, and the cord is safely in place. You are still fully closed, with no signs of early labor or anything like that. Of course, I'm not an OB, but as far as general physician knowledge, I would say you have a very healthy baby."

Sofia let out a deep breath and smiled. "So, being infected for that short a time didn't affect anything?"

Dr. Ozu shook his head. "Nope. Doesn't seem to have left any marks behind on either of you. Now, if you start to experience anything you deem strange—any pain, labor pains, tightness in the stomach, bleeding, or any of the common or uncommon warning signs—I want you to contact a doctor right away. You should be able to call your doctor, and they will be able to refer you to someone out here."

Sofia lifted an eyebrow. "What about cravings? I mean, nothing weird like dirt or laundry soap like they ask, but I have cravings for apple fritters that are so bad sometimes that I feel like I could kill someone for one."

Dr. Ozu laughed. "That's perfectly normal. As long as you are eating enough other foods too, there is nothing to worry about. Of course, if you commit homicide we may have to run some tests, but those types of cravings come and go through the pregnancy. You have nothing to worry about."

Sofia put her hand to her chest. "Oh, good. I was starting to think I was losing it."

Dr. Ozu smiled, chuckling. "No, not losing it. You can eat as many apple fritters as you want. Within reason, of course. Make sure you are getting protein, vegetables, fruit, and all your basic nutritional needs as well. And make sure you are taking a prenatal vitamin. If you don't have one already, you can pick some up at Walmart or any pharmacy. They are pretty much the same as prescription brands unless you needed one specific kind of supplement."

Sofia nodded. "I've been taking them every day."

Dr. Ozu patted her knee. "Good. Let me just collect a couple of things, and I'll let you get dressed. Then you are free to go. Do you know your way back through the barracks?"

Sofia nodded. "Yeah. I've had more than a few boring nights walking the halls."

Dr. Ozu turned to pick up some paperwork and Sofia bit the inside of her lip. Finally, she decided to just go for it. "Uh, Doctor, I actually had some other questions, but they aren't related to me. I am studying genetics in school."

He lifted both eyebrows. "You are? That's great. We need more people in that field. What were your questions?"

Sofia thought about it for a moment. "Well, Calvin said you are the one who worked with Juntto. Can you tell me about that?"

The doctor grabbed his stool and took a seat, thoughtfully considering his answer. "That was difficult, I can't lie. It was not just genetics, but psychology as well. You know as well as I do that we can have the best genes in the world, but our psychology often makes the path to successful use of those genes difficult."

Sofia nodded. "Right, but how did that relate to Juntto?"

Dr. Ozu looked up, taking a deep breath. "You have to remember that we aren't just dealing with a normal human from Earth. We are dealing with alien or maybe even supernatural forces when it comes to the Leviathans, most of which we don't understand. Until now, there was no ability to study this kind of thing. Geneticists worked with human genes, not aliens or people from other dimensions. We are also not talking about creatures that are two planets over. We are talking about dimensional shifts. We could travel the galaxy forever and never find them because they are not in this time or this place."

Sofia nodded. "Okay, and that did cross my mind when I was thinking about all this. Before I left San Diego to come here, I was learning about adding traits not found in an organism to improve them. For example, giving plants resistance to disease."

Doctor Ozu smiled slightly. "Right."

Sofia shook her head, hopping down from the table and starting to pace. "That got me thinking. When it comes to Leviathans, we don't know how much we don't know, right? I mean, they could be anything. Their entire structure and makeup could be something completely foreign to us from their genes to the follicles of their hair. We could be looking at creatures who have no corollary at all in this world and in this time."

Dr. Ozu crossed his legs and put his finger on his lip. "That is very true. At this point, we don't have a clue as to what new things, or things not known to us, are circulating and creating the Leviathans. Or what out of those things will give us clues to other dimensions."

Sofia shook her finger, still pacing. "BUT...we know what they're *not*. We know one hundred percent that they are not humans. So, since we know what they aren't, we could still use Timothy's tech for locating incursions but adjust it."

The doctor tilted his head and stared thoughtfully at her. Sofia nodded at him. "Just try to follow me for a second. I know it sounds strange now, but there is a point to it in the end. I've been putting a lot of thought into this over the last few days. Right now, when we use the system, we are looking for one type of energy: demonic. That means we have to search for human energy too because of the Damned. But what if instead of searching for demonic energy, we scan the planet, eliminating the humans from the search?"

The doctor grinned. "Basically, you are saying that you want us to look for everything that *isn't* human? You have to stop and think about how the scan works. Everything that gives off energy can be picked up by it. Animals, and even some plants, have been seen. We witnessed that when we were scanning the oceans and picked up energy coming off a specific type of algae that grouped together in the Atlantic. What you're proposing here is that we not only adjust the program for every human, but it would have to be adjusted for every living thing *in the entire world.*"

Sofia sighed as the doctor spoke. She hadn't thought about that.

Doctor Ozu could see she was trying. "Think about science and technology. Think about our capabilities within the time frames that we are given. It would be incredibly complex and have too much data to compress the search into such a small sector, and we would be looking for an energy where we don't even know how it is emitted. If we had, say, twenty years to perfect it, we could definitely work out a system for that. We would input every species of living thing on the planet."

Sofia glanced at him. "But we don't have twenty years. We barely have twenty hours, and most days it's down to minutes or even seconds."

Ozu tapped his pen on his notebook. "Exactly. It would be like looking for a needle in a haystack. The world is just too big for anything like that to work in the time we would need it to, not to mention the many species of animals in places like the Amazon and the oceans that have not even been identified yet. People don't realize we are still discovering species on our own planet."

Sofia paced faster, rubbing her temples. She knew she had the answer to the problem; she *knew* it. She walked back and forth for another couple of minutes, then heard the doctor stand. Suddenly she stopped, her eyes darting around. "Wait. Wait. So the system might not work for finding *new* Leviathans, but what about finding ones that we know about already?"

The doctor took a seat again. "Go on. That has merit."

It was warmer outside but the wind was still wild, blowing sand all around, even into the small courtyard in front of the barracks. On that day, even the large buildings didn't keep the sand from swirling in and slamming into anyone who happened to be walking through. The soldiers were all wearing bandanas tied around their mouths, hoping the gusts would slow down soon. Eddie, Turner, Brock, and Sean came into the courtyard, putting the guys on a break to get something to eat.

Turner pulled his bandana up over his nose. "This shit is crazy. I feel like I could pour out my fucking lungs and make a damn sand castle with what's inside."

Sean pulled his coat collar up and hunkered down. "The wind blew my wheelchair sideways. I thought for sure I was going to end up crawling back here."

Eddie chuckled, punching Sean on the shoulder. "Don't worry. Your friend Timothy would surely carry you back."

Brock smiled. "Be careful. The last guy who showed he was a homophobic douche-canoe, Sean punched straight in the face."

Pandora and Katie walked out of the barracks and up to them, the sand and wind not seeming to bother them in the least. Katie nodded. "Hey, guys. So, we've been working on it, and I think I can open a portal to hell and Pandora and I can bring back demons for you guys. I know we've been promising it, and Pandora and I are both feeling better, so we didn't want to leave here or be called away without having at least dropped your demons."

Eddie rubbed Turner's shoulders excitedly. "What do you think, boys? Is it time to get the band back together and get out there to kick some fucking demon ass? Huh? I got mine ready and rolling. You just need to amp up and get yours."

Turner lifted his eyebrow. "Does Eddie's even count as a demon? I feel like he could fit two in there, as small as his is."

Eddie slapped the back of Turner's head. "Not what your mom said. She was begging for me to slow it down, she just couldn't take the massive size of the thing."

Pandora chuckled. "Please, I can tell a big dick a mile away, and brother, you are not on the list. But don't fret. Neither is Tucker."

Tucker stopped laughing and frowned. Pandora patted Sean's shoulder. "But old Sean here—he could rival some of the guys in size. That's for damn sure."

Sean shook his head, his cheeks red. "Not even sure if it works anymore."

Pandora winked at him. "We could take it for a test drive later, if you know what I mean."

Turner sighed. "Okay, enough about Sean's dick. I am ready to go and all about it. I have been only human for far too long, and I'm tired of the weakness."

Katie smiled and looked down at Sean. "How about you? You want big and hefty or slim and fast? Or are you more of an intelligence guy? That could take a bit to find down there."

Sean shook his head, looking up at the guys. "Sorry, guys. I'll always be on your team, but I'm not interested in being Damned again. At least not right now. I have really enjoyed having my body to myself these last few months."

Eddie bent down next to him. "Just one thing. It's your choice, of course. But what about your legs? A demon could jump in there and have you healed up in two hours. You could be sprinting around the course like you used to, beating all of us by at least a lap."

Sean nodded. "That's been my biggest thought about not getting a demon. But when it all comes down to it, I want to be me. I want to be in control of myself, whatever that means. If it means being stuck in this chair, then I'm fine with that. I might change my mind later, but for right now, I'm solid."

Eddie smiled at him. "Then I support your decision one hundred percent. It's your choice. We'll miss you in the field, but we want what's best for you."

Turner fist-bumped Sean. "Yeah, man. I'm down with whatever you need. And shit, if you get a hankering to go out in the field, I'll strap you to my shoulder and you can just blast the demons down like a fucking turret."

Brock laughed, patting Sean on the shoulder. "Me too, buddy. I'll support whatever it is you choose. We only get one life up here, and you have to decide how you want to live it."

Eddie tilted his head to the side. "Well, we kinda got two since we can be Damned again and all, but I get what you're saying."

Pandora took a deep breath. "Boys, one thing I've learned after being here for centuries is that humans have short, fragile lives. Some die miserable, and some die happy. The ones who are happy, they've made decisions in their lives that were exactly what they wanted. They didn't back down."

Katie clapped her hands. "Okay. Then Brock, Turner, Eddie, you guys pull out your weapons. Sean, I would suggest you move back a bit. I don't want the demon I grab to go running right into you as soon as it hits land. They don't really care; they just look for a body to take."

Sean nodded and wheeled his chair back, moving as far as he could and still have a shot if the demon got wild. This wasn't going to be the safest thing in the world. Katie and Pandora pulled open a portal after some effort, and Katie glanced at Pandora. "All right, let's jump in and get this shit done."

16

The cinders that were rolling down the volcano shimmered brightly before bursting into flames. The heat was pumping strong, and the smell was something along the lines of ten-year-old rotten eggs mixed with the sweat of a wildebeest. Pandora wrinkled her nose as she climbed through the portal. "Ugh. What the fuck? I don't remember it smelling like this in here before. What, I lose my demon powers and suddenly my fucking nose works?"

Katie put her hands on her hips, squinting at the waves of heat. "Ah, hell. It's not great to be back. No. Not at all."

Pandora shook her head and dove into Katie, already having had enough. *I have complete faith that you have this. You know something smells bad when you prefer the aroma of live human kidneys and liver, not to mention the bowels, over the outside air.*

Katie smiled. *Don't worry. Just going to snag one of these morons and we can be out here lickity-split. I'm sure they will come to see me any moment...*

Katie kept the smile plastered on her face and her hands

on her hips, robotically turning back and forth to look for any sign of a nearby demon. *Yep. Any second...*

Pandora groaned. *I know this seems like a bright idea, but they apparently aren't in this area.*

Katie dropped her smile. *Fine. Then I guess I will just have to bring them to me or go hunt one of these sonsofbitches down. What is it with this place? You don't want to be detected, and they come in droves. You do, and they are all somewhere picking their fucking asses.*

Katie loosened up, shaking her arms by her sides. She wrinkled her nose as she slapped her hands together, a whirlwind of air swirling up from her feet into the dark sky. Her armor appeared, clamping hard to her body. When she reached up, her angel sword slammed into her hand. She switched hands and shook it, snarling. *Okay, angel-armor-giver guy. No need to fucking throw it at me like a damn bus. Now, this should bring them.*

She stood there for a second before looking down to see a few pebbles bouncing. Pandora chuckled. *I think you are going to get your wish.*

Katie looked up to find a pretty big demon racing toward her. *Nice. That's a big fucker. Come to Momma. We got places to be and people to infect.*

She took off, flying straight for him. She could see him flinch, waiting for the punch, and she laughed as she whizzed by him and quickly turned, taking off again. She flew toward his back, not wanting to be anywhere near his jowls. As she approached, her feet touched down. Katie took two steps and leapt into the air, going full wrestling on his ass.

Her legs wrapped tightly around his torso and she put

one arm around his neck and the other on his forehead to keep his head from dipping down. She forced him down on one knee and released her right hand. Pandora popped out and took it, and together they opened another portal. Katie did a backflip off him and grabbed him by the back of the neck to toss him through the portal.

The demon was highly confused. "Hey! Wait! What the fuck? Ahhhhhhhhhh!" He shot through the portal and went rolling across the sandy ground. He slid on his face until coming to a stop in the middle of the courtyard.

The demon grunted, then put both hands down and pushed himself up. He spat right and left, trying to get the sand out of his mouth. Standing up, he brushed the sand from his body and looked around. Standing around him were the guys, their guns cocked and pointed at his head. The demon threw out his hands. "What the hell? I didn't even do anything."

First Pandora and then Katie stepped carefully through the portal, steam rising off their shoulders. The portal slammed shut behind them and Katie slowly raised the tip of her sword, pointing it at the demon. "I've got a deal for you, demon. Turner, come here."

Turner hurried over, keeping his gun pointed at the beast. Katie nodded, pushing down on it. "It's all right. I think we got this."

Turner nodded, putting his pistol in the back of his pants. He stood tall, looking the demon up and down. The beast raised an eyebrow, looking from Katie to Turner and back again. "Uh, what's the deal?"

Katie smiled. "Well, you can either infect this strong young soldier here…"

The demon gagged. "Gross. Just gross."

Katie gave him a deadpan look. "…or I'll kill you. Forever. You see this armor and this sword? I am an angel. Do you know what that would mean for you?"

The demon let out a deep sigh. "Completely dead. Like never coming back. Poof."

Katie nodded, flicking her sword up and down. "Very good. We might have a halfway-intelligent one here."

She stared at the demon as drool dripped off his bottom lip. "Okay…or not. So, what you're going to do is team up with Turner here. You guys are going to be best buddies. You'll get to live on Earth, and fight and fuck to your heart's content."

Eddie lowered his gun a bit, laughing. "Just so you know, Turner hasn't been laid since he paid that hooker in Columbia. He's still got dick-pox, but he can fight."

Turner flipped Eddie off and looked back at the demon. The beast sighed, realizing that he had no choice. He waved his big hand at the sword, rolling his eyes before taking off at high speed straight for Turner. About halfway there he jumped, his body becoming translucent and shrinking a bit, then he slammed into Turner's chest and disappeared into him. Turner went over backward and hit the ground.

Everyone ran over, bending down next to him. Katie shook his arm. "Turner, can you hear me?"

Turner took a deep breath, scaring everyone, then began to laugh loudly. He opened his eyes, and they shimmered red. "Fuck yeah, boys. I'm back in action."

Angie clapped her hands excitedly as she turned the large desktop computer screen an inch to the right. "This is so exciting. I've always wanted to do Twitch, but I never figured I would have a chance. I really hope I get some subscribers. This shit could be so awesome. I could become famous on the internet. Can you believe that?"

Juntto grunted, his tongue out of his mouth, staring at several bright lights they'd purchased to make everything look really good. He had the instructions in one hand and about five cords in the other, trying to figure it out. "Why do humans make things so hard? Just fucking have one plug and one switch. Light. Done."

Angie giggled at him as he fiddled around, knocking over one light but catching it before it fell. He twisted the cords together, then ran them across the room and plugged them in. The lights came on, and Angie squinted. Juntto stood up and put his arms out. "Ta-da!"

Angie nodded. "That's great. It's like the fire of a thousand suns, but hey, maybe I'll get a tan while I'm doing it."

Juntto kissed Angie. "That's right, look at the bright side. Get it…"

Angie rolled her eyes as he sat down in the chair in front of the computer. He pulled out the camera and situated it on top, moving it until he had a good clear picture. "This was expensive, but I look good."

Angie laughed and came over to him. "What are you doing now?"

Juntto typed on the keyboard, shrinking a bit so his hands weren't so big. "I am just connecting your computer so that it will stream the game. Then you will have the live stream and the cam. You will be a cam girl!"

He got up and went back over to the lights, looking at the stream as he tried to turn down the brightness. Angie sat down grumpily in the chair and pulled up Twitch so she could open an account. "For the last time, I am not a cam girl!"

Juntto growled as he tried to fix the light. It blinded Angie for a moment, and she glared at him, annoyed. "Why don't *you* set up the account and *I* will fix the lights?"

Juntto took the pencil out from between the lights and nodded. "Probably a good idea. I will screw it up. Can't screw up setting up a Twitch account."

Angie shook her head, chuckling as they switched places. She pulled a chair over and stepped up on it as Juntto sat down, cracking his knuckles and beginning to fill in the information. Angie smiled as she turned the lights down. "I could be finding a career here. This could be the start of my empire. It's been a long time since I've tried to do something without everything crashing down immediately around me."

Suddenly the computer blipped, and the screen began filling up with ad after ad. Juntto raised his hands up and pushed back the chair. "Uh, Angie?"

She looked at him, smiling. "Yeah?"

Another three pop-ups appeared, and the computer made a series of beeping noises. Her smile faded and she turned back, climbing off the chair. She walked over and hit the escape key a couple of times, but nothing happened. "Did you forget to turn on the ad blocker? Sometimes these sites can be insane."

She skimmed the mouse up to the side of the toolbar, but it wouldn't let her click on anything. She furrowed her brow and hit control, alt, and delete. She let go and waited, but still nothing moved on the screen. Slowly she turned her head toward Juntto. "Please tell me that you remembered to put Norton Anti-Virus on here before we started."

Juntto blinked. "I thought you did it."

Angie stood up, grabbing the sides of her head. "Holy shit. Not even five minutes into it and we have some sort of virus. Well, at least I didn't have any personal information on here yet. We'll just have to wipe the thing clean and start over. Damnit."

Juntto raised a finger and grimaced. "Actually…"

Angie's face fell. "Juntto! What did you do?!"

Juntto's shoulders went up and he gritted his teeth, giving her a forced smile. "Well, I just entered your social security number. You know, like it tells you to do when you are filling out the forms?"

Angie stood there frozen, staring intensely at Juntto with a look of anger and confusion. "My social security number? How do you even know that?"

He chuckled nervously. "You said it one time with the bank and I read this article that said one sign of being in a serious relationship is knowing your partner's social, so I thought it was a human thing. They need it, don't they?"

Juntto gasped, looking at the screen as more pop-ups filed in, the mouse now moving on its own. "Wait! Are we Twitching now? Is this what Twitching feels like? It's so comfortable and magnificent. Look at how the screen changes so fast, and it looks like the Twitches move your mouse for you. That's great customer service."

Angie stood up, slamming her hand to her forehead and snatching the mouse from Juntto. "NO! *FUCK!* This is not

Twitching. This is a fucking virus. Someone hacked into our computer, and you just gave them my social security number."

Her phone buzzed, and she groaned as she pulled it out of her pocket. There was a notification on her screen that someone had opened up a new credit card in her name. Before she could even respond, she got another one, and then another.

Angie threw her arms up in the air and plopped down in one of the chairs. "Great. Someone stole my fucking identity."

The semi had passed the sign for Utah a while ago, and they were traveling through the state, not sure where exactly they were. There was no plan to stop there, though, so it didn't really matter. Not many cars were on the road, which was a good thing since the 18-wheeler wove back and forth across the center line repeatedly.

Inside the cab, sweat was pouring down the foreheads of the Damned guys, and their hands shaking. The driver gripped the steering wheel tightly. "I don't know, man. There is something not right about all this. It's a fucking conspiracy, I'm telling you."

The other guy scratched nervously. "You think so? I should have known, man. We shouldn't have gotten involved in this. We should have just stayed where we were and enjoyed the spoils of being infected."

The driver stared at the road ahead for several moments before jumping and scaring the other guy. He reached across and grabbed his companion by the collar. "Dude, did you hear about the angels?"

The other guy whimpered. "What? No. What about them?"

The driver let go of him and shook his head, his voice breaking as he talked. "I heard there's an army of angels coming to Earth. They're going to kill all the Damned. I just know it."

The other guy gasped. "That's not true."

The driver nodded, looking at him with wide, scared eyes. "It's true. Beelzebub told me."

The other guy shook his head wildly, looking around and scratching the back of his neck. "No, he didn't. I was there; I was right there with you. He didn't say that."

The driver jerked the wheel again, getting back on his own side. The bed of the truck swerved before straightening out again. Inside, calm as could be, Kabbus writhed, his tentacles beginning to move wildly again, slapping the floor of the truck. Suddenly everything on his huge body stopped thrashing and he muttered something under his breath. His tentacles began to move again, and the fog crept to the doors. He let out a deep menacing laugh.

The driver slammed his hand down on the steering wheel over and over. "I'm telling you, man. Beelzebub told me that shit. He said they could already be on Earth and people may not even know that shit. We are fucked, man."

The guy in the passenger seat froze, looking at the driver and turning his head from side to side. "Uh, bro?"

The driver glanced at him, confused, and then stopped, looking at the angel armor on his arms and chest. He turned his head back to the passenger and froze. Then, with a shaking finger, he pointed. "Dude!"

The other guy looked down at himself, and then over his shoulder, seeing wings sprouting from both of their backs. Their eyes met and held briefly before both started screaming wildly. The driver jerked the wheel again and glared at the passenger, animosity moving through his chest. The other guy slowly lifted his head, giving the driver the same look.

Without warning, the guys lunged at each other, wrestling in the front seat of the semi. The driver left one hand on the wheel, swerving as his foot left and went back to the brake. The driver gritted his teeth. "Just give in to it, man. You aren't meant to be here. God told me himself."

The other guy strained against his hold. "No, *you're* not supposed to be here."

They continued to wrestle. The driver finally took his hand off the wheel and got onto his knees in the seat. He pulled his fist up and threw himself at the other guy, punching him until blood ran down his face. The other guy grabbed the driver by the hair and yanked his head back, grabbing his neck with his other hand and choking him.

The truck swerved in and out of the lanes, passing cars honking and maneuvering around it as it sped forward with no one behind the wheel. The driver managed to get his hands around the other guy's neck and they sat up on their knees, choking each other. The sound of tires on gravel caught their attention, and they both looked through the windshield as the truck smashed through the guard rail and flew over a small cliff.

Both screamed as it plunged into the woods below,

turning over on its side and sliding to a halt against a large tree. The men no longer made a sound, the truck's engine sputtered, and smoke rose from its hood. Trees that had been in the truck's path tumbled over, and their branches rustled as they hit the forest floor. The smell of diesel wafted through the air.

The back doors of the truck blew completely off their hinges, slamming to the ground. The black fog crept over the edge, followed by Kabbus. Long tentacles extended as he lowered himself to the ground and moved through the debris. Suddenly the passenger door flew open and the two guys climbed out and fell flat.

They were both covered in blood, and they breathed heavily as they tried to figure out exactly what had happened. Kabbus turned and began to slither toward them, and the driver put his arms up and shook his head. "Why? We were helping you! Beelzebub, remember? We are your allies."

Kabbus gurgled and grumbled as he slithered toward them quicker, finally descending upon them. Both Damned shut their eyes tightly and put up their hands, screaming as his mist completely covered them. Kabbus lingered for several moments before making his way out of the woods. As his large body moved, and the fog cleared, the two Damned sat frozen against the overturned semi, their dead gray faces frozen masks of fear.

17

Sean rolled into the dungeon, wiping the sand off him before he entered. He went to his area and began working again, scrolling through the recent data. Timothy was sitting on the desk to his right, filing his nails. Timothy glanced at him a couple of times before asking, "Turner get his demon?"

Sean nodded, staring at the screen. "Yeah. Real big gnarly dude, but he was actually halfway-intelligent. Didn't put up a fight either. Turner was fucking stoked."

Timothy pursed his lips, nodding his head. "Good for him."

There was silence for a moment and Sean smiled, turning toward Timothy. "No, I don't have a demon in me."

Timothy looked around and then back at Sean. "So, were there not enough? Or do you not want a demon?"

Sean sighed. "I don't want one. I haven't wanted one since mine left."

Timothy slid down in his chair and turned toward

Sean, putting his chin in his hand. "So, let me ask you this. You're in the chair, and…"

Sean tapped the armrests of his chair. "Yeah, I am. What does that even mean? I can still kick fucking ass if I need to. You've seen me demonstrate that. And I still make amazing Korean fried chicken."

Timothy nodded agreement. "Yes to both of those. Good. I'm glad you did what was best for you. Your hacker skills need work, though."

Sean rolled his eyes, turning back to the screen. "Demons don't hack. I'm learning."

Timothy chuckled as Doctor Ozu and Sofia walked into the room. Timothy stood up, and Sean spun his chair around. Sofia smiled. "Hey, guys. This is Dr. Ozu. Doctor, this is Sean and Timothy. They're our tech masterminds."

He shook their hands. "It's good to finally meet you."

Sofia excitedly put her hands out. "So, the doc and I were talking about this tracking problem, and we think we might have found something that could solve it."

The doctor nodded. "We are thinking that if you do a reverse search, a backward system, then you will be able to find the anomaly."

Timothy's eyes shifted between the two of them for a moment. "Reverse search. A backward system. Are those technical terms or…"

Sofia chuckled, shaking her head. "No, I guess they aren't. Instead of searching for demons, you go in and search for the Leviathans."

She put her hands out. Timothy took a deep breath and scratched his head. "So you're saying the answer to tracking the Leviathan is tracking the Leviathan. Which we aren't even sure has a chemical makeup originating from this planet."

They both nodded. Timothy blinked at them and clicked his tongue. "You know, I… Okay, I don't understand a damn thing you are talking about. What kind of plan is this, people?"

Sofia pulled up a chair and sat down, rubbing her hand over her belly. Timothy looked at her frantically. "Oh, girl, do not go into labor in here. That is a fifteen-hundred-dollar chair."

Sofia narrowed her eyes at him. "Only twenty-two weeks at this point, buddy. I think you're safe. So, you are going to use your equipment to check out San Antonio and Sonora, Texas. Pull up the last few days. That should be a small enough sample. Then you want to look at everything. Take all the selections off. Look at humans, deer, rabbits, whatever."

Timothy stared at them, raising an eyebrow. "The whole damn thing will be a collection of rainbow dots. Now, I am all for painting Texas in the colors of my people, but this is just going to make everything horribly confusing. And if I know what they are, why would I want to look at them?"

Dr. Ozu smiled. "This is good. I like that you ask questions. It's going to help you work on it when you are ready. So, as you take away the knowns, you are going to notice an anomaly—something that is the same in both locations. Something that is not a demonic incursion, but not registering as Earthly either. It may not be at the same time on both days. It may not even be entirely the same shape, but it will be very similar."

Timothy sighed. "And what will that be?"

Sofia chuckled. "That will be your Leviathan, Kabbus."

Timothy leaned back, looking at the ceiling and tapping his chin. "I get what you are throwing down there, human incubator. That is a very simple way of doing it, but sometimes the simplest answer is the best. We were over here trying to reinvent the damn wheel. Hmmm. But... Hmmm."

Sofia could already see his wheels turning. She pulled a flash drive from her pocket and handed it to him. He took it with two fingers, holding it up and looking at it as if it were diseased. "Is this the virus that got you pregnant? 'Cause if so, I don't want it."

Sofia scoffed. "No, that was the Calvin Plague. Don't think you can catch it. That is Juntto's genetic makeup. It might help you to have data on something not from Earth. You know, so you can calibrate your readings."

Timothy eyed it again and dropped it into Sean's hand. He shrugged and crossed his arms, giving them both a smile. "Okay, let me think about this a few minutes, and then I'll write up a plan. Shouldn't take me too long. You know, since I am a genius and everything."

Sofia and the doctor laughed. The doctor got up and reached out to shake Timothy's hand again. "I was told I was coming here to work with the best."

Timothy flung back his imaginary hair and pursed his lips. "You know, I have fans worldwide. When I had nothing to do as a kid and wanted to not get beaten up on the corner, I turned to computers. They have become my life. You, sir, are in good hands."

The doctor helped Sofia up and she leaned forward,

kissing Timothy on the cheek. "Sometime soon we need to go shopping. I am basically living in stretch pants."

Timothy gasped. "Yaaassss, queen. Don't you worry. We will get that taken care of real fast. Can't have you walking around like you're doing aerobics."

Timothy and Sean watched as the two left. Timothy immediately sat down and went to work on the project while Sean checked the other radars, making sure they weren't missing any incursions or major battles. The phone rang and Timothy sighed, picking up the receiver and putting it to his ear. "Yes?"

"Oh, thank God," Angie said, letting out a deep breath.

Timothy raised an eyebrow. "I don't know if he will take the praise for me, sister. I am a problem child."

Angie chuckled. "No, I need your help. My identity has been stolen. I need you to track down the assholes responsible."

Timothy rolled his eyes. "I'm busy now, but my protégé can help."

Timothy held up the handset and yelled for Sean. "Sean, help Angie get her life back together."

Juntto and Angie sat in the back of a New York City cab as it hurtled through the city on its way to Wall Street. Angie had Sean on the phone, and he was tracking their movements through their GPS. The cab finally came to a stop outside a tall mirror-fronted building and Angie squinted up, looking out the window at the top of the building, which was high in the sky. Juntto, having shrunk enough to fit in the cab, was busy cracking his knuckles.

The cab driver looked nervously in the rearview mirror. "This what you are looking for, yes?"

Angie put the phone to her ear. "Is this right?"

Sean sighed. "Yes. This is the address linked to the IP address that's linked to the bug that stole your stuff. Eighth floor, end of the hall. That's as far as I can track it."

Angie wrinkled her nose. "All right. That's a lot of links. Thanks, Sean. We'll let you know how it turns out."

"Mmhmm," Sean replied dryly before hanging up.

Angie turned to Juntto and nodded as she handed the driver money. "Thanks."

They both got out of the car. The driver watched as Juntto grew to his largest size and started pounding his fist into his hand. The cab took off, its tires squealing. They walked toward the tall entry doors, and Juntto ducked as they entered. He snarled at the secretary at the front desk and pushed through a group of stock market bros standing around drinking lattes and comparing their dick…er, wallet sizes.

They took the stairs since Juntto was too heavy for the elevator in this form. On the fifth floor, Juntto stopped and picked Angie up so she wouldn't die from the climb. On the eighth floor, he put her down and she smiled, straightening out her clothes. Juntto pushed through the door and shrank just enough to not hit his head on the ceiling. He stomped down the hallway, Angie jogging to keep up with him.

They got to the entry of a large office with a bank of desks all through it. Angie caught her breath and gave the people who had turned and looked at them as they opened the door an awkward smile and a brief wave. She really fucking hoped that Sean was right; otherwise, they might just end up in jail.

Juntto didn't give it a second thought, though. He just burst in, several people gasping and everyone now giving him their undivided attention.

He snarled. "I am looking for the asshole who stole her identity. We want it back. I don't want you to be her. She must be herself. I make love to her. I don't want to make love to you."

Several of the women raised an eyebrow and nodded. Angie scooted forward, tapping his elbow. "Uh, sweetie? Sweetie, they don't actually become me."

Juntto furrowed his brow. "What?"

Angie shook her head. "Never mind. Continue."

They stood there scanning the room when all of a sudden, a guy near the back jumped up from his desk. He grabbed his jacket and stared at them for a few moments before taking off at a sprint out the side door into the hallway. He was obviously scared to death, given the look on his face, and the wet spots on the front of his pants.

Angie chuckled nervously as they backed toward the door. "Thanks for your time. You can go back to whatever it is you're doing now. Sorry for the intrusion."

They left the office, turning right and stopping. They stared at the guy and he stared at them, realizing he was in a dead end. Angie and Juntto began to walk slowly forward when he took off again, slamming through a door to his right and running through the office. Juntto and Angie followed, leaping over desks, papers flying everywhere while the people screamed. They burst through the other door and ran after him down the hallway.

The guy reached the stairwell and hurried into it, Angie and Juntto on his tail. Juntto took four steps at a time, trying to catch up with him as fast as he could. When he reached the top of the next flight of stairs, he dove head-first, tackling the guy to the floor and pinning him down. Juntto breathed deeply and Angie hurried, running down the steps and coming up behind Juntto. She stared at the guy, who was thrashing on the floor.

The guy looked up at them angrily. "What do you want? I don't fucking know you."

Angie chuckled and bobbed her head. "Fuck you. Your name is not Angie. Mine is. You stole my fucking identity, opened up credit cards, and took money out of my bank account. Who the fuck do you think you are? Make money the honest way instead of stealing from others."

The guy shifted his eyes from Juntto to Angie and started to struggle again. "Fuck you two. You don't fucking have proof of shit. I don't have to do anything you tell me to do. Let me go before I fucking press charges."

Angie moved back as Juntto sighed, grabbing the guy by the neck and lifting him into the air. He walked back up the steps and through the door to the fifth floor, then stood in front of a window. "I will personally open up this window by smashing it with my fist. Then, if you do not stop doing this shit, I will hang you out and drop you to your death. Do you understand what I am telling you?"

The guy glanced at the window and peered over the edge at the drop to the ground and swallowed hard, blinking his eyes hard. "Yes, yes. I won't do it anymore. No more. I'm done. Please. *Please* don't drop me out the window."

Juntto slowly lowered him back down and pushed him hard against the glass. "You have stolen my woman's identity. You stole her money. She works hard as a mercenary to protect your stupid ass, and you stole her money."

The guy looked at Juntto and at Angie, realizing who they were. "I know. *I know*. I'm sorry."

Juntto shook him hard. "You will give the money back to her now."

The guy put his hands up. "It's… It's…gone. It's gone."

Juntto gritted his teeth and brought his huge fist up to the guy's face. "Then you will pay her back with your own money."

The guy nodded nervously. "Yes. My wallet is upstairs. It's in my desk drawer."

Juntto set him down. "Let's go get it."

They walked back up to the eighth floor behind the guy, who shook all the way up the stairs. When they reached his office, they followed him to his desk. The guy took out his checkbook and wrote them a check, his hand shaking the whole time. Juntto pointed to his computer. "Is this the one you use?"

The guy flinched. "Yes."

Juntto nodded and smiled as he smashed his hand into the tower over and over. He kept his eyes locked on the guy's as pieces flew everywhere,. When it was completely destroyed, Juntto grabbed the cord and unplugged it. He walked over to one of the windows that was open at the top and pushed it through, giving it a heave and watching as it plummeted past the window and down into the alley.

He dusted off his hands and went back to the desk, patting the guy on the shoulder as he left. "Now, be nice."

———

You could have heard a pin drop in the hall where the dungeon was located. The door was shut and the lights were dim as Timothy worked his magic. He sat at the front with multiple computer screens going. His head turned right, then left, then right as his fingers moved at a rapid pace on the keyboard. Suddenly he stopped and slid his chair back, nodding his head.

He looked over his shoulder. "Okay, Sean. Come see how Momma works her magic. First, we look at Sonora, Texas and San Antonio, Texas. I mean, come on. Just look at all these living and breathing things."

Sean wheeled over to Timothy and squinted at the screens. Timothy pressed two buttons, and the view switched to the large main screen overhead. Sean leaned back and shifted his eyes to Timothy. "And what am I looking at?"

Timothy put out his hand. "Life itself. All of those glowing blue dots are living, breathing Earth creatures. Now, let's just adjust the readings. Take away anything that looks human."

He typed quickly on the keyboard and looked up. A bunch of the blue dots had disappeared. Timothy smiled and turned back to the keyboard, typing again as he spoke. "This is freaking genius, although I can't take all the credit. That Sofia is a bright one. Now we take away your common animals. Dogs, cats, cows…"

More blue dots disappeared off the screen over their heads, only leaving the small animals and plants he couldn't take away from the view. Amidst the array, it soon became obvious that there was one red dot in Sonora and one in San Antonio.

Timothy finished typing and backed up next to Sean, crossing his arms. When the screen beeped, he grinned. "Well, looky here. Which one of these is not like the other? That little red dot is our alien. That's our cute little Nightmare from hell, Kabbus."

Sean smiled and then wrinkled his brow. "How did he end up in two places at one time?"

Timothy shook his head, wiping his brow. "Seriously, you would think this was your first day in the dungeon. Follow along here, Sean, follow along. These dots are at different times, and if you look at the times, you can see it is not unreasonable to think he made it to San Antonio from Sonora."

Sean clapped his hands, nodding. "That is fucking impressive right there. I thought the demonic incursion system was good, but this? This is finding something when you can't even begin to know what type of energy it puts out. That is some fantastic work."

Timothy bowed. "Thank you."

Sean looked at the screen again. "What now?"

Timothy grinned evilly. "Now we isolate the fucker and see if the same energy signature is floating around anywhere else. Then we send Katie in to kick its ass back to whatever cold, dead dimension it came from."

18

"Come on, pussy, one more rep. Just one more," Pandora said, her hands under the bar as Katie pushed up, grunting.

Katie chuckled as she brought it back down. "Just one more? I thought you were a tough bitch."

Pandora snickered. *"That's* what I'm talking about."

Katie strained hard, pushing the bar up and resting it on the rack. Her head fell back and she breathed deeply, shaking her head and laughing. "Okay, maybe I should have stopped at the last one."

The door to the gym burst open with a bang and Katie and Pandora glanced over to see Timothy running in. He put his hands on his knees and breathed heavily. Katie lifted her eyebrows. "Uh, you okay?"

Timothy nodded, putting up one finger. Katie and Pandora waited until finally he stood up and put his hands on his back. "I found it."

Pandora smirked. "The male g-spot?"

Timothy gave her a "Yeah, right" look. "No, honey, I

found that years ago. I found Kabbus. He's in Utah, of all places."

Katie stood up quickly and looked at Pandora, both of them getting very serious very quickly. Pandora gave her a nod. Katie smiled. "Okay, let's go get the boys."

Eddie walked behind the line of soldiers, watching as they lay in the sand, their eyes to their scopes. "You want to connect yourself with the target. You want to anticipate its movement, feel the wind, and think of how that bullet will fly when it leaves your gun. Then, and only then, you take a deep breath through your nose and release it out of your mouth. As you release, pull the trigger."

One of the soldiers laughed, shouting, "And pray."

Eddie smiled. "You won't need prayer if you are a professional."

Brock and Turner walked over to him, their faces serious. Eddie glanced at Brock and Turner. "What's going on?"

Brock smiled and patted Eddie on the chest. "We've got a mission."

Eddie leaned back and whistled loudly. "Let's do this thing."

The guys behind him all fired at the same time, which didn't faze the team. Eddie turned around to find that every one of them had hit their mark. He clapped and licked his lips, wagging his eyebrows at the guys. "Told you I was good."

Brock and Turner chuckled. "Time to load up and move

out, dude. We're gonna get our hands really dirty on this one."

Eddie turned to the guys. "Uh, you guys are dismissed for now. Clean your weapons and return them to the armory in the barracks. Schwartz, you're in charge. Wish me luck, boys. We are going to kick some ass."

The same soldier as before yelled, "You shouldn't need luck. You're a professional."

Eddie laughed, pointing at him. "Damn straight."

Eddie took off at a jog, trying to catch up with Turner and Brock. He headed inside and down to the armory, where they were pulling out the weapons they wanted to take. Brock looked at him. "Only what you can carry today, boss. We are moving through a portal on this one. No time for the plane."

Eddie took a deep breath and grabbed two pistols. "You know I like it when we run things last minute like this."

Katie and Pandora came through the doors with Dr. Ozu trailing behind them. Katie put up her hands. "Dr. Ozu wanted to talk to us about this really fast. He is the most knowledgeable scientist we have when it comes to the Leviathans."

The doctor smiled and stepped forward. "Gentlemen, ladies, you are walking in on a beast that none of us know very much about. We don't know what weapons will be useful against him. Bring different ones. Even though the special metal always works on demons, it doesn't have any effect on the Leviathan."

Pandora scoffed, flicking her thumb over the blade of her sword. "Angelic swords can cut through anything. If we can't shoot it, we'll slice it up."

The guys cheered. "That's right, whack that bitch down to bits."

Eddie looked up as he pushed two daggers into his shoulder sheaths. "I heard the thing has tentacles. I always did like fried calamari. We could be eating seafood tonight, folks."

Pandora sneered. "I promise you, this is one mother-fucker you do *not* want to ingest. In fact, I suggest you steer clear of the tentacles altogether. They have a tendency to snap necks."

The team finished loading up in the barracks armory and headed outside. They all gathered in the courtyard, where Katie would open a portal. She slid her angelic sword onto her back and snapped it in place before turning to the group. Brock shifted his stance, never having seen that level of seriousness on her face. Everyone noticed—all the guys, Pandora, even the doctor, who had walked out to see them off.

She took a deep breath, collecting her thoughts. "Pandora and I have faced this thing before, and I'm going to tell you right here and right now that it is no joke. It is one thing to mess with your body, but this thing—it can twist your mind. There is a reason they call it the Nightmare."

The guys glanced at each other and pulled out their guns, pointing them at the ground. Katie shook her head. "This thing, it…it preys on your fears. Out there, when you are fighting it, you might experience things. Visions almost, but they are dreams. They're going to seem very real, and they're going to fuck with you beyond belief."

The guys instantly started to get nervous. Katie could see it in all of their faces. They had seen her when she had returned from her first encounter. They knew if it could take *her* down, it could do the same to them. Katie pursed her lips. "Look, the most important thing for you to do when you face it is to keep your mind focused on what you are there to do. If you think the situation you are in is completely unreasonable, look to me. If you're not dreaming, I'll be there to reassure you. It's important that we all stay together. If I move, you move, and the same goes for Pandora. Stay close to one of us, so if we see you fall to his tricks, we can pull you out. We are one another's strength, okay?"

Katie looked around at everyone, anxiety growing in her chest. "Okay?"

The guys all pumped their fists, nodding. Katie stared at Brock for several moments, talking to him through her gaze. Finally, she broke eye contact with him and clapped her hands. "One last weapons check. Make sure you are loaded and secure. You have to be ready to go as soon as we get through the portal. We don't know what we are walking into."

The guys checked their weapons again one at a time, making sure they had the proper ammo for each. Brock walked over to Katie and put his hand on her shoulder. "Who's gonna look out for you if you're looking out for everyone else?"

Katie turned and looked at him seriously. "That bastard took me down once. I won't let him do it again. If he does, then we are dealing with something far worse than I imagine."

Pandora walked up to them, shaking her head. "Don't think you are immune, Katie. Question everything. Question everyone. And most importantly, fuck that bastard up."

Katie bumped fists with Pandora and turned to the rest of the team. "Are you ready?"

The guys cheered. Katie shook her head, putting her hand to her ear. "NO, I ASKED, ARE YOU MOTHER-FUCKING *READY*?"

The guys gritted their teeth and pumped their fists in the air, cheering loudly. The trainees and other soldiers on the base had lined up in the distance and were standing in ranks, watching them as they prepared to leave. Stephanie and Korbin walked out, each of them giving Katie a nod. Timothy came out too, waving wildly at them. Sean was behind him, rolling across the sandy ground up to them. "Keep your shit together out there, you hear me?"

The guys all smiled at Sean. "I know you're real broke up that I won't be there with you, but just know I'll be here thinking about fucking your moms while you're out there fighting this bitch."

They all laughed, and each one fist-bumped Sean as they lined up behind Katie. She glanced over her shoulder, and Pandora stepped up beside her. They pulled open the portal together and took a step through.

The team stepped through the portal one by one, and it snapped shut behind Turner. They paused, looking around them. Eddie frowned. "Uh, where the fuck are we? Since when does Utah have three moons and a pink sky?"

Katie smirked. "We have to go through another dimension to get to Utah. I haven't perfected the jump straight to the location thing yet."

Eddie stared at her in shock. "*What?*"

Katie patted him on the chest. "It's quicker. Just trust me."

Turner chuckled, shaking his head. "Shit, I knew Utah was another fucking dimension."

Everyone burst into laughter.

Katie and Pandora stepped through, waiting for everyone to exit the portal behind them. They held their swords down and out, unsure of what they were walking into. Pandora looked at Katie. "This shit looks a lot like the last fucking time, and you know what kind of fond memories I have of that."

Katie bit the inside of her cheek. "Just keep your eyes open and look for me if you question it."

Pandora nodded. "You do the same. I'll slap you back to reality."

Katie smirked. "Welcome to Provo, Utah where the Leviathans reign, the angels slap the fuck out of each other, and everyone is lost in their own damn minds."

Eddie looked around. "It was much cooler in the last dimension."

Pandora excitedly turned to him. "Wait till you go to the naked one."

Katie shook her hand in the air. "Enough. Pandora, don't tell him that. And didn't you have some pullback after the nightmare you had?"

Pandora scoffed. "Please. A little nightmare won't keep this girl from finding sexy naked men."

Brock turned in a circle and stopped, his mouth dropping open. "Wow. Who knew Utah was this nice?"

They were at the edge of a large, shimmering lake that backed up to tall, jagged mountains with snow-capped peaks. To the left was a small city. The tallest building was no higher than five stories, but the place was clean and glistening.

Pandora shook her head. "I know everyone is else is all fucking caught up in the beauty, but does anyone else see a problem with a nightmare-inducing Leviathan this close to a fucking city? Lots of people live and congregate in fucking cities. In fact, I am pretty sure there is smoke coming up from the streets in that pretty little city. Apparently, even Armageddon looks nice from a distance when you're in Utah."

Brock shook his head. "Don't jump to conclusions. The city seems quiet. There is a possibility that this Leviathan isn't as tough as we think he is. Otherwise, we would be staring at a whole lot of really scared people right now."

Eddie had turned back around. He tapped Brock on the shoulder and pointed behind them. "You mean those people?"

Brock frowned and looked behind them. Dozens of people were screaming and running all over the place.

There were men, women, children and every age in between freaking out. They were grabbing their heads and pulling their hair while screeching and fighting invisible forces. The group seemed to move like a flock of birds, staying together despite changes in direction.

Pandora sighed. "Well, that's very unfortunate. Looks like Kabbus doesn't like the idea of getting the fuck off our people."

Brock narrowed his eyes and stepped forward. "It looks like our people are heading straight the fuck for us right now. All their eyes are shut, so how can they even see us here? This is nuts."

Katie backed the group up. "Nuts or not, it is what it is. I suggest you buckle up because you ain't seen nothing yet."

The crowd of people ran straight for them. The team put up their arms as they attacked, punching and hitting the team every way they could. Brock got down on one knee and put his arms out, catching fists as they flew toward him. Turner pulled people off him and turned them around, facing them back toward the city. Some fell for it, wandering off like zombies, while others spun back, throwing punches at his face.

Eddie groaned, wiping blood from the corner of his mouth. Coco perked up. *Uh oh. Let me take care of that really fast. Wait, these aren't demons. Oh, no. Oh, shit. He's here. I can feel him.*

Eddie ducked, letting a punch fly over his head. *Coco, take a deep breath. I need you to stay in this with me.*

Coco was terrified. *I'll do what I can, but if he mesmerizes you, it works on me too. Just know we will be completely without defenses.*

Eddie didn't like the sound of that. *Have you faced Kabbus before?*

Coco laughed. *No one faces Kabbus and lives to tell about it. And no, it's always been this scary story that we were told. An enigma. We never thought that Kabbus was real. Not until now. I will tell you, though, if you don't get these humans off your ass, you better believe you are going to fall victim. You won't even hear it coming.*

Eddie groaned, looking at Katie. "Dude. What are we supposed to do with all these motherfuckers rolling in on us like this? We cannot get stuck in the crowd with these fools. This Leviathan could be anywhere, and I would like to find him before he finds us. Apparently, according to my demon, it could mean life or death. So, are we shooting these motherfuckers or what?"

Katie shook her head as she pushed a woman to the ground. "We are not using lethal force on these people. They aren't even Damned. We have no cause to kill them. We are here trying to save their asses."

Eddie stopped and glared at one who was lunging for Turner. "They are fucking fighting us. They are trying to rip us apart."

Katie shook her head. "No. You don't understand. It's not really them fighting you. They're having waking nightmares. Remember, Kabbus draws on your worst fears, so they are stuck inside the thing that scares them more than anything in the world. We are here, so Kabbus is incorporating us somehow, but they have no idea who we are. They don't even know they are fighting. We have to be gentle with them."

Eddie sighed, pushing another back. "I would have

brought rope if I had thought this would be the case. Tie them up, and they can't hurt us or anyone else until we figure this shit out."

Brock bent down, catching a charging man on his shoulder and lifted him into the air. He carried him over to the grass and dropped him. "Don't you guys have some sort of angel powers? Can you help pull these people out of this?"

Katie and Pandora looked at each other, and both sprouted their wings. Katie nodded at Brock. "We do, but the last time, it only calmed them a little bit. I'm not sure if it will work at all this time, but we'll give it a shot. Something has to give or we'll be fighting these humans for hours."

Katie and Pandora took off into the air and circled around in front of the mob. As soon as they took flight, they began whistling wildly to get the people's attention. The nightmare-hazed group followed the sound, their eyes still clenched tightly closed. They stopped attacking the team, giving them a reprieve to back up and ready themselves if it didn't work.

Katie reached out and took Pandora's hand. They pulled the energy from their chests and let it build and build, the bright glow radiating around them. Pandora kept her eyes shut, her body pulsing from the energy. "You ready?"

Katie nodded. "On three. One, two, *three!*"

Both of them released the energy that had built up in their chests and it exploded from them in a wave of light, moving over every single person below them before dissipating. They floated for a moment, waiting to see what would happen. The people began to calm, some even coming out of it. Katie put her hand to her chest and breathed deeply.

Pandora laughed, surprised that it had actually worked. "I'll lead them out of harm's way."

Pandora began to whistle again, regaining everyone's attention. She kept backing up from the lake and the city. Timothy had detected nothing outside the city, but no one really knew. The group followed, walking almost like zombies as they followed her away.

As Katie slowly floated down to the ground, the team all checked in, letting each other know they were good to go. Pandora watched as the familiar black fog showed itself again. It was rolling down the street toward them.

Pandora landed next to Katie. "Kabbus has arrived."

19

Angie sat on the couch, one leg underneath her, turned toward Juntto. He sneered at the pizza she was holding over her plate. It was a huge slice of New York-style with extra cheese and pepperoni. "Open up and eat some real pizza."

Rolling his eyes, Juntto opened his mouth and took a big bite. He chewed and swallowed, watching the news out of the corner of his eye. Angie smiled. "See, *that* is pizza."

Juntto lifted an eyebrow. "It's pizza, yes, but is it *enough* pizza?"

Angie opened her mouth to argue, but Juntto's phone went off before she could speak. He grinned, holding up a finger, and put the phone to his ear. "This is Juntto."

The general didn't even greet him. "We have a problem. I need you on a plane to Provo, Utah. Kabbus the Nightmare has resurfaced."

Juntto jumped up with a serious look on his face. "Yes, General."

Brushwood let out an exasperated sigh. "You have to hurry."

Eddie's hands shook and he held them in front of his face, peering at them. He blinked. Everything felt like it was going in slow motion. The entire scene was completely chaotic. Kabbus lurked in front of him, his tentacles flying everywhere. Eddie raised his gun and adjusted his sight. He blinked again, trying to get the blurriness to dissipate. Letting out a deep breath, he pulled the trigger.

The bullet ricocheted off of a sign two feet to the left of Kabbus. He lifted his head, furrowing his brow, and staring at the distorted metal, the bullet lodged in the building behind it. He had been so far off on his shot that he might as well have closed his eyes. He shook his head to clear it before trying again.

He took the shot, and it hit the brick wall to the left of Kabbus. The brick it struck disintegrated, chunks flying everywhere. "What the fuck?"

Eddie looked down at his gun, making sure that everything was in order. There was nothing on it that seemed like it could cause such a huge difference in aim. He shook his head and rolled his shoulders. Kabbus had slithered toward a woman on the ground who was having a nightmare. Eddie gritted his teeth and aimed again, this time sending the bullet straight into the woman's head.

He froze, his eyes wide, realizing he had just killed someone by accident. *Coco, what the fuck are you doing? I need your goddamn help. I am all over the place, and I can't figure out how to fix it.*

Eddie could almost feel Coco's deep fear. The demon whimpered, but he didn't say a word. Eddie shook his head. *Coco, snap out of it. Kabbus is going to kill all these people.*

A soft cry came from Coco's mouth, echoing through Eddie's head. *Please, Eddie. Please don't do it.*

Eddie pulled his brows together. *Don't do what? Kill Kabbus? I thought we talked about this, Coco. You work with us now. You defend the innocent and the Damned. Why are you doing this?*

Coco sniffled. *Not Kabbus. Please, Eddie, don't send me back to hell. I promise I'll be a good demon. I'll do whatever you like.*

Eddie couldn't understand what was wrong with Coco. *Coco, why would I do that? I have been waiting to have a demon again. Get it together!*

Coco shrieked, *PLEASE don't send me back. PLEASE! I promise to do whatever you want me to. Coco is a good demon.*

Eddie shifted his eyes back and forth, looking for anyone else on the team. They must have all moved into cover. He pulled up his gun, realizing that Coco was going to be absolutely no help. He aimed again and again, blasting away at Kabbus. Not a single one of them came anywhere close to the Leviathan.

Eddie slammed his fist down on his leg. "Fuck fuck fuck!"

Brock rubbed his eyes, gripping the M-16 in front of him tightly. He had to get himself in a good position. He took a deep breath and opened his eyes, his mouth falling slightly open. He glanced around him, finding himself on a stage with a band behind him. He grabbed for his gun, but in its place was a guitar—his old guitar. He ran his fingers down the strings, hearing the sweet tones echoing from the speakers to his right and left.

In front of him was a sea of people, all laughing and cheering, putting their hands in the air. Brock let go of the guitar, leaving it hanging from him. He turned in a circle, slightly confused. *Wasn't I just fighting something?*

His old bandmate came up and slapped him on the back, putting his hand over the mic. "Hey. You okay, dude? We are kind of at a show here."

Brock looked at him frantically. "Where is Katie?"

His bandmate looked at him strangely and then laughed. "Oh, you mean the hot blonde? Don't worry. She'll be waiting in your trailer. Right now, you have a house to fucking rock!"

Brock smiled, turning back and looking at the thousands of screaming fans in front of him. He pulled his guitar back up in front of him and stepped to the microphone. "HOW'S EVERYBODY DOING OUT THERE?"

The entire stadium erupted in screaming. Brock strummed his guitar. "Here's a little ditty I just recently wrote. It's for you."

The crowd cheered and Brock wiped his arm across his forehead, feeling his long hair flowing over his shoulders. He chuckled and began to play, leaning forward and singing into the mic. The song wasn't one that he could remember ever playing before, but for some reason, it streamed out of him like he had played it a thousand times. Even the band was backing him up on it.

Brock shrugged and looked back as he rocked into a guitar solo. His bandmates screamed, giving him the rock and roll sign with their hands. He closed his eyes and let the music just flow out of him, every strum, every note, melodically flowing like it was the most natural thing in the world. He put his lips to the mic and sang out the last line of the song, finishing up with a deep strum of the guitar.

He kept his eyes closed, the band's last notes vibrating through him. He knew it was the best song he had ever played or would ever play again. It had exploded from his soul like a train. When he stopped to listen to the fans, the entire stadium was silent. A smile pulled on his lips, just knowing they had all been shocked and amazed by the tune.

Slowly he opened his eyes, staring out at the sea of faces. The reaction wasn't exactly what he had thought it would be. Everyone was just staring at him, some in disgust, others in confusion. There was one clap way out in the back, and then the crowd began to boo. They hated it. They hated *him*.

Brock shook his head and put his hands up. "Wait! I can do better! Wait!"

It was no use; he knew there was no way he could do any better. Still, with the crowd turning, he panicked and tried to strum the guitar, but his fingers no longer worked…

Turner kept low, moving around a large piece of debris in the street. The people were getting more and more destructive in their terrified haze. He couldn't shoot them, so he had to just let them continue until they could get it all under control. It was difficult concentrating on a Leviathan when the very people he was there to save were beating him mercilessly everywhere he went.

As he walked around the corner, he paused, tilting his head to the side. Standing halfway down the block was Eddie. At first, he was going to call to him, but then he realized that something was definitely not right. He was standing a few feet from a brick building, firing his gun into it over and over again. He would pause, pound his leg, and shout, "Fuck fuck fuck!" Then, after a moment, he would raise his gun and fire again.

Turner started to walk toward him but stopped again, turning to his right to find Brock. He glanced up and down the street, but there was no one else. Brock was standing with his nose just inches from the wall, completely zoned out. His eyes were glazed, and he had a look of anguish on his face as he moved his hand up and down over his gun like it was a guitar.

"Fuck," he whispered to himself, turning to find Katie.

She wasn't on the block; he could only assume she had taken flight with Pandora. Either way, they had to fight Kabbus. He ran over and grabbed Brock's shoulder, shaking him lightly. "Snap out of it. We have to finish this thing!"

Brock began to weep, shaking his gun up and down. "It was the best I'll ever do, man! The best I'll ever do."

Turner backed up and ran for Eddie, but he couldn't pull him away from the wall. "Guys! Get your shit straight. We need to…we need to… What the fuck is that?"

Turner backed into the street, looking right and left, hearing giggling. He paused, slowly lowering his head and looking down at his pants. They moved wildly around his crotch. He jumped, dropping his gun on the ground. He unbuttoned his pants as fast as he could, pulling one leg out. As he pulled the other, he fell to the ground, shaking his leg to get the rest of it off of him. "Fuck, shit, fuck. There's something in my pants. Something in my pants."

He looked down at his boxers, where everything had gone calm. Turner looked around, but there was no one there except Eddie and Brock, and they were too obsessed with their own thing to pay any attention. He could still hear the giggling. Anxiety bubbled in his chest as he slowly reached down and began to lift up the front of his boxers.

"Holy fuck!" he screamed as little green goblins began jumping out, running up and down his chest, snarling and giggling.

He tried to knock them away, but they seemed to multiply. One stopped on his chest and let out a high-pitched squeal of excitement. "We're the dick pox! We're here to eat your dick!"

Turner screamed, clenching his eyes shut as hard as he could.

Katie flew over the streets of the small city. Everywhere she went there were people screaming and freaking out, caught in their own heads. She kept sending out calming waves, at least quieting them down for a few moments so they wouldn't hurt themselves or each other. Pandora had gone the opposite way and was doing the same thing. She had to get to Kabbus and stop the madness before he ended up taking out the whole town.

She glided around the corner and flared her wings to slow her down. In the street below were Turner, Eddie, and Brock, and they were definitely not okay. Brock stood crying as he stared at a wall, strumming his gun like a guitar. Eddie was shooting at a brick wall over and over, even after there were no more bullets in his gun. And Turner, he was lying on the ground in the middle of the street clutching his crotch and screaming at the top of his lungs. It was obvious that they were in their own nightmares.

Katie flew up higher to see if Pandora was close, but she couldn't spot her. She bit the inside of her cheek and shook her head. "If I don't save them now, they're going to be fucking frozen dead gray Kabbus meat."

She took a deep breath and dove, wishing she had some sort of telepathy with Pandora or at least a fucking comm, so she knew what was going on. But Katie knew Pandora had her own issues to deal with. She had been chivvying people down the street toward a large warehouse on the outskirts of the town. She was trying to get them to safety, figuring one warehouse would be a lot easier to protect then miles of city streets and residences. Still, Katie really needed her help.

Katie stood in front of the guys and let out a calming wave. She needed to get them away from the city; only then could they kick the dreams out of their minds. Eddie began to relax, dropping his gun and just standing there. Brock's arms fell, and his shoulders relaxed. Turner let out a deep breath and stared aimlessly at the sky.

She took off toward Turner, grabbing him under the arm. "I can get you to safety."

He stood up, whimpering. "They're eating my dick. Eating my dick."

Katie blinked. "Right. Okay. We'll stop them, buddy."

Walking over to Brock, she took him by the hand. He said nothing, just followed her, tears still staining his cheeks. Last she grabbed Eddie, who kept shaking his head. "I just keep missing. I keep missing. Coco, where are you?"

Katie pressed them together and opened a portal before guiding them to some sort of dark, shadowy world. She didn't even take the time to look around. She had to get the guys back to the base. She opened another portal and walked out, determining that the base was pretty close. She hadn't planned to open her portal this close, but that was okay. They were only a few hundred feet from the front gate.

Katie heard the portal snap shut behind her and she bent over, breathing heavily. "We are really close, guys. You should be feeling better already. I told you it would be tough. It's hard to escape Kabbus and his nightmares. It will take practice for us all. I'm just glad I was able to stay upright to get you guys…"

Katie turned around with a smile that quickly faded. "Out…of…there…Oh, fuck!"

Instead of Brock, Turner, and Eddie, Kabbus let out a deep laugh, his tentacles writhing as he slithered straight toward the base. Katie froze for a moment, trying to figure out where the guys had gone and how he'd gotten through a portal that small.

Suddenly it clicked, and rage blew through her. She was absolutely horrified. She had been so busy trying to save the guys that she hadn't even realized that Kabbus had lured her right into a fucking trick. She slammed her hand against her legs and screamed. She had spent all that time killing demons and defeating the masterminds behind the hellish movement, and in the end, she had been tricked by some multi-tentacled slob who didn't even have the decency to bullshit her with words.

She ran her hands through her hair, tapping her foot wildly on the sand. She stared down at the granules as they began to blow around her. Suddenly she realized something. It wasn't just the fact that she had been tricked. It was the idea that instead of saving her team, she had endangered everyone at her base. She had brought Kabbus right where he wanted to go. Right where the demons would have wanted him to go.

"The base is in danger, and no one even knows Kabbus is near," Katie whispered to herself, pacing back and forth.

She stopped and looked at Kabbus, who was still slithering toward the base. "I can't let this happen. That motherfucker has to die."

She reached down, running her hand over Tom in his holster. She pulled it out and took off, running straight for the Leviathan. She aimed at him, slowing down to make sure she got off a good shot. She pulled the trigger once, but it clicked. She stopped, pulling the trigger again and again, but her gun was empty. She reached down for more ammunition, feeling in the pouch, but she was out.

She shook her head and kept pulling the trigger, but nothing came out of the barrel. Katie reached over her shoulder and patted her back, but she couldn't feel her sword. "No, this can't be happening. Where is it? *Where is it?*"

She whirled around to keep her eyes locked on Kabbus, but when she did, he was gone. She stared at the base, but there was no one out and about, no vehicles running, no training going on. The wind blew hard, pushing sand across her face, but Katie didn't flinch. She knew what she had to do. She had to get to the base and warn them before all hell broke loose.

She started to run, but all her feet did was sink into the sand. She screamed, using everything she had to pull her leg free and take another step. Her eyes shimmered with tears as she pressed on, looking at the base—her home, where everyone she loved was waiting without warning.

Pandora put out her hands. "Everyone stay here, and you will be safe."

All the people nodded, surprising her. For some reason, they had almost all snapped out of it. She closed the doors and took off, flying fast across the city. She spotted the guys below her, so she did a quick scan and landed. Turner was sitting on the ground patting his crotch, Eddie was backing away from a wall and looking down at his gun in confusion, and Brock had walked out into the street, scratching his head.

Pandora looked around for Katie but didn't see her. "We need some fucking comms. Brock, what happened?"

Brock was still coming out of it. He looked at Pandora strangely. "She…she opened a portal."

Pandora's eyes went wide. "Shit."

Brock shook his head. "I don't know where she went."

Pandora pressed her lips together. "I have an idea, and I hope to hell I'm wrong."

20

Timothy yawned, covering his mouth as they watched the screen. He glanced at Sean. "Do you miss going into the action like Rambo?"

Sean shrugged. "Sure, a little bit. But I've still got a part to play, and I want to be what I am supposed to be, not amped up by a demon."

Timothy chuckled and looked up as a red dot appeared on the screen. He leaned forward and narrowed his eyes. "That's Kabbus. He's moved locations."

Sean furrowed his brow. "Where is he?"

Timothy shook his head, typing as the screen zeroed in on the location. He stood up quickly, knocking his chair over behind him. "Shit. That's here. He's here."

Turner rubbed the side of his face and shook his head, goosebumps running up and down his arms. "It was terrible. You should have seen it. There were these little green goblins. They were everywhere. They were giggling and screeching, and then my dick…"

He looked up at Pandora with sincere worry. "My fucking dick."

Brock sat down on the curb, his face sullen and lost. "There were so many of them. My life's work. The most amazing piece I have ever written. The piece I had been trying my whole life to find, and nothing. They hated it. They hated *me*. They could have killed me at that point. There were so many of them. They were everywhere."

Eddie reloaded his gun and looked through the scope. "It was like the bullets had a mind of their own. They went everywhere but where I aimed. Then there was the woman. She was so scared. So scared, and I killed her. It was an accident, but I killed her right there in the street like an execution."

Eddie put his head in his hands and began to sob. Pandora stood with her hands on her hips, watching the guys. "I need to get you guys back together. This fight isn't over."

She took a deep breath and pressed her palms together. Rubbing them fast, she pulled the energy from her chest, down her arms, and into her palms. When the light was bright enough, she pushed it out, aiming the full effects at the three guys. She held on to it for as long as she could before letting the leftover energy seep back through her body.

The guys all looked up, Eddie confused as he wiped his tears. They walked over to Pandora and nodded. "Thanks for that. That was terrible."

Pandora squeezed Eddie's shoulder while she looked at the other two. "We have to move, and fast. Are the three of you okay to keep going?"

They all nodded and pulled out their guns, double-checking that they had ammo. Brock took a deep breath. "Let's do this."

Pandora smiled. "All right. Stay close, and remember, don't let your mind get away from you."

She gritted her teeth as she used every ounce of her energy to open a portal. She was damn glad she had been practicing since Katie was nowhere to be found. She looked at the open space in front of her and breathed heavily as she stepped through, allowing the guys to follow her before closing that portal. They stepped quickly into an alternate dimension, looking around.

Pandora raised an eyebrow. Everything there was spotless, and even though she had not seen that part of the city, it looked very familiar to her. Standing on the sidewalk and glancing at the newcomers was a parade of beautiful naked people. Some sneered at them, while the rest looked at them both longingly and curiously. Everything sparkled brightly around them.

Brock looked at the people and then at himself, making sure he was still fully clothed. He leaned forward, clearing his throat. "Uh, Pandora? This is an alternate universe, correct? I'm not in another dream, am I?"

Pandora closed her mouth, having let it drop open when they first stepped through. She swallowed and glanced back at the guys. "Nope, this is definitely an alternate universe, and it happens to be one I've been to a couple of times before."

Turner turned his head, watching a beautiful redhead walk by. She glanced over her shoulder and winked. "Why does that not surprise me in the slightest? I feel like we may be overdressed for this occasion. Should I begin to disrobe?"

Brock put his hand on Turner's as he reached for a button. "In case you hadn't noticed, this is a dimension of beautiful naked people, not creepy, hairy, naked people. You might get us thrown in some kind of prison if you do that."

Turner narrowed his eyes at Brock. "You are no fun, not even a little bit. Is this what we get when you have a girlfriend?"

Brock patted him on the shoulder. "This is what you get when I'm looking out for your safety and our eyes."

Eddie was ignoring everyone, standing a few steps away and watching everyone who passed. "Woah. Where the hell are we, and can we please stay here, just for a little while?"

Pandora snickered. "This is my happy place."

She opened another portal and grabbed Eddie by the collar. "And no, we cannot stay. Remember, we have to save our friends, planet Earth, and all humans? You know, the ones who are facing a Nightmare Leviathan?"

Eddie sighed. "If only I didn't have any morals or a conscience. This would be the place for me to call home. I wonder if we could vacation here?"

Angie and Juntto stood in front of the jet in the hangar bay, looking around at the crew trying to prep the plane as fast as they could for take-off. They had just finished the routine maintenance when they had gotten the call to fuel up the jet. Juntto set his heavy bags of Juntto-sized weapons on the ground with a clunk.

One of the crew members walked by, and Angie reached out to clutch his arm. "What are we looking at here? We need to get in the air."

The crew member nodded with a serious expression. "We're finishing up the fueling now. Shouldn't be more than ten, maybe fifteen minutes. We are going as fast as we can."

Angie gave him a forced smile and nodded her head. "Of course you are. Sorry, it's kind of our job to push people."

The guy patted her hand. "I know. I'll grab you both when it's ready."

He walked off and Angie looked up at Juntto, making sure he didn't take the whole grabbing comment literally. Normally she would have to explain that he hadn't meant it in the literal sense of the word, but she realized that he hadn't even heard the guy. He was staring out of the hangar with a very worried look on his face.

Angie rubbed his huge arm. "Juntto, are you all right? I've seen you worried before, but never to this level. Katie is there. She is keeping things under control."

Juntto let out a deep sigh, shrinking as if he were deflating. He turned to Angie and looked her in the eyes, taking her hands. "When I was a young boy in my dimension, we heard all the stories of our people. Some were bright and heroic, and some were sad but taught important lessons. Then there were the ones that gave us kids dreams that would wake us through the night. There was a story about the Nightmare Man. It was about the things that came in the dark. The creatures that lurked close, pushing you into your darkest nightmare and then draining your body dry of not only your fear but your soul as well."

Angie swallowed hard. "We all had stories like that. For us, it was the boogeyman."

Juntto wrinkled his nose. "He came for your boogers?"

Angie giggled. "No, it was like your story, only humanized."

Juntto nodded, flashing back to his memories again. "This Nightmare Man… He was the worst of all of them. As warriors we feared very little, knowing our weapons and our sheer strength could overcome any foe that tried to attack us. But this one…he was different."

Angie furrowed her brow. "How?"

He took a deep breath, glancing down at his weapons. "Because the Nightmare Man was a thing that no sword could kill and no shield could protect you from. He killed you all right, but not before he took over your mind."

Angie bit her lip, watching Juntto's frightened face. Her phone buzzed in her pocket, making her jump. She let go of Juntto and reached in, pulling it out. "It's a text from Timothy."

She opened the screen and looked at the message, her face going pale. She reached up, shaking Juntto's arm. "It says, **He's here. He's here. The Leviathan is**, and it ends there."

Juntto's face fell and he turned, pointing at one of the crew. "You. How long a flight is it from here to Vegas?"

The guy thought about it for a moment. "About six hours."

Juntto turned back to Angie with frustration on his face. "Six hours is too long. They could all be dead by the time we got there, not to mention that the pilot could be affected and crash the plane right into the base. We have to figure out another way to get there."

Angie was stunned, still staring at Timothy's message. Juntto grabbed Angie by the shoulders and shook her slightly. "Angie. I need you to stay with me right now. Our friends and family are in danger. I can't have you freezing up."

Angie took a deep breath and nodded. "Right. Sorry. It's just…it's such a cryptic message, and it cut off. We need to get there. Okay. I'll call Katie. Maybe she can portal us in. She has to know that he is there."

Juntto nodded as Angie pulled out her phone. "How did it get from Utah to Vegas so fast? As far as I know, it doesn't have teleportation powers."

Angie shook her head as she pressed Katie's number and put the phone to her ear. "I don't know, but we have to do something."

Katie turned the corner in the training barracks and ran down the hall, pulling hard on all the doors. No matter where she turned, she couldn't seem to find a single soul. She knew they had to be there, but where? She turned and headed back out, taking off across the courtyard and heading over to the armory. It hadn't been put on lockdown yet, so that had to mean they didn't know what was going on.

Katie flung open the doors and looked around, but there was not a single person inside. All of the machines sat perfectly still, and open boxes of ammo lingered like they had been abandoned. She backed out, rubbing her hands over her face. "Think, Katie. What is going on?"

Suddenly her phone rang, and she patted her pockets until she found it. She felt like she was in slow motion, her emotions hanging in the wind. She pressed the Answer button. Angie's voice spilled through the speaker. "Katie! It's Angie! Come to the airfield in New York and get Juntto. The Leviathan, it's at the base. I got a text from Timothy."

Katie looked around, not saying a word. Angie cleared her throat. "Katie? Are you okay?"

The sound of Kabbus' tentacles slapping against the smooth floors inside the base echoed like bare feet on a wet floor. The fog cascaded both in front and behind him, searching out any of the people still on the base. He didn't sense their fear just yet, meaning he had made it inside without anyone knowing he was there. That was exactly what he needed—a sneak attack so that everyone would be down before they even had a chance to fight back. Katie had played perfectly into his scheme.

Stephanie leaned back against the pillow on their bed. Korbin slid in at her feet, pulling them into his lap. "I find it thrilling that even as a badass mercenary, you still find time to paint your toenails."

Stephanie laughed. "I just did it before you came home."

Korbin smiled. "Sorry. It was busy at the fort, and I lost my polish."

Stephanie smiled. "So where is the next fort going to be put up? I'm expecting they will be all over the world, and will eventually be a mainstay in most places. Hopefully even in small towns."

Korbin nodded. "That would be preferable. They would really protect small towns well. As far as the next ones, we are looking into Russia. I thought somewhere in the islands, but it's also looking like possibly Brazil, which is at least warm. We will see. I just want to make these people safer and to make their lives a little better when they go to sleep at night. Wherever I go next is going to be right, because regardless of the geography, they are going to need the fort. I guess that's all that matters."

Stephanie nodded, rubbing her hand over her chest. She cleared her throat and pulled her feet out of his hands, sitting up cross-legged. He looked at her, confused. "Are you all right?"

She cleared her throat again, pressing her hand to her chest. She got up from the bed and walked in a circle. "Yeah. I just feel so…so…"

Korbin watched her as she turned around, her eyes flashing red. He stood up. "What's wrong?"

Stephanie pursed her lips. "I just don't understand why you feel you have to be away all the time. You could send someone else to do this. You come back here thinking it will be all fine because you are visiting. Well, that's fucking bullshit. Sending me flowers? Fucking bullshit."

Korbin rubbed his chest, his brow lowering. He pointed at Stephanie, narrowing his eyes. "Really? Well, that's just typical of you to say that. It's fucking typical of you to play the me me me card, isn't it? I want to help other people, and there you are, trying to control every aspect of my fucking life. Would you like to dictate my bathroom schedule? When I take a sip of water? When I breathe?"

Stephanie gasped. "Oh, okay, so now it's me being selfish. Turn it around on me."

Korbin scoffed. "Can't turn something around if it's only facing one direction."

Stephanie rolled her eyes and laughed. "You idiot, you can too. Good lord, how do you even know which way to point the fucking guns on your precious forts? I...I..."

She gritted her teeth and looked down at her shaking hands. Her eyes shifted around the room and back to Korbin's face. He looked at her angrily, putting his hands on his hips. "Well? You what?"

Stephanie put up her hand and shook her head. She could feel fear building in her chest. It was so powerful that she was on the edge of letting it take her over. "Do you feel that?"

Korbin looked her up and down. "Feel what?"

Stephanie walked over to him and put her palm flat on his chest, taking his hand and putting his on hers. "The fear. It's bubbling up more and more with every second that passes. We aren't really angry at each other. We are arguing out of fear—fear that wasn't there just two minutes ago. We were having a normal conversation and then there it was, erupting like a volcano."

Korbin's face began to relax as he realized that what she was saying was true. He put his other hand over hers and shook his head. "This isn't us. We don't ever speak to each other in this manner."

Stephanie shook her head, looking at him sadly. "This is what Katie was talking about. It's what she was warning us about. We're experiencing our fears and manifesting them into anger, arguing with each other. It's turning us against one another."

She stood there for a moment, grasping her chest, her breathing picking up. Her head shot up, and she looked Korbin in the eyes. "He's here. Kabbus is here."

She turned to run for the door but Korbin grabbed her arm, bringing her in. He put his hands on her face and kissed her softly. "No matter what this beast brings, no matter how it makes us feel, we need to stay strong. For us. For the base. For our family here."

Stephanie nodded in understanding. "Right. Of course. For our lives."

He let go of her, and she ran to the door. Looking back at Korbin with love in her eyes, she slammed her palm against the panic button on the wall, activating the emergency alert. Immediately all the red lights began to blink, and a siren blared overhead. She pulled her phone out and dialed the tech room, tapping her foot as it rang. After a few moments, she slowly lowered it, looking at Korbin.

She blinked several times. "There's no answer."

The alarm blared across the base, breaking the silence and pulling everyone from their heads. War had come to them. A war of the mind.

21

Doctor Ozu put out his hands, He was sitting on the edge of the desk. "Take dinosaurs, for example. We have been trying to extract their DNA for decades. Making attempts to replicate long since extinct animals. It is difficult because their DNA had that different link. However, we have recently realized that we can work backward from living creatures like chickens. Unfortunately, with the Leviathan, we don't have samples. If we did, we could not only replicate but alter, creating forces for defense."

Sofia and Calvin glanced at each other and back at Ozu. "Wouldn't that be dangerous? I mean, why would we want to bring unpredictable creatures here?"

Ozu shrugged. "Personally, I don't. But you have to understand the mind of the defense world. To create a creature that could do, say, three times the killing of Juntto but has never gone through the negative aspects of his time on Earth? It would be pivotal to defense efforts."

Sofia smiled. "That's really amazing, that in such a short time span compared to how long humans have been alive, we have become that scientifically capable. I would have thought it would have taken much longer."

Dr. Ozu chuckled. "That, my dear, is only the tip of the iceberg in genetics. We are seeing breakthroughs no one ever thought possible. You know, if you are interested, I could help arrange an internship. They…"

Suddenly Dr. Ozu stopped speaking and stared off in the other direction. Sofia looked that way and then back at him, unsure of what he was staring at. Calvin stood up, peering around. The doctor was acting very strange, and it seemed to have come out of nowhere. Calvin walked forward and put his hand on the doctor's shoulder. "Are you all right?"

Ozu got off the desk and took a couple of steps forward, one arm crossed over his chest and the other pointing at the desk. "Did you see that? There was a…"

Sofia smiled. "Yes? What was it?"

The doctor rubbed his hand over his chest and took a step closer. He narrowed his eyes and went down on one knee. Calvin and Sofia watched him warily. He crept slightly forward, his eyes growing frantic. Suddenly he jerked away, falling on his back and throwing his hands all over the place. Sofia gasped and Calvin stepped in front of her as he flopped around, finally jumping up and crawling onto the desk. He sat on all fours, his eyes combing the floor and then looking up at the ceiling.

Calvin put his hand up. "Doctor, what do you see?"

Ozu began to sweat, shaking his head wildly. "The snakes! The snakes! They're everywhere. Don't you see them? They're hanging from the ceiling, and they're all over the floor, and in the drawers too. Oh, God! They're going to bite me. Swallow me whole."

Sofia's eyes grew wide, and she swept the room with her gaze, trying to locate what he feared. She shook her head at Calvin. "I don't see anything."

Calvin glanced back and forth. "I don't either."

Sofia hopped out of her chair, standing behind Calvin as they attempted to calm him down. Sofia spoke in a gentle voice. "Doctor Ozu, I think you might not be feeling well. Why don't you let us give you something to calm you down? We use it on soldiers all the time. Maybe the trip and the stress are starting to get to you."

The doctor picked up a letter opener and swung it around. "Stay back! They're coming for us. We have no chance. Save yourselves!"

Sofia grabbed onto Calvin's arm. "What's wrong with him?"

Calvin shook his head. "I don't know. He is hallucinating or something."

Suddenly the alarm began to blare out across the base, the lights flashing red. Calvin frowned, watching Ozu carefully. "The base has been breached."

Soldiers and mercs began to run wildly around, most of them preparing for something they didn't even know was a threat. As the sirens echoed across the base, the weapons for a normal attack were deployed. Little did they know this would be no ordinary fight. There were no demons to physically ward off, no bullets to pierce the enemy. He was large but stealthy, getting to the people before they saw him coming.

On the bottom floor, down the hall and in the dungeon, there was nothing but stillness. The computer beeped wildly and alarms were buzzing all over, trying to get Timothy and Sean's attention. Even though they were sitting and standing right there in front of them, they had no idea that the full-on attack had begun.

Timothy's face was straight and stern, his hand holding a cup of coffee. Slowly it tilted, trickling the hot liquid onto the floor in front of him. Sean sat perfectly still as well, his hands just inches from the keyboard, his eyes glazed. The phone rang over and over, and the comm beeped. The soldiers' voices rang out over the speaker, calling in for confirmation. Calling in for warnings. Calling in for help. But the room remained perfectly still, a haze seeping through the entire place.

The coffee began to puddle, and a single stream ran across the floor beneath Timothy's loafers, over the threshold of the door and out into the hallway.

Sean blinked, clearing the haze from his vision. He stretched his back and looked up, expecting to see Timothy. "Weren't we just..."

Timothy wasn't next to him. He turned in his wheelchair, looking around, but he was no longer in the dungeon. Instead, he sat at a long wooden table, candles lit in the center and dozens of dome-covered dishes all over the surface. When he looked down, he was wearing a chef's coat and hat, and his tennis shoes had been replaced by non-slip Crocs.

He frowned, touching his black and white checkered pants. Suddenly the domes began to lift from the dishes one at a time, floating back toward the kitchen. In front of him was the largest display of his favorite foods he had ever seen. The fragrant aromas were so strong that he felt as if he could already taste the food.

There was kimchi, bulgogi, samgyeopsal, and many more of his favorite childhood Korean dishes. There were also roasted turkeys, stuffed ducks, and desserts as far as he could see. To his right was his absolute favorite, homemade eclairs, with the chocolate just applied. His stomach began to growl and he laughed, feeling as if he had hit the jackpot.

He reached up and took the napkin from his plate, tucking it into the front of his shirt. "If I can't walk, I might as well eat."

With a smirk, he reached over and grabbed an éclair and set it on his plate. He then filled the other half with a taste of about twenty different dishes. He felt as if he hadn't eaten in a week. Grabbing his fork and knife, he held them up, ready to dig in. He smiled as he lowered them to the plate and cut a savory and juicy strip of samgyeopsal, holding it up in front of him and licking his lips. However, as he went to put the meat to his mouth, it disappeared in a puff of smoke.

Sean furrowed his brows and looked down, making sure he hadn't dropped it. He sighed and tried again, but the same thing happened. Every time he got the food to his mouth, it just dissolved into smoke. Even the scent was gone. He tried over and over, stabbing the food on his plate and lifting it to his mouth. Smoke drifted off and circled around the room as the sound of his knife and fork scraping the plate vibrated around him.

He threw the silverware down and tried to grab the food with his hands, but it was gone immediately. "No. No. Noooooo!"

Timothy shook his head, opening his eyes as if he had fallen asleep. He looked around him, finding himself standing in the middle of a bar. He wrinkled his forehead and glanced down at his clothes to see he was wearing the finest couture. He wiggled his eyebrows. "Don't know how I got here, but hellllo, Armani."

A girl walked past him in a tight leopard skin body con dress and black platform heels. Around her shoulders was a black feather boa. Timothy put his fingers to his lips, trying not to laugh. "Oh, sweetie. We are going to need to have a really long talk about picking your clothes from the zoo. That is not cute."

The girl sneered at him and huffed, strutting off.

Why did you just let her walk off like that? It was your fucking chance.

Timothy stopped and looked around nervously. "Uh, who said that? Y'all must be fucking with me, because I know I didn't just hear that."

The voice laughed deeply. *I know you missed me. Trust me, I did not miss you.*

Timothy put his head down and strode to the corner of

the bar. *No. No. No. How did you get back in my head? You were gone. Long-fucking-gone.*

The voice chuckled again. *Or was I? The most important thing now is you stop acting like a goddamned pussy and go out there and grab some instead. Be a fucking MAN!*

Timothy stood straight up, putting his hands over his ears. "NOOOOOOOO!"

"Everyone to their stations! The ship is going down," a marine yelled into his hand, although it looked as though he thought it was a comm.

He dipped around the corner, dodging and weaving. Another guy screamed, tumbling through the doorway, running his hands wildly through his hair. There was smoke coming from the second level of the barracks, but no one seemed to notice.

Down the hall, deep in the recesses of the building, Kabbus filled a corridor, laughing heartily. He moved toward the door, leaving a trail of soldiers in his wake, all gray and dead from fear.

The courtyard was a mess, soldiers running everywhere. Some were under Kabbus' spell, while others attempted to prepare for the coming fight. The loudspeakers squealed before Stephanie's voice came out of them. "Stay calm. Battle stations. Kabbus the Leviathan is in the base."

Joshua and Wanda stood at the armory doors, waving

in several of the injured soldiers and pushing the girls to the back. They were getting ready to lock it down, trying to keep as many as safe as they could.

Brock, Turner, Eddie, and Pandora ran through the basement halls, calling Katie's name. They turned a corner and Brock pointed. "There she is!"

They ran up to her and grabbed her by the shoulders. She had been standing still and staring at one of the gray cinderblock walls. She blinked at Brock, not knowing whether she was dreaming or awake. Suddenly the vision of Kabbus posing as the guys went through her head and she grabbed her sword, backing up.

Brock put up his hands. "Katie, it's me. We've been looking everywhere for you. You were with us, then you opened a portal, walked through, and was gone."

Pandora walked up and put her finger on the sword, slowly pushing it down. "All right, ninja warrior. I know you're confused, but Brock is not the enemy. Besides, I don't want to spend the next year consoling you because you accidentally stabbed your boyfriend while believing he was a murderous Nightmare Leviathan."

Katie loosened her shoulders and looked at Pandora. "What was the song I sang you at night when you wouldn't go to sleep?"

Pandora glanced at the guys, embarrassed. "That is really rude. Why would you call me out like that?"

Katie gritted her teeth and raised her sword again.

Pandora put her hands up. "Okay, okay. It was the theme from the Power Rangers."

Several of the guys chuckled, and Pandora threw them an angry glare. Katie put her sword down and rubbed her head. "God, I'm sorry. I just didn't know what was real anymore. I did this, Pandora. I fucked up, and now Kabbus is on the loose in the base. I thought I was running around warning people, but apparently, I was here staring at this wall instead."

Pandora rolled her eyes and looked at Brock before diving head-first into Katie. Katie stumbled back and held her chest. *You really need to warn me first.*

Pandora chuckled. *Yeah, well, right now you need to get out of pity-party mode. There is no time for that fucking shit. You're the world's biggest badass, and it's time to go after that fucker.*

Katie swallowed hard, her breathing heavy and her heart beating fast. *I don't know. I don't know if I can do this. He gets in my head and I don't even know where I am.*

Pandora worked her magic, slowing down her heartbeat. *Calm yourself. Take a deep breath and close your eyes. Everything is as it should be. We pulled you out of it.*

Katie nodded, following Pandora's orders for a moment. When she opened her eyes, she was still there with Brock and the guys, and Pandora was sending calming vibes from inside her.

Pandora knew Katie had to get it together. *You feel better?*

Katie looked down at her armor. *Yeah. I think so. Yeah.*

Pandora talked in a relaxed tone. *Good. Very good. Now, I need you to think. You have got to stop and think as hard as you can. Clear your mind. The Leviathan is trying to fuck with you, but you aren't going to let him. You are stronger than that moth-erfucker. You know that. Your mind is stronger than that.*

Katie cleared her mind and rolled her shoulders. Pandora gave her a second to collect herself. *Now, is there something you were supposed to do? Someone you should be contacting or somewhere you need to be?*

It only took Katie a minute. She patted her pockets, pulling out her phone. *Juntto! I have to go get Juntto. He is at the airport in New York, and we need to bring him back here.*

Pandora clapped her hands. *Yes! Good. Then go get him.*

Katie looked at the guys. "I'm going to grab Juntto. We'll be right back. Get the men together and help whoever needs it. Don't face Kabbus on your own."

The guys all nodded and started to run off. Brock stared at Katie with a smile. He walked up and kissed her cheek. "I knew you were still in there. I could see it in your shimmering blue eyes."

He headed toward the courtyard. Katie opened a portal and rushed in, not even noticing which alternative universe she had stepped into. As soon as she was through, she opened a second one and bolted through into the hangar bay.

Angie let out a deep sigh and hurried over, wrapping her arms around Katie. "Oh, my God. We thought… I don't know what we thought. You sounded so strange on the phone, and then you were gone. Are you okay? What's going on?"

Katie looked at Juntto, who had his bags in his hands. She felt terrible that Angie looked so terrified, but there was really no time to explain. Time was of the essence, and Katie had already taken up enough staring at a cinder block wall. "I don't have time to explain. Kabbus is at the base. I'm all right. It's a mess, though. Luckily, Pandora and the guys found me before I became his victim too."

Angie clutched her phone to her chest. "I tried to get hold of Timothy, but there wasn't an answer."

Katie looked at her worried face and took a deep breath, putting a hand on her shoulder. "I'll make sure they are checked on. Everyone is scrambling right now. I came straight here when they woke me up. Juntto, we need you."

Angie looked at them frantically. "I want to help. I can help."

Katie glanced at Juntto, who shrank and took Angie by the shoulders. "You remember the stories of the Nightmare Man?"

Angie looked at him, worried. "Yes."

Juntto chewed his lip for a moment. "I don't want you anywhere near him. We don't even know at this point if we can kill him. You are going to be safest here. If he gets into your mind, your worst fears will come true. That is very hard to get over after you experience it."

Angie's eyes teared. "I know, but what if you…"

Juntto shook his head, putting his hand to her lips. "I am Juntto, king warrior. I fear nothing. If he gets into my mind, it will be clear as day. You have nothing to worry about."

Katie could see Angie's face softening, and she realized for the first time just how close Angie and Juntto had become. Angie lunged forward, hugging Juntto tightly and clenching her eyes shut. "If it tries, just think about Hygge. That is a good place to be."

Katie smiled and cleared her throat. "I'm sorry, guys,

but we need to go. Juntto, are you ready for this? I don't know how other Leviathans are affected by Kabbus."

Juntto shrugged. "I don't either, but like I just told Angie, I fear nothing. His games will not work on me. All he will find is a spear in his heart. He will not be able to torture us then."

Katie smiled, knowing he was mostly saying it for Angie's sake. Juntto picked up his bags and kissed Angie on the forehead. "Go get your followers on Twitch. I will be back soon."

He disappeared through a portal with Katie and Angie crossed her arms, still worried. "You better be, you big-ass frost giant."

22

The base was still in chaos, and the armory was still not completely secured. There were just too many people, and Joshua could not leave them behind. Half of them were in living nightmares, running around screaming or crouched in the corners of shadows, rocking. On top of that, no one knew where the team members were since they were all in different places trying to get the situation under control.

In the center of the courtyard, the air swished and the edges of a portal shimmered as Katie forced it open, grunting loudly. She stepped through, pulling her guns. Juntto stomped through behind her, already screwing his spear together. They looked around, finding Brock and the guys running toward them, loading their weapons.

Brock shook Juntto's hand. "I'll be the first to say it's good to see your big blue ass."

Juntto chuckled. "Your pasty white ass is something I'd rather not see."

The guys all laughed, but quietly, nervous that their reality would be twisted upside down at any moment. They were all becoming more resistant to it, though. That, or Kabbus was focusing his hell on the other soldiers running around instead. Either way, it gave them a window to work.

Pandora sniffed. *I would be careful if I were you. I can smell the tentacles getting closer. It's like a mixture of fish soup and ball sweat. Bro needs to take a fucking bath.*

Katie wrinkled her nose. *So glad I can't smell him right... Wait, what is that smell?*

Pandora laughed. *You're welcome. Just making sure you can track him too.*

Katie slammed a mag into her gun. *That shit's wrong, dude. Just wrong.*

Eddie tapped Katie on the shoulder. "Uh, what is that?"

To their right, in a medium-sized building where the teams stored their gear after training, a black fog began rolling out of the door and across the sand. Katie sniffed the air and snarled. "Here comes our monster now."

As she spoke the words, Kabbus emerged from the building, using his tentacles to bend the doorframe back for him to fit through. Turner's lip twitched. "That's one big fucking dude."

Juntto threw down his bags, holding his spear by his side. "And he has no manners when visiting someone else's house."

Pandora scoffed. *Wow, who taught Big Blue over there manners and etiquette? I'm impressed.*

Juntto growled as Kabbus bounced out of the building, looking for his next victim. Juntto tossed his spear up, grabbing the middle and taking off at a bounding run. His large feet hit the ground, shaking everything around him, and he let out a deep battle cry.

Brock, Eddie, Turner, and Katie could only watch as he ran toward the Leviathan, ready to end the feud once and for all. When he got closer, he leapt into the air, bringing his special-metal spear up over his head and thrusting it down as he fell toward Kabbus. The beast waved his tentacle at him with force. He could see the suction cups on the bottom moving in and out as if they were alive.

Juntto gritted his teeth and put his arm up to block it, not feeling the wet stickiness of Kabbus' body.

As Juntto dropped, something hit him hard in the stomach. He grunted, coming to an abrupt stop, the wind knocked from his lungs. He put his hands up, feeling a solid wood surface in front of him. Slowly he opened his eyes to find himself sitting in a rolling chair in front of a mahogany desk. He looked at his raised right hand where the spear had been, only to find a pen instead.

He lowered it and clicked the end. As his chair rolled slightly, he looked at the floor, finding it similar to what he remembered from various government office buildings he had visited. The room was bright white, with nothing on the walls and no doors to be found. "What the fuck is this?"

Juntto whirled his chair back around to the desk and froze. Where once there had been nothing but a blank desk now sat stack and stacks of papers, files, and folders. His eyes grew wide and he tried to push away, but his chair spun him back to the desk. "Oh, God. Paperwork! No! No! No!"

Pages began to flood onto his desk, piling higher and higher. Sheets fluttered around him, falling from the ceiling. Every page was filled with questions, none of them yet answered. All of them had one thing in common, though: a single line at the top reading, Must be completed by Juntto the Frost Giant under penalty of law.

Juntto pushed the stack back and stared at it as it teetered back and forth on the desk. He put his arm up as it crashed down on him like a wave. There was a constant sound of typing echoing around the room, and a typewriter now sat in front of him on the desk. He went to press a key, but his fingers were too large, and he couldn't get himself to shrink no matter how hard he tried.

Between the fluttering of papers and the click of keys he could hear Katie's and Pandora's voices somewhere in the background,. They were shouting, but he couldn't understand what they were saying. Their voices faded in and out as if they were being pushed and pulled inside his paperwork hell.

Another wave of papers flooded down on him, and he pushed back with all his might. His chair finally rolled back, but only for a couple of feet before slamming into something. Juntto turned quickly, his eyes growing wider by the second. In front of him was a filing cabinet, and it kept growing taller and taller.

He put his hands over his eyes and shook his head. "I don't deserve this. It is not my turn to do the paperwork. We had a deal. I have been good. I played by the rules."

He opened his eyes and looked down, finding himself

shin-high in paper. He stood up as the papers got higher and higher, quickly reaching his waist. In his hand was another pen, something he didn't even remember picking up. He screamed, throwing the pen into the continually growing piles of paper. They reached his chest, then his neck, and he had to keep his head tilted back to keep it above the paper.

Juntto clenched his eyes shut, hearing gunshots ringing out.

BANG! BANG! BANG! The gunshots were loud, ringing bells in Juntto's mind. He gasped and opened his eyes, trying to find out where they came from. "Don't shoot me, I'll do it. I'll do the paperwork."

He shook his large head and blinked, snapping out of his nightmare. It had all seemed so real to him, but at the same time, now that he was out, he knew it had just been a dream. It was the strangest thing he had ever experienced, and his heart was beating so fast he could hear it in his ears. Then again, it could have been the gunshots going off near his ears.

"Juntto. You're okay," Sofia's voice said softly from his right.

Suddenly, Juntto's vision cleared and he could feel the scratchy sand beneath him. He looked at her and then around the courtyard. Standing nearby with worried looks on their faces were his friends. Brock nodded at him, and Eddie held his gun closely, almost hugging it. Turner let out a deep breath, putting his hand to his chest. Standing above him was Calvin, his gun smoking in his left hand and his eyes glistening red.

Calvin reached down, and Juntto took his hand. He shrank his body to make it easier to stand up, and when he straightened, he was eye to eye with Calvin. "Thank you. Gunshots whipped me out of that terrible nightmare. What kind of monster is this? It should be put down immediately."

Calvin chuckled. "That's the plan, buddy."

Katie nodded to Calvin. "Here's your chance."

Calvin put his hand in the air to hold the others back. Sofia ran up beside him, and they each raised the guns they were gripping tightly. They put their arms out and fired at the same time, riddling Kabbus with bullets up and down his body. One of them caught his tentacle, and he whipped it down to his face. Sofia snarled. "Got you, you sonofabitch."

The Leviathan seemed to study the hole in his tentacle and the orange blood dripping out. He looked back at the team, and for the first time, he opened his mouth wide. The sound that came out was from another world. The pitch was high and sharp, fading in and out as if it were vibrating. Everyone covered their ears and watched as Kabbus took off, slithering as fast as his tentacles could carry him in the other direction.

Eddie lifted his eyebrows. "Don't ever let anyone tell you they are too fat to haul ass. That dude might give himself a stroke, though. I can't imagine his cholesterol is very good."

Katie glanced at Eddie and laughed. "Well, if there is cholesterol and fat in fear, then he will definitely be going on the Keto Diet sometime soon. No carbs for him."

Eddie snickered, giving Katie a high five before they turned back to Calvin. "Come on, let's get to the armory. We can regroup there and see who we can help inside. There are a lot of messed up and scared people on this base."

Brock sighed. "I don't blame them. This is definitely not in the Army training manual."

Turner shook his head as he followed them toward the armory. "The real shit never is, brother. It just never is."

The armory was jam-packed with people. The machines had all been turned off, and the boxes had been shoved to the back to make more room. Joshua, his girls, and a large number of affected soldiers were taking refuge on the main floor. Those who hadn't been affected attempted to see to the others, doing everything they could to calm them down. Gasps, cries, and sounds of general discomfort permeated the building. It looked like an infirmary in a war zone, only the injuries weren't easy to see, having left no outward wounds or blood.

Joshua stood near the entry as the others came in, wiping his forehead. Katie put her hand on his shoulder. "Are you all right?"

Joshua smiled. "Yeah. I haven't been affected yet. Maybe the weird are immune."

Katie laughed. "I don't know. We're all pretty weird."

Joshua looked around. "We're doing our best to calm

people down, but some are still going in and out of their nightmares. Others are so affected that they can't seem to snap out of them in between. All we can do is keep them comfortable and safe from hurting themselves or others by accident. We just weren't equipped for something like this. How do you treat a wound you can't see?"

Katie let out a deep breath. "I think our angel powers can help with that."

Pandora pulled herself out of Katie and grabbed Joshua's arm, trying not to fall. She squeezed his arm and smirked. "Been putting in some time at the gym, there? Nice job, dude. Nice job."

Katie tapped Pandora on the shoulder. "I hate to interrupt your game, but can we maybe calm all these people down?"

Pandora rolled her eyes and turned to Katie. "Of course. By all means."

They took each other's hands and built the energy up in their chests, then pushed it down and out their palms, letting a wave of light wash over the soldiers and girls. Slowly the ones still stuck began to come out of it, and the others could feel calm rush over their fears. The armory began to quiet down, and Joshua started handing out orders to the girls to help those who had physical injuries.

Wanda, the soldier with a thing for Joshua, walked up to Katie and Pandora. "We don't know how to fight this thing. It feeds on our fear. We watched so many soldiers out there just get run over by the Leviathan, leaving cold gray corpses. We don't know. We just don't know how to handle this."

Katie nodded at her sympathetically. "I understand.

Even for us, we are struggling with how to get close to him. He didn't like the bullets, but I don't know if they did any real harm."

Pandora turned to Calvin and Sofia. "Hey, you two baby makers. How did you guys fight it off?"

Calvin looked at Sofia and stepped forward. "We didn't. It's just…we're going to have a child we love. Because of that, family and friends, we honestly have nothing but hope in our hearts. Demons are coming to Earth and there's a walking nightmare outside my door, but I'm going to raise my child to have hope. Never-ending hope."

Sofia walked over and put her arm around Calvin. "It's really no different than surviving the world in all its chaos even before the demons. You have to hope for a better tomorrow. Hope that things will change, and hope you can show them the beauty between the ugly."

Pandora made a gagging sound. "That is the most made-for-tv bullshit I have ever heard. Did someone pay you to say that to fuck with me?"

Juntto stood up and put out his hand. She could see the tears in his eyes. "No, they are right. They are exactly right."

Pandora groaned. "Okay, here we go. Now Frosty is in on this too. Am I having a nightmare? Katie, pinch me."

Katie gave her a blank look and slugged her as hard as she could. Pandora winced and rubbed her arm. "Okay, unfortunately not dreaming."

Juntto came toward them, looking at his hands as he walked. "Of course. That makes so much sense. How could I have not thought of it before now? Ugh."

Katie wrinkled her nose. "So, he doesn't like hope, or does it kill him? What are we talking about here?"

Calvin glanced at Juntto. "I think it might work as a defense mechanism."

Juntto pointed at Calvin, nodding. "That's right. Kind of like that. Kind of a shield or brick wall in your mind."

Eddie chuckled, rapping Tucker's head. "Then you should be good to go, because it's nothing but fucking rocks up there."

Tucker snarled, pushing him to the side. Juntto was caught in his thought, not hearing what they were bickering about. He stepped over to Katie. "Let me explain this to you. I used to be a conqueror. I used to take what I wanted, kill who I wanted, pillage anything I wanted. I was the king in my own head, and there was no conscience involved. Then, when I went into my freeze-sleep in your homemade freezer…"

Wanda raised an eyebrow. "His *what*?"

Katie shook her head. "Just go with it. It's a very long story. Best freezer you could ever have, though. In went a bastard of a Leviathan, out came the teddy bear one."

Juntto smiled. "I learned compassion. I learned to love someone else, sometimes even more than I love myself. I learned to love all of you that way. To protect, not destroy. When my body recognized the positive my brain effects was receiving from that, it changed. It rewired itself to run on compassion instead of destruction."

Katie thought about it for a moment. "But how do you rewire your own brain like that? I don't think any of us are really thinking like old Juntto right now. We are thinking like the people we have always been."

Juntto looked pleased with his revelation. "That's right. But the trick is not to rewire it. Kabbus is trying desperately to rewire us to run on and act from places of fear and anger. He is the one doing the rewiring. Instead of allowing that to happen when you see him, when he is close, you do the opposite. You act from places of love, bravery, and hope. Once that is done and we can get close to him, we might have a standing chance of taking him the hell down before he kills anyone else."

Katie and Pandora left the armory and shut the doors tightly behind them. They looked out across the base, but there was no sign of the Leviathan. Katie wrung her hands in front of her. "Okay, we know what we need to do. And don't act like it's so hard. I know that deep down, you already act out of those places."

Pandora sneered, pushing up her tits. "Fine, but you don't need to go telling people that. I have a street rep I need to keep intact, bitch."

Katie chuckled. "Our secret. So, love and hope, Pandora. Love and hope."

Pandora's lips bent down on each side and she strutted forward. "I can do that."

Katie closed her eyes for a moment. "Whatever you need to do to get into that headspace."

Pandora smiled. "A three-some with…well, I'll keep that to myself."

Katie raised her eyebrows. "Thanks. Appreciate that."

They clapped their hands loudly in the air, and their

armor snapped to them, their swords appeared in their outstretched hands. Katie smiled and spread her wings, flying to the middle of the base. "Kabbus the Nightmare Man! Come face *your* worst fear! Face *me*, fuckwad!"

Kabbus appeared to her left, smacking his lips. His body was even more disgusting now that it was bloated from feeding on fear.

23

Pandora took a deep breath, feeling the confidence building inside her. She smiled as she reached up, holding her sword high up into the air. "I will strike with force. I will strike true. I will strike…"

She looked up at her sword and stopped, staring at a pitchfork instead. She tilted her head to the side, suddenly feeling a blast of heat surrounding her entire body. Glancing around curiously, she lowered the pitchfork and rubbed her hand over her chest.

A volcano erupted in the background, and the bubbling rivers of lava sizzled and glurped. She was back in hell. "Huh. Home, sweet home?"

Hearing the familiar sounds of whimpering and crying, she whirled around, immediately balling her hand on her chest. Chained to smoldering crosses along the front of a tall lava-rock cliff face were her friends. Katie was in the middle, her smoking wings spread behind her. To her right were Calvin, Korbin, Sofia, and Stephanie, and to Katie's left were Brock, Eddie, Turner, Sean, and Timothy. Their skin was blistering and red, and they groaned as small demons raced around them, cracking whips at their knees.

She stepped forward and opened her mouth but paused, hearing someone exhale behind her. Slowly Pandora turned and saw Lucifer with a huge smile on his face. He put out his arms and bellowed, "My queen has returned. I knew your heart was forever with us."

Her feet were moving before her mind could catch up. She galloped across the hot stones and wrapped her arms around Lucifer, kissing him. Stepping back, she spread her arms out, looking down at her body. She was no longer the beautiful, voluptuous angel she had been on Earth. Her scales had returned, moving up her body and over her neck. She glanced over her shoulder, looking for her wings. Instead, she found blackened and charred bones where they had once been.

She gasped and put her hands to her mouth. "My wings."

Lucifer laughed loudly, the sound mixing with the chorus of screams and agony from her friends. She turned toward them, shaking her head, tears pouring from her eyes and sizzling down her cheeks.

Lucifer walked over to her and put his arm around her shoulder. "You knew it was in you the whole time."

Pandora shook her head. "No! I became an angel again. I was meant for good."

Lucifer guffawed loudly, holding his stomach. "Were you? Think about it."

Pandora stared at her friends, feeling the bones of her wings cracking and disintegrating on her back. Her heart sank. "I'm afraid this is who I am—evil through and through. There never has been, and there never will be, a chance at redemption for me. How could I have ever seen through the dark? It was all a shadow. It was a trick. A punishment for choosing this life, a life I could never live. A life that defines exactly who I am."

Pandora groaned and wailed, running toward the river of flowing lava. She stopped at the edge and cried into her palms. She pulled her hands away and watched as her tears turned to steam rising from her black skin. "My heart is the color of my body. My soul is dark, and my appearance reflects that, no matter how much I wanted it to be different."

Lucifer walked over and rubbed her back with his long black talons. "There, there. Come, look at these people you thought were your friends. They saw right through you. They were the ones who delivered you back to us. They didn't want you, because they knew your true nature was nothing but dark."

He turned Pandora and walked her over to them, lifting her chin so she could stare into their eyes. She combed over their faces until she reached Katie's. Her eyes started to close but then opened, the blue in them still shining brightly. Even though she was being tortured and her wings were aflame, she shook her head with force.

Pandora's mouth opened slightly, and she pulled away from Lucifer. She walked up to the cross and put her hands on Katie's feet. Katie groaned as she bent her head forward, looking down on Pandora just as God had looked down on her the day she'd left her post above.

With chapped lips and a mangled body, Katie spoke

with strength and courage. "No. Your words are not true, and you know they aren't. Darkness is a choice, and you chose long ago, even before us, that it was not the place you wanted to be. Remember, there is hope. There are people who love you."

Pandora looked at the guys, all of whom had their eyes focused on her. She turned the other way, watching as Sofia cradled her hands around her belly, the only part of her not burned, singed, or whipped.

She looked back up at Katie, who forced a smile. "Be brave. Be righteous."

Pandora looked down at her hands on Katie's feet, and the scales began to retract. She could feel the warm glow of her angel powers begin to spark again in her heart, and her eyes faded from red to blue. She closed them tightly, hearing Katie's words over and over in her head.

Tears poured down her cheeks as she remembered that there was, indeed, hope. "I can be righteous and brave."

When she opened her eyes again, there was no more fire and brimstone. No more lies and deceit. She was back on the base with Katie reaching down to her. "Are you okay?"

Pandora took a deep breath and got to her feet. She looked down at her body, finding her golden angel armor shimmering brightly. She looked in her hand, which was clenched tightly. Not on the handle of a pitchfork or whip, not to Lucifer or any demon. Instead, she held her sword firmly in her one hand and her shield in the other.

Pandora stretched her wings out wide behind her, full of feathers and glory. They were still black and silver as she had wanted but didn't represent evil, not in the least. A smile moved across her lips and she looked at Katie, no longer suffering. "I'm okay. Thank you."

Katie gazed back at her, slightly puzzled. "For what?"

Pandora chuckled as she folded her wings back. "Because even in my dreams, you doled out useful tidbits of courage."

Katie smiled. "Glad I could be of service. Now, can we take care of this bitch?"

Pandora looked at Kabbus, his tentacles wildly cascading around him. "Yes, please. Ursula over there is starting to get really fucking old."

Katie and Pandora spread their wings and took off. They sped forward, beating their wings hard. As they got closer, they split off in separate directions, circling around and swiping their swords down and through the Leviathan's nasty jiggling body.

They turned and circled again, this time bobbing and weaving through the maze of tentacles that whipped through the air, trying to take them down. Pandora whirled around, folding her wings in and holding her sword out. She clipped the tip off of every tentacle that got anywhere near her.

Katie laughed as she did the same, putting her shield in the air with one leg bent like a ballerina. "Who knew slashing and hacking a dickwad Leviathan could be so feminine and demure?"

Pandora soared up and back down, continuing to slash at the beast. "A night at the ballet. You shouldn't have."

Katie smiled. "Wine and roses after?"

Pandora sneered.

Katie rolled her eyes. "Fine. Donuts and milkshakes after?"

Pandora's sneer turned up. "Now you're talking my language, bitch."

They flew in opposite directions again, meeting back up in front of the monster. They hovered there for a moment, hands clasped. The Leviathan screeched again, writhing in its pain and suffering. Pandora hated to admit that she was enjoying it. "I guess this kind of torture is not so bad."

Katie shrugged. "I wouldn't mind watching this sonofabitch be torn tentacle from tentacle by Lucifer. I'd make some sugar popcorn for that."

Pandora oohed. "The green and purple kind? I love that."

Katie shook her head. "You know it all tastes the same."

Pandora scoffed. "I don't care what anyone says—the blue M&Ms taste better than the others."

Kabbus slammed his tentacles on the ground, shaking the buildings. He wailed, blood squirting from his injured appendages. He tried to pull himself along, but he was seizing up, the pain too much for him to bear. Pandora wiggled her eyebrows. "Apparently angel swords mixed with hope and love actually *do* make good weapons against these morons."

Katie brought her fingers to her lips and tapped them, narrowing her eyes. Pandora glanced at her. "Uh oh. I've seen that look before. You are planning something evil yet pure at the same time. Spill it. I love plans like that."

Katie smiled, shifting her eyes toward Pandora. "I have

a question. Kabbus can give demons nightmares too, right?"

Pandora looked at him, then back at Katie, then back at Kabbus again. "Oh, this is good. This is really good. Why, yes, as a matter of fact, Kabbus can give demons nightmares. In fact, he used to do it on a regular basis. I remember when he first came here, I was in a ball shaking after picturing newborn babies surrounded by kittens and puppies. It was terrible."

Katie lifted her eyebrow. "Oh, yeah. That's the pits. Why don't we give someone else our problem for a little bit?"

Pandora smirked mischievously. "In the words of Timothy, 'Yass, queen, yass.'"

Pandora and Katie used their joint magic to open another portal to hell. As soon as the heat hit them, Katie poked her head in just to make sure. She nodded at Pandora, and they drove Kabbus through the portal and slammed it shut, leaving him with the rocks, the lava, and most importantly, the demons.

The next day was hard. There was debris everywhere, and although the bodies had been removed the night before, there was still an eerie and chilly feeling where they had been found. It was as if some of their fear still lingered in the air. None of the soldiers could go anywhere close. Instead, they spent the day clearing up the base. Fortunately, not too much had been damaged, but now that Kabbus was gone, they did a full deep-cleaning and repaired the few things, like the doorway, that he'd ruined.

Everyone chipped in, from the soldiers to Dr. Ozu. Much to Calvin's dismay, Sofia was right there with them, doing whatever she could to make the base a home again. "I know what it feels like to have a nightmare hanging over your home. I won't let that linger here."

From the front hangar, the jet, which had arrived early that morning, had been moved out to the runway. In it were over a dozen coffins, lined up perfectly straight and draped with the flags of country and service. It was their memorial to the dead; their way of honoring their sacrifices in a war that had appeared on their doorstep without warning but with full consequences.

The guys all tried to keep the mood alive, playing music over the speakers and doing their best to smile at the other soldiers, but still, everyone was somber and wrung out from the day before. None of them had realized just how taxing it was to have their minds attacked and then have to handle the aftermath. Eddie, Turner, and Brock had volunteered to collect and arrange the bodies, trying not to put any more on the soldiers than they had already borne. As it was, they should have been in bed resting, but cleaning up the base was important to them all.

Stephanie put down her broom and walked over to Korbin, clasping his arm. He stared around the base, watching the flags that hung in front of the hangar flapping in the breeze. "It's terrible how that feeling of fear can linger with you."

Korbin nodded. "It is. I just hope they are at rest now."

Stephanie patted Korbin's arm. "I think the base needs something."

Korbin smiled, kissing Stephanie on the forehead. "I think you're right."

"Put all of the tables right there in the center of the courtyard," Stephanie yelled.

The soldiers all carried tables out of the storage area for Stephanie. One by one they set them up, taking tablecloths from Timothy and giving them a colorful and festive feel. One by one the chairs appeared, and the tables began to fill with the food that Sean and Katie were working on in the kitchen.

Brock walked over next to Stephanie. "This is a really perfect plan. These guys have been through hell and back, and that isn't even literal this time. We needed something to pep them up and get them back in the groove of being a family. Many of them lost friends for the first time."

Stephanie crossed her arms over her chest. "It is a loss that we will feel for some time, but we have a job to do, and we need to be bonded to do it."

Brock smiled. "Just like the old days."

Stephanie patted him on the back. "That's exactly right. No matter what our personal feelings were, we came together as a family and worked as a unit. I think the new guys are really starting to get that. At least, I hope they are."

They both chuckled and went over to the tables, helping the soldiers set up the last few. Brock leaned his head back after the last one was in place, closing his eyes and taking a deep breath of fresh air. The sky was a brilliant blue, with large white fluffy clouds passing slowly overhead. It was a little chilly, but bright and beautiful nonetheless.

The last of the food was brought down and all of the soldiers and mercs gathered together, taking seats next to their fellow soldiers. They filled their plates with good old comfort food, the kind you would find at a reunion or a picnic. They had baskets of fried chicken, bowls of potato salad, Jell-O molds, and pasta salad. There were huge platters of cookies, and brownies too. They hadn't been able to cook all of it, Timothy running out at the last second to get a bunch more, but the soldiers didn't care.

It was refreshing, but with the weight of the dead just across the courtyard, they were still quiet and somber. When they had settled into eating, Korbin stood and stepped up onto the bench. "If I could have everyone's attention?"

Everyone turned and looked at him. Korbin was glad to see their faces. "Yesterday was hard. Harder for some than others."

Korbin raised his Coke in the direction of the hangar. "But I want you to all realize something. Every single one of you faced your fears last night, and you did it with confidence and valor. We celebrate you today. We celebrate those brave souls who did not make it out alive, and we celebrate our family, all one unit, all fighting for the world, and some of the best goddamned soldiers I have ever had the privilege of working with."

Everyone cheered and raised their sodas. Korbin smiled and looked down at Stephanie, who reached up and took his hand. "I'm so proud of you."

Korbin chuckled. "I haven't heard that since I was a kid."

Stephanie pulled him down to his seat. "Well, maybe I should tell you more often. You are the bravest man I know, and I love you so much for that."

Korbin sighed and leaned forward, kissing her forehead. "How did I get so lucky?"

Stephanie snorted. "You came into my whorehouse. Lucky you. You hit the jackpot."

Korbin laughed. "And I get it for free."

Stephanie clapped her hands. "Damn right."

Turner cleared his throat and stood up, looking around at the troops. "Shit. I don't know if this is appropriate, but fuck it. Y'all, I saw little dick goblins trying to eat my fucking dick. No lie. Little green goblins trying to devour my dick."

One of the soldiers in the crowd yelled, "I bet they're still hungry."

Everyone burst into laughter and Turner's mouth fell open, then he smirked. "Whichever dickbreath just said that, trust me; I will find you, and I will bury you."

Brock chuckled. "I think it might have been worth it to him. If it means anything. I'm glad you don't have dick goblins anymore."

Turner nodded. "Thanks, buddy."

Brock swallowed a bite of his food. "Because if you did, I was going to have to kick you off the team. No one wants goblins running around, especially ones that are so into dicks."

Timothy leaned toward them. "Don't knock it until you try it, ladies."

Katie took a deep breath and stood up, stepping onto a chair. Everyone quieted down, not used to her speeches anymore. She raised her glass in the air. "I think we all saw something we'd rather not see, but we have to remember to have hope."

She pointed at Calvin and Sofia. "Hope for the future."

She pointed at Juntto. "Hope for redemption."

Then she smiled and turned to Pandora. "And faith in one another."

24

Hell was as miserable as it had always been. Demons were scurrying around looking for something to scavenge and the heat index was beyond belief, especially the deeper you went down into the rings. No one had noticed the portal Katie and Pandora had created; they had done it so fast it didn't have time to register. Still, there he was, the Nightmare Man, slithering over the lava rocks. Sweat poured down his tentacles, which had by that point mostly regrown. Still, Kabbus seemed to be weaker than he had been when he got there.

Between the temperature, the pollution in the air, and the hot stone below, Kabbus was using up much more energy than he did on Earth. Even after devouring a dozen soldiers at the base, he was almost back to where he started —which was not good news for the demons, although they had no idea.

Kabbus approached a long stretch of open stone. To his left, he heard the scurrying of claws on rock. Two demons, both low level and relatively stupid, charged at him, ready to attack. The biggest problem for them was that they'd had no idea what they were getting themselves into when they chose that target. Even weak, Kabbus was capable of crushing the toughest imbecilic opponent.

The two demons leapt at him, yelling in their little demon voices. As they came down on Kabbus, they opened their eyes, finding themselves standing in a green field. One gasped in horror. "Huh? What this?"

The other demon scratched his head. "We jump dimension?"

The first demon grabbed the second and turned him around, pointing with shaking fingers. From the edge of a lush forest, several unicorns trotted out, swishing their bright white tails in the sunshine. The demons clung to each other, backing up. The second demon looked at the sky, swallowing hard as he stared at the large, vibrant rainbow overhead.

The demons moved quicker, backing farther and farther away. But the farther they moved away, the closer the unicorns got. As they approached, the first demon tugged on the second's arm. "What on back?"

Narrowing their eyes, they both gagged, shaking their heads. Riding on the unicorns' backs were small, adorable squirrels, their big bushy tails flirting. They wore uniforms on their bodies and held tiny little swords. "That worst thing ever seen."

The demons began to run away and scream, hating every blade of bright green grass their feet touched. As they ran, small furry bunnies popped their heads up, their pink noses moving as they chewed. Rainbow after rainbow cascaded overhead, shining multi-colored reflections down over the demons. Butterflies flew alongside them, and they could swear they could hear some sort of group singing in small voices.

Panic had struck the demons, and they didn't know whether to keep running, vomit, give up and let the unicorns take them, or just off themselves. However, the choice was not going to be theirs. Kabbus was enjoying watching them suffer, letting their fear build up as high as it could. At the same time, though, he was wasting away down there in hell.

His tentacles began to move again, sizzling and smoking as they slapped the smoldering lava rock. He moved over the demons, who were clinging to one another on the path. He lingered there for a moment and then slithered off, leaving the demons' gray husks.

Timothy sat back in the chair in the dungeon, staring up at the screen. "That was horrific. Like completely and terribly the worst thing. I'm really glad it's over."

Sean pouted. "I know. It was the worst torture I could have ever been put to."

Timothy looked at him with pity. "Sean, I'm so sorry. Were they demons?"

Sean wiped his teary eye. "No. There was all this food, all my favorites, but every time I tried to put a bite in my mouth, it turned to smoke."

Timothy put his hand on his chest and gasped. "My lord, that *is* terrifying."

The phone rang, and Timothy patted Sean's shoulder as he answered. "This is Timothy."

"Timothy. Good to hear that you are alive and well. This is Brushwood."

Timothy sat down in the chair. "Oh, you know me. Takes a lot more than a creepy mind-melding Leviathan to get rid of me. What can I do for you today, sir? I have not seen a single blip on the screen so far today. Even the Earthbound demons seem to be staying low-key."

The general chuckled. "I would too if we had just been visited by that thing, but that's not why I'm calling. I was actually calling to tell you that I wanted to use your tech to look for the remaining Leviathans. Figured I should call you before you get rid of it or something."

Timothy bit his lip, swirling his finger around in a circle on the desk. "General, I'll be honest. I'm not sure if that is a good idea. I think I need to run it by Katie first. She is the leader, and she should be the one to make that decision."

The general grunted. "Is there any specific reason you don't feel comfortable? Could it just be residual from what happened?"

Timothy wrinkled his nose. "I guess it could be. It was pretty damn traumatic, and we lost a lot of men from that incident. But at the same time, I felt that way before I built this system. I'll be honest with you: I don't know if it is such a good idea poking around the world trying to find these guys. especially when they are in more remote areas. You never know what they can sense."

Brushwood heard him out and responded, "I under-stand your concern, but this is also a little bigger than that.

We want to be protected, but also in the know and ahead of the times."

Timothy pursed his lips. "Right, but this system might actually find those Leviathans, and then what? We waltz in their bedrooms and flip on the light? I think we've seen that it's not a good thing when Leviathans wake up. They tend to get up on the wrong side of the ice shelf. The only one we got a positive return on was Juntto, but he almost cut Pandora's head off at first. Not that I hold it against him; just worthy of bringing up at a time like this."

The general pursed his lips. "Timothy, I completely understand your concerns. This is very dangerous territory. You are the only one with a tracker, but if you talk to Katie and decide not to do it, I will respect your choice."

Timothy breathed a sigh of relief. "Thank you, General. I really appreciate you being understanding."

He smirked. "I've been in this business long enough to know that some things are risky, and sometimes that risk is not worth it. Just do me a favor; talk it over with Katie, and let me know as soon as you can."

The general waited until Timothy had hung up before carefully setting his phone down. He pressed his lips together, staring down at the table. He definitely hadn't seen that coming. Usually, Timothy was all gung ho after bad fights. This one must have been very serious. He raised his eyebrows and looked up, shrugging his shoulders.

Dragos and the rest of the World Council looked at him, waiting to hear what the final outcome had been.

They could tell from his strained look that it might not be a good report, but anything that wasn't exciting and new to the council was considered not good, so it didn't really matter.

Dragos cleared his throat, staring at Brushwood. "So, will this Timothy on Katie's team use the technology or let us use the technology to track down the rest of the Leviathans?"

The general took a deep breath, smoothing his jacket as he sat there. He glanced from one council member to another, hating the idea of being the point man on something they were not going to like in the least. "I'm not sure. They have concerns. Timothy is going to roll it over with Katie. On that note, though, the bond between them is strong, and I suspect that Katie will take Timothy's advice over mine."

The council immediately began whispering loudly to each other. Some of their faces were understanding, while the majority looked enraged. These leaders were not told no very often. Usually that would entertain Brushwood, but on that specific topic, it really didn't.

Dragos banged his gavel on the desk, and everyone began to quiet down. He kept his eyes locked on Brushwood until there was no more sound in the room. "I don't think I need to talk about the urgency of finding these beasts. They have proven to not be the most Earth-friendly creatures. I would rather accidentally wake one than have it surprise us. Their system is the only one that can track them. No one else has been able to replicate it."

The general shook his head. "I don't know what you want me to tell you. Right now, they are not sure. Long term, it will probably be a no. These things are what they are."

Dragos scoffed. "Nonsense. We'll have our people look into hacking their equipment. We need the information one way or another. If they will not cooperate, we will take what we need."

The general shook his head, standing up. "Hold on. Hold on just a minute here. We just got our positive relationship back with Katie, and you want to jeopardize that by not only misleading her into trusting you but stealing from her? She has gone above and beyond to protect the people of this world, including every single person in this room. She is one of God's angels, in case you've forgotten. That is not the kind of woman I want to run into when she is pissed at me."

The council members whispered some more, and Dragos rolled his eyes. "We aren't stealing the secret to the universe, just to where the Leviathans are. It is Katie's job to forewarn us, in this and in attacks. What would you like us to do instead?"

The general gritted his teeth, tamping down his frustration. "I have told you that I will speak to her. We cannot do that to Katie. It will completely ruin the relationship, and she will become one of our enemies. I would much rather have her as a friend than an enemy."

The general sat back down, giving the council a chance to talk the decision over. Dragos was insistent, and he had a feeling it was because of something that probably didn't even have to do with tracking the Leviathan. That wasn't a surprise, though. Even the people closest to him didn't trust him. He was always out for himself in one way or another.

One of the other council members flicked on his mics, talking in place of Dragos, who looked angry. "We have decided, General, that you are correct. We do not want to abuse Katie's trust. We want to keep her on our team. Therefore, we will not do anything without your approval."

The general nodded in thanks. "I appreciate your decision."

The council moved on to other matters, but the general knew he could not trust what they had to say.

"Move faster," one demon snarled to another.

The other demon grunted. "They're heavy, okay?"

The first demon rolled his eyes. "Like our master will care. He will already be pissed at what we have found."

The other demon shivered. "It isn't our fault. I hope he doesn't remove my legs again. It took two decades to regrow them, and I still don't have a pinky toe."

The two demons dragged a third, terrified demon up to the doors of Lucifer's throne room. The guard looked at them and then at the demon. He swallowed hard and grabbed the rings, pulling the large doors open. The demons nodded and continued inside, making their way across the vast marble floor.

Lucifer was sitting on his throne, giving his demon servant instructions. "So, I don't want Calichon sitting next to Triumph. They had a love affair, and it's not pretty when they get too many glasses of scotch in them. Total catfight."

The whimpers of the demon being dragged echoed through the room. Lucifer snarled and looked around. "What is that fucking noise? If it is one of the demons missing a limb again, tell them to deal with their shit on their own time. I am not a damn surgeon."

The first demon cleared his throat. "Your Grace. We are sorry to interrupt. We found him out by the lava quarries. Total mess. We weren't sure what to do, so we brought him here. Especially after the others were discovered."

Both demons bowed low, shaking. Lucifer looked at his servant and waved his hand. He stood, pushing his sleeves up and walked down the steps to the floor. As he approached, he waved the two demons to the side and looked down at the one they had dragged in. He pushed on him with his claw and snarled.

Wrinkling his snout, he glanced around and raised his eyebrows. "Well, fuck! This is not good. I was hoping I would never have to deal with that fucking Leviathan again. Fuck my luck!"

He looked at the two demons and wrinkled his nose in disgust. "Do whatever you need to with him, just get him out of my throne room." He turned dramatically, snapping his fingers. "Get my walking jacket."

He slipped his sitting jacket off, and the servant caught it as it fell. They knew not to let his clothing hit the ground. The last time it had happened, a demon had lost his dick and ended up in five pieces mounted around the castle for crying about it.

Lucifer rolled his shoulders and strode around the corner from his throne and down a long stone corridor. When he reached the end, he pushed on the door and waited for it to creak open. Stepping inside, he put his claw to his chin and stroked the hair hanging from the end of it. He walked around the armory, running his fingers down his different weapons.

He paused, then shook his head. "Meat mallet won't work. I would have to touch the dirty bastard. Let's see… Sword, no. Spear, boring. Ax has potential. Oh, wait. Yes, this is perfect."

Lucifer smiled excitedly as he reached up and pulled down a pitchfork. He touched the tips of the tines, wincing at their sharpness, and then bellowed his laughter. "This is exactly what I was looking for."

He sauntered out of the armory, stopping for the servants to help him into his jacket, then headed out, taking a stroll into the lava plains and molten mountains. He hadn't been that far out since Katie and Pandora had been messing around in hell planning their attacks. As he walked up a small hill, he spotted Kabbus. "Oh look, he's blobbing about as he always has. Some beasts never change."

Lucifer cleared his throat and yelled, "Kabbus! Nightmare! Lord of Terror! Get the fuck out of my house! I thought I told you that you were not welcome here? I swear, you are like an insolent child, just doing whatever you like, then someone else has to come along to dispose of you. I had a perfectly nice afternoon of dismemberment planned, but now I'm out here shooing you off my property like a stray fucking dog."

Kabbus slowly slithered around to face him and made a succession of noises. Lucifer rolled his eyes. "Yes, I *am* pissed you are eating my demons, dammit, not to mention leaving your tentacle slime everywhere. You don't just march into someone else's dimension and do whatever you like."

Kabbus raised his tentacles into the air and lashed out at Lucifer. They flew past him, blowing open his jacket. Lucifer spat, pulling his jacket closed and buttoning it. He stared at Kabbus with a blank face for several minutes. "I was afraid for maybe a millisecond, or it might have been indigestion. I had a terrible slice of baby fat for lunch. It always sits wrong, especially when I have to go for a long-ass hike through the lava fields afterward to take out the fucking trash."

Kabbus made more noises, and Lucifer looked at him, surprised. "That isn't very nice. Do I come to your home and call you names like that? No, I do not. And I also do not eat your servants. I told you that if you came back here, you would be finished. So sad you didn't listen to me the first time around."

He grew very large and lifted his pitchfork, slamming it down into Kabbus. The beast roared, and Lucifer chuckled as he picked him up and flung him into the fiery pits. He watched until he could no longer see him and then turned away, wiping the single bead of sweat from his forehead.

Lucifer shrank back down and tossed his pitchfork to a servant standing by. The servant handed him a towel to wipe his hands with. "Fucking Katie and Lilith had me take out their trash? Beelzebub will answer for this."

25

Brock stuck his hands in his pockets and looked out the window of Joshua's office. Calvin and Korbin were sitting in the chairs, and Joshua was behind his desk. "It sure was weird being in here the other day when all these machines were off. I don't think I've ever seen them not running."

Joshua smiled. "That was only the third time they have all been turned off at once in the middle of a production cycle, but we caught up on that one and put it all back together. It was worth it. The sound would have been terrible, with everything else going on."

Brock looked at Joshua and nodded. "Agreed. Quick thinking. I like that."

Korbin chuckled. "I do too, especially when it comes to the men and women on this base. And your girls! They were on it, helping whoever they could. I appreciate that."

Joshua sat up proudly. "I will tell them you said that."

Korbin looked over his shoulder at Brock. "You said you wanted to talk to all of us together?"

Brock rubbed his hands together. "Yes. I have been doing some thinking, actually. We all know that Calvin is going to be staying here so he can be with his wife and for his baby, who will be here before we know it. Everyone on this base has a place, and I have just kind of filled in where I was needed, or sometimes not needed, but they took me anyway. I would like to replace Calvin on the fort sites. Do training and building—whatever needs to be done."

Calvin was impressed. "This is good, Brock. Teamwork. I very much appreciate it."

Brock squeezed his shoulder. "Of course. Everyone has done something similar for me at some time or another. I need to start paying those dues back. I want you to be with your family. I know how important family is, or at least I remember from when I was just a human trying to get through life. Hopefully one day I'll be in the same situation, or somewhere around there, and someone will do the same for me."

Calvin shook his hand. "I'm sure they will."

Brock shrugged. "Besides, I want to build forts. I've heard great things about them, and if it's something Korbin is this passionate about, I want to know more. I want to learn about it from the ground up. I like training Damned too, so that would be a great way for me to get my hands dirty."

Korbin stood up and put his hand out. "This sounds fantastic. I was worried that I was going to have to call out to other mercs not on teams to see if anyone wanted to come. That would have been hard for me, because I have to know that I can trust them, and that they're going to do the best job they can out there. Lives depend on it. On all of it."

Calvin shook his finger in the air. "You know what else it will do? It will take a load off of Katie. Between the Leviathan, the problems in New York, and the forts, she has really been running herself into the ground. She shouldn't have to do everything on her own."

Brock snickered. "I tell her that all the time but she just laughs."

Korbin smiled. "Yeah, well, she's the kind of superhero where you have to take some of her jobs without asking in order to get her to slow down. She won't argue if you just do it, so this will be good. And Brock, it will give you some really good experience working with Damned who haven't been military. Basically, training a civilian from the bottom up in a short amount of time. You have to find your rhythm."

Brock was excited. "I'm looking forward to it, and to telling Katie that she can take a deep breath and slow down until the next disaster surfaces. She may fight me, but I know she is going to be happy about it."

Joshua tapped his hands on the desk. "Well, this is perfect. Plus, we did an inventory, and I won't be as short as I thought on the forts. Not as much as you want, but we have enough to make everyone happy."

Korbin shook his head. "No sweat. We'll work with what we have. That's what we've always done. They will be protected to start out, and after that, we can send them whatever they need."

Joshua pulled out his paperwork and began filling in different sections. "I will get the team working right away on setting you up with special metal bullets, grenades, missiles, and possibly some bigger guns. I want you to be able to either take them with you to your next location or at least know they will be there within a couple of days of you getting there."

Brock stretched his arms over his head. "So, where are we going for the next fort? Have you decided?"

Korbin looked at Calvin. "We did, actually. To take the guesswork out of it, we had the council come up with a list of countries we wouldn't have to wait for. Then we talked about which ones they were really hoping for us to get into."

Calvin smirked. "That's right. They told us Antarctica, but we said we'd just send Brock."

Brock stared at them for a moment before Calvin began to laugh. "Dude, I'm fucking with you."

Brock sighed in relief. "You don't even know. I would freeze out there. I would need a fur-lined parka and about twelve scarves."

Korbin laughed loudly. "Actually, we decided that we are going to head over to the Middle East. Bahrain was one of the places on our list, and it's also pretty well protected. There is an ancient burial site located there that has been of interest to the demons on occasion. The ancient burial site needs a fort over it no matter what. It will be the first place a portal will open if they target there."

Brock nodded, listening to Korbin. "So we will be out there until it's done. Will we need to recruit Damned?"

Korbin wasn't sure. "Sometimes they come to us, sometimes we have to attract them to us. Some are coming with us from France, too. I'm sure there will be more than enough Damned for us to find some decent ones who want to serve. It's heroic in their minds, and it gives them something to do that isn't destructive."

Joshua stood up and smiled, letting his hands swing at his sides. "You guys can talk all you want in here since it's nice and quiet. I have to get on the floor, though, if you don't mind."

Korbin patted him on the back as he passed. "Of course, dude. Do your thing. We will get out of your hair. And thanks for getting us these bullets so fast. They are much needed."

Joshua headed out onto the armory floor and started checking clipboards. When he got to the third row, he glanced at Wanda, who was moving back and forth, boxing bullets. He bit the inside of his lip and put the clipboard back. His feet shuffled back and forth, not quite sure which way to head. Finally, he made a decision.

Wanda looked up and smiled as he approached. "Hey, you. What's up?"

Joshua swallowed hard. "I was wondering if you would like to go to dinner with me?"

Pandora and Katie sat on the edge of the barracks roof. They swung their legs back and forth in sync, as if they were on the same wavelength. Katie leaned forward, staring down at the courtyard below.

Pandora put her arm around Katie. "Don't go falling off the roof. Not enough time to sprout those wings. I don't feel like having to mend a fucking broken back."

Katie shook her head, leaning back. "That would be quite the inconvenience, wouldn't it?"

They both smiled, staring at the sun setting in the distance. It was beautiful, painting the sky in shades of pink and blue. There was just something perfectly calm and quiet about it. No demons, no raging Leviathans, just a normal sunset on a normal evening out in the desert. Katie had forgotten what those were like. She was always so busy doing a million things that she didn't take the time for this type of thing anymore.

Pandora tilted her head to the side. "This reminds me of a sunset I watched in Egypt a very long time ago."

Katie smiled. "Aw. A moment of self-reflection?"

Pandora scoffed. "No. Please! Do I look like Buddha? I was with this really hot royal type, and he was pleasing me in ways the Egyptians never taught their descendants, if you know what I mean. Still pretty, though."

Katie stared at her for several moments, blinking. "You always tell the worst stories."

Pandora shrugged. "What? I can't help it. Hey, do you know what my first nightmare was?"

Katie grimaced. "You already told me."

Pandora sighed and repeated it anyway. "I didn't have a fucking cooch. My coochie…it was gone. Done. Plastic like a fucking Barbie doll. That's the kind of shit that makes me thankful for fucking Egyptian sunsets."

Katie tilted her head back and started laughing. At first, it came out with no sound, then it burst from her like fire. She held her stomach as she giggled, tears rolling down her cheeks. "Oh…oh, God, it hurts. You know, if I didn't know you, I would be confused. But since I know you, that night-mare fits you perfectly."

Pandora curled her lip and crossed her arms. "It's really not that funny. It was some scary shit, okay?"

Katie shook her head. "I was having nightmares about not being able to save people or the world. *You* were having nightmares about not being able to get the big D anymore. You could have always scissored a Ken doll."

Pandora pursed her lips. "If I could, I would turn you plastic for one damn day. I bet at some point you would feel that hard shiny layer and think to yourself, "Where am I going to put the dick?""

Katie smiled and patted Pandora's hand. "You know what? I think it's good that we're so different in that sense. We would kill each other, always trying to be the person who saved everyone."

Pandora swung her legs. "Yep, and if we were both like me, we would get nothing done. Shit, the human race would be half-gone and we'd still be in that alternate universe with all the naked people."

Katie wrinkled her nose. "I feel like it's not as glam-orous as it looks. There have to be saggy old people around there somewhere. They probably put the ugly people and the old people into like naked sweatshops."

Pandora laughed. "To make what? They don't wear any clothes."

A strange wind suddenly gusted up the side of the building and swirled around them. Their hair blew around them like a tornado, and they felt goose bumps up the backs of their necks. Pandora sniffed the air and narrowed her eyes. "I smell...a stick...up an ass."

Katie and Pandora turned to find Gabriel standing behind them in his robes. His white hair glistened in the setting sun, and it almost looked like he was covered in glitter. He stretched his long silver wings out behind him, the first time Katie had seen him with them.

Katie stood up and turned around, wiping the dust off her ass. "Hey, you always show up to the party about three minutes late."

Pandora rolled her eyes. "Try, he shows up after everyone else leaves and the trash has been collected. Then he makes you feel uncomfortable, and you sit there talking to him until he finally leaves."

Katie pointed at Pandora. "But it's all in riddles."

Pandora nodded her head. "Yeah, of course."

Gabriel smiled. "I'm glad to see you two getting along and working side by side so well lately."

Pandora shrugged. "I'm too awesome to always be hitching rides."

Gabriel chuckled. "I came for a couple of reasons. Did you send a Monster of Time to hell?"

Katie pursed her lips and shifted her eyes to Pandora. Pandora shrugged, and Katie turned her gaze back to Gabriel. "Uh, were we not supposed to? We did it before."

Gabriel blinked at her for a couple of moments before shaking his head. "It's not looked too highly, no. We don't have a lot of angel mercenaries and random Leviathans walking around. But now that you've done it twice, we'll have to write something in about it."

Katie grumped. "Great, so I'm basically the girl who got the sticker put on Tide Pods telling people not to ingest."

Gabriel covered his mouth, letting out a small chuckle.

Katie's eyes went wide, and she and Pandora looked at each other in awe. "Holy moly, he just laughed at one of our jokes!"

Pandora crossed her arms and looked at Gabriel with amusement. "Where is this good mood coming from? Did you start dating again in heaven?"

Gabriel shook his head, straightening his face. "Just thought it was funny. Now, I don't have very long."

Katie sighed. "When do you ever? I feel that's like the mantra in our lives."

Gabriel tilted his head from side to side, agreeing. "Anyway. I came to tell you something. Hell wants to come to Earth. Trust your friends, Katie, but know that a friend of your friend can be your enemy.'

Katie looked at Pandora. "Does that count as a riddle?"

Pandora put her hand out and tilted it from side to side like Gabriel had done with his head. "It could be, or he could mean exactly what he is saying."

Katie narrowed her eyes. "Isn't that in and of itself a riddle?"

Gabriel put his hands out and then dropped them to his side. "Why do I even come?"

Katie smirked. "Okay, okay. I'm sorry. We like to bust your…chops. Anyway, my answer to that little tidbit of depressing news is that I have hope, Gabriel."

Gabriel looked at her with pride on his face. "Good, because you'll need it."

Suddenly there was a loud bang behind them, and both Pandora and Katie spun. One of the soldiers had knocked over a stack of crates he was trying to move. Pandora snickered. "Hey, Gabriel, I remember when you…" Pandora let her voice trail off as she turned back around.

The angel was gone.

***

Katie leaned against the headboard, her hair pulled up on top of her head in a messy bun. She was wearing one of Brock's old band t-shirts, and sat with her legs straight out in front of her, crossed at the ankles. There were lit candles all over his room, flickering in the darkness. The shadows danced, creating a visual effect that set the mood. Brock smirked as he scooted off the end, pulling his boxers up.

He glanced over his shoulder at Katie. "I like having you here like this. I know it's not forever, but it's really nice for a little while. I don't have to guess where you are."

Katie smiled. "Before long, *you'll* be the world traveler. You and Korbin are leaving Stephanie and me here to pine away in our flower beds, waiting for our men to come home."

Brock laughed. "Yeah, right. I can't imagine you pining for anyone at any point."

Katie put her arms over her head and shrugged. "Who knows? I could lose my angel powers and Pandora could run off, and I could be left here."

Brock gave her a look. "You still wouldn't be pining."

Katie wrinkled her nose. "No. No, I wouldn't."

Brock chuckled, walking over and opening his closet. He pulled his guitar down from the hook on the back of the door and walked over, taking a seat on the edge of the bed. "So, when you thought you were saving us in the street, I was actually having a nightmare."

Katie reached out and touched his hand. "What about?"

Brock strummed his guitar once, slapping his hand to the strings to stop the sound. "I opened my eyes, and I was standing in a stadium in front of thousands and thousands of fans. My band was there behind me, and I just started playing. I played the best song that I had ever written. I knew it without even thinking about it, and my band knew it too. Anyway, I sang my heart out, and when I was done, I stood there for a few moments with my eyes closed."

Katie wrinkled her forehead. "That doesn't sound like a nightmare."

Brock sighed. "It wasn't. Not until I opened my eyes and saw the absolute hate and disgust for me and my music. Nobody liked it, and that was the best I was ever going to give them. I tried playing something else, but my guitar made no sound. My hands just stopped working."

Pandora groaned inside Katie. *Really? I decide to stay with you tonight, and this is what I get? Is he going to play? This song better not be sappy or I will come out just to puke in his guitar.*

Katie growled at her. *If you're staying, shut up.*

Brock began to strum the guitar. "In my dream, it was almost like they couldn't hear me."

Katie pulled her knees to her chest and put her chin on them. "I hear you, Brock."

So he played.

And they listened.

AUTHOR NOTES - MICHAEL ANDERLE

FEBRUARY 20, 2019

THANK YOU for not only reading this story but these *Author Notes* **as well.**

(I think I've been good with always opening with "thank you." If not, I need to edit the other *Author Notes*!)

RANDOM (*sometimes*) THOUGHTS?

You ever have too many things you want to accomplish?

Besides too many books to read, I mean ;-)

I am having to learn how to cope with too many fun projects where the interest in one project is causing me to enjoy doing this other project less than I should or could if the new bright shiny wasn't calling to me.

Whispering sweet nothings in my ear...

I'm fifty-one years old. While I've suffered from this issue before, it usually hasn't been with ten projects; it was with maybe two. Thank God that I'm having this challenge when I'm this old or I would have substantially hosed myself decades ago.

Now I have the maturity (sort of and don't snort, Stephen Campbell, when you read this; it is unmanly) to temper my desire to start too many projects.

Actually, I'm trying to finish up some projects and reduce the total as LMBPN Publishing moves forward.

I can't say that I'm too successful at reducing projects, but life is a marathon, right?

That is what I keep telling myself as I go to sleep, dreaming of another ten projects to tempt me to start the next day.

For me, "No" is the most liberating word I have in my vocabulary. Perhaps I translate it as "Not Right Now."

AROUND THE WORLD IN 80 DAYS

One of the interesting (at least to me) aspects of my life is the ability to work from anywhere and at any time. In the future, I hope to re-read my own *Author Notes* and remember my life as a diary entry.

Las Vegas, NV—in bed typing these notes because the tv is on in the living room.

It snowed last Sunday night and is possibly going to snow tonight here in Las Vegas.

(UPDATE! – It snowed like crazy!)

I've visited Las Vegas at least twenty times in my life, and this is the first week I've ever encountered snow on the Strip.

It feels like it should be Christmas time... But it is February.

I know from reading that it snows in the desert, but now I am experiencing snow in the desert, and I come away confused.

It's the desert. Sand, rocks, and cacti are what I think belongs here. The white stuff just feels so wrong. Enough about the snow (all 1/32" of it (maybe) that immediately melted when it hit the ground. I imagine I have readers in REAL snow places that are looking outside at four feet wondering if I'd like to change places?) No, no I wouldn't. I am allergic to the nasty cold, and I don't think I could type new stories and messages if I was freezing.

You know, that 44-degree weather?

FAN PRICING

$0.99 Saturdays (new LMBPN stuff) and $0.99 Wednesday (both LMBPN books and friends of LMBPN books.) Get great stuff from us and others at tantalizing prices.

Go ahead. I bet you can't read just one.

Sign up here: http://lmbpn.com/email/.

HOW TO MARKET FOR BOOKS YOU LOVE

Review them so others have your thoughts, and tell friends and the dogs of your enemies (because who wants to talk to enemies?)... *Enough said ;-)*

Ad Aeternitatem,

Michael Anderle